SHE'S
TOO
PRETTY
TO
BURN

PRAISE FOR *SHE'S TOO PRETTY TO BURN*

"A smoldering, hypnotic thrill ride. Heard's YA debut
crackles and pops with electric psychological suspense."
—**KIT FRICK**, author of *See All the Stars*,
All Eyes on Us, and *I Killed Zoe Spanos*

"An expertly plotted deep dive into a complex
web of friendship, desire, and murder."
—**MINDY McGINNIS**, author of *The Female of the Species*

"An anxiety-ridden ride as two girls' lives crash together
through secrets, love, and danger. Captivating and stunningly visual."
—**AIDEN THOMAS**, author of *Cemetery Boys*

"Heard paints a mesmerizing portrait of love and
betrayal amidst a slow-burn thriller . . . and once the
murders begin, it's impossible to look away."
—**DIANA URBAN**, author of *All Your Twisted Secrets*

"A gritty, compulsively readable thriller
that shimmers with California heat."
—**HANNAH CAPIN**, author of *Foul Is Fair*

"A powder keg of psychological suspense that
recognizes the dark side lurking within all of us, this thriller
had me riveted right from the very first page."
—**CALEB ROEHRIG**, author of *Last Seen Leaving* and *White Rabbit*

"*She's Too Pretty to Burn* holds you by the throat until the very last page. Heard has written a perfect, ultra-modern teenage noir of early queer love and the battle to resist our most destructive impulses. Ambition is truly a killer."

—ADAM SASS, author of *Surrender Your Sons*

"Veronica and Mick's complex, compelling relationship grounds this intense and unrelenting thriller, full of impossible choices, betrayals, mistakes, and danger."

—KATE ALICE MARSHALL,
author of *I Am Still Alive* and *Rules for Vanishing*

"Gorgeously written and expertly paced, *She's Too Pretty to Burn* is an intense, wild ride that keeps the reader on the edge of their seat until its stunning conclusion."

—LIZ LAWSON, author of *The Lucky Ones*

SHE'S TOO PRETTY TO BURN

WENDY HEARD

SQUARE
FISH

Christy Ottaviano Books

HENRY HOLT AND COMPANY • NEW YORK

SQUARE
FISH

An imprint of Macmillan Publishing Group, LLC
120 Broadway, New York, NY 10271 • fiercereads.com

Our books may be purchased in bulk for promotional, educational, or business use. Please
contact your local bookseller or the Macmillan Corporate and Premium Sales Department
at (800) 221-7945 ext. 5442 or by email at MacmillanSpecialMarkets@macmillan.com.

The Library of Congress has cataloged the hardcover edition as follows:
Names: Heard, Wendy, author.
Title: She's too pretty to burn / Wendy Heard.
Other titles: She is too pretty to burn
Description: First edition. | New York : Henry Holt and Company, 2021. | Audience:
    Ages 14–18. | Audience: Grades 10–12. | Summary: When seventeen-year-old Veronica's
    photograph of her introverted girlfriend goes viral, they are sent into a spiral of fame
    and lethal danger as they navigate the turbulent waters of their relationship, secrets,
    acclaim, and the underground San Diego art scene.
Identifiers: LCCN 2020020581 | ISBN 9781250246752 (hardcover)
Subjects: CYAC: Lesbians—Fiction. | Photography—Fiction. | Art—Fiction. |
    San Diego (Calif.)—Fiction.
Classification: LCC PZ7.1.H4314 Sh 2021 | DDC [Fic]—dc23
LC record available at https://lccn.loc.gov/2020020581

Originally published in the United States by Christy Ottaviano Books/Henry Holt and
Company
First Square Fish edition, 2022
Book designed by Mallory Grigg
Square Fish logo designed by Filomena Tuosto
Printed in the United States of America

ISBN 978-1-250-82126-3 (paperback)
10 9 8 7 6 5 4 3 2 1

IN MEMORY OF VETA DENTON,
WHO GAVE ME SAN DIEGO.

Art, like nature, has her monsters.

—Oscar Wilde, *The Picture of Dorian Gray*

CHAPTER ONE

✧✧✧

VERONICA

THE DESERT SKY IS HOT AND BRIGHT. BIRDS FLIT back and forth, oblivious to the smell of my blood as it soaks the dirt and rocks.

Woozy thoughts snake through my brain. Why did I never notice how many different birds there are? I bet Mick notices birds. She sees all the quiet, important things.

A new wave of pain rampages through me. I think I'm going to black out, but an image seizes me—high above, on the cliff, a silhouette—a thin, slinky shape. Someone is standing there, looking down at me.

He's watching me die.

CHAPTER TWO

◇◇◇

MICK

TEN DAYS EARLIER

COACH MORRIS BLOWS HER WHISTLE, SIGNALING THE
end of practice. The team swims to the edge of the pool, Liz
beside me. "Are you going home to get ready?" she asks.

"I'll just shower here. My mom's picking me up for that
dinner thing, remember?" I wriggle up onto the concrete deck,
which is hot even though the sun is going down. Liz pops up
next to me, and we walk to the bench where we left our towels.

"I can't wait," she bubbles. She's looking forward to tonight's
party, a feeling I cannot relate to.

"Who's driving us again?" I ask, drying my face.

Liz pulls her swim cap off, and her thick, wavy brown
hair tumbles around her shoulders. "Those girls I met from
Bonita. We'll pick you up after your dinner."

Internally, I shudder.

She reads my expression. "Don't be weird tonight."

"I won't."

"I'm serious."

"I'll keep a smile plastered onto my face." I demonstrate, baring my teeth like I'm at the dentist.

"I can't, like . . ." She looks up at the darkening sky as though she's searching it for the right words. "I can't be your only person. You have to get out there. When was the last time you made a new friend?"

I shrug, stung. This is part of a larger conversation I really don't feel like having right now. She sighs and heads for the locker room, leaving me behind. I follow, my shoulders heavy. We used to have our own two-person parties, sleeping over at each other's house every weekend. Now I feel like an intruder into this new and exciting social life she's organized for herself.

My steps slow, and I stop to look at the sunset glowing red-orange behind the palm trees. I wish I were at the beach right now, or hiking through the forest. I'd rather be doing anything other than what I have planned for tonight.

A huge Cooper's hawk glides down and settles onto a telephone pole, disrupting a cloud of blackbirds. They scatter, twittering, into the blood-and-fire sky.

Their echoed birdsong sends a chill through me, but I don't know why.

* * *

I feel my mom's exasperated eyes on me as I walk across the parking lot under the fluorescent overhead lights toward her leased Nissan Altima. When I get in, she says, "You couldn't have worn something nicer?"

I look down at my jeans and white T-shirt. "I'm going out with Liz after this. I didn't want to be too dressed up."

"You're going to a *party*."

"Don't remind me."

"You have incredible legs. You should wear a skirt, or some shorts. Or a crop top; show off those abs. It's such a waste."

"Mom, stop, please."

She digs around in her purse and extracts a cosmetics bag. "At least put some makeup on." She dumps the bag in my lap and pulls out of the parking lot onto the street.

I hate it when she says things like this. How is my own private human body a waste?

It's not worth fighting about, so I click on the dome light, flip down the sun visor, and start applying mascara. "Why do you care what I wear for dinner, anyway? Where are we going?"

"We're meeting Andrew."

"Your agent? Why?" I put the makeup away.

"He just wants to talk. Don't forget your eyebrows. They're super blond right now from the sun. You should go all the way blond with your hair."

Like you? I want to say. She's been trying to get me to bleach my hair since it darkened to light brown in middle school.

It doesn't matter. I only have one more year here. I'm working hard on swimming; I want to get a scholarship and go somewhere far away, far enough that I can barely make it home for Christmas. I've already been scouted for a school in New Hampshire. I don't even know if it's a good school, but it's far, and that's what matters.

I fill in my too-blond eyebrows. She pulls up to a red light and looks me over. "Your lips look dry. Use some of my lip gloss. It's in the side pocket of my purse."

"Ughhhh," I groan, frustrated and hangry. I pull random crap out of the pocket—a bow tie from her catering job, a server's folio full of receipts, a wine key, a pair of earrings— and yank the lip gloss out.

"Don't even start with me, Micaela. And you better put all that stuff back in there."

I glare at her profile, return everything to her purse, and check my phone. No new texts. I don't know what I'm hoping for; it's not like Liz is going to cancel and say she'd rather stay in.

Anxiety sits like a cannonball in my gut. I wish I could find a way out of this party. It sounds like it's going to be a bunch of rich kids drinking beer and—

"Why are you staring at your phone like that?" my mom asks, half laughing. "It's a blank screen. Are you trying to make someone text you with telekinesis?" She slides into a parking spot. We're at the restaurant; I hadn't noticed.

I feel myself flush. "I was just spacing out." I shove it back in my purse and get out, slamming the car door behind me. The evening air is close and hot, and I suddenly can't remember if I put on deodorant.

We approach the restaurant. It's a California Italian place my mom likes for their low-calorie salads. The swinging brass-and-glass door opens, and Andrew steps out. "Look at you gorgeous girls."

My mom beams. She's wearing what I call her *Real House-wives* outfit: designer jeans, flowy boob shirt, and the fake diamond engagement ring she bought so people will think she's married to a rich guy. Andrew is a good-looking man a decade younger than my mom, with light brown hair and a fake tan. He seems shinier than most people, like he's been buffed and polished. I fade into the background as she gives him a pair of cheek kisses and he gushes more about how pretty she is. He turns his attention to me after a minute and says the obligatory look-how-beautiful-and-grown-up-your-daughter-is things, and then a hostess my age is leading us to a table in the middle of the room. The air-conditioning is strong, bringing goose bumps up on my arms. Andrew sits to my left, and my mom sits to my right. When the waitress comes, I order an iced tea and pray they bring the bread soon; I'm starving.

A small votive candle sits in the middle of the table. I find myself transfixed by the dancing flame, and I reach out and dip my fingertip in the melted wax. I bring it to my nose and sniff. Vanilla. As my mom and Andrew chat, I make a little wax finger glove, then melt it in the flame. The fire bites at my skin. I like the little stings of heat.

With our food ordered and cocktails in front of my mom and Andrew, they exchange a meaningful look. Andrew says, "Let's toast. To the two of you." He lifts his glass.

My mom beams and clinks her wineglass against his tumbler. I'm not sure what we're toasting.

Andrew says, "Do you want me to tell her? Or do you?"

She grins and says, "You tell her."

"Tell me what?" I ask, suspicious.

He says, "So, as you know, your mother has been doing work for Sunbrella for years."

Of course I know what he's talking about. My mom never

shuts up when she lands a modeling job, and she's been getting steady work from Sunbrella for two years. They always take pictures of her sitting on decks drinking things out of tall glasses.

"Yes. I am aware," I reply.

"And you know your mom is the most beautiful woman on my list."

"Stop it," she protests, but she loves it.

"She doesn't look a day over thirty," he continues.

She bats her eyelashes. "Okay, fine, go on."

This whole conversation is making me want to crawl inside my own skin and die. I pull the candle closer to me and stick my fingertip into the wax again.

"So anyway," Andrew says. "Your mom's success with Sunbrella has drawn the interest of Inner You, an interior design company in La Jolla."

"Very upscale," my mom interjects.

"But what they want is a mother-daughter shoot. They had a list of girls in mind to cast your mom with, but we showed them your picture, and they were so jazzed about the idea of an actual mother-daughter team that they ate it up on the spot. Picture this." He holds his hands up like he's visualizing the advertisement. "Poolside. Two California girls enjoying their infinity pool. I'm thinking a boho-inspired string bikini on Mick, and something with a deep V on Mom." He grins like this is the best news he's ever delivered.

I freeze. Inside and out, I am frozen. The fire chomps on my finger; I've let it drift right into the flame. I yank it back, knocking the candle over.

"Are you kidding me?" I say, shaking my hand out. I look at my mom. Her face tells me she is not kidding. "This has to be a joke, though. Because you know there is nothing on earth that is getting me into a bikini and in front of a camera."

The waiter arrives with a basket of bread. He sets it on the table with a stack of small plates. "How's everything?" he purrs. "We still doin' good over here? You need any refills?"

We stare at him in silence. At last, Andrew says, "We're fine."

"Mmmmkay." The waiter sees the candle, sideways in a puddle of hardening wax, and takes it away with him.

My mom takes a deep breath and blinks at me. This means she's trying to be patient because we're in public. "This is a paying job, Micaela."

"Mom, no." To Andrew, I say, "I can't do this. You don't understand. It's physically impossible for me to do this."

Andrew's tone is warm and comforting. "You don't have to worry about *anything*. These are professional photographers. They know how to make you look good. I promise, you're in excellent hands."

"You don't understand. This *isn't me*."

He pats my hand. "Forget the boho bikini. We'll find something sporty, andro chic, maybe boy short bottoms or something with a racerback—"

"I'm not asking for the gay version," I snap, pulling my hand away, fighting the urge to flip the table and fling dishes at the walls. "I'm telling you *no*. I am an athlete. I don't train six days a week to prance around in an *andro bikini*, whatever the hell that is."

My mom's cheeks go bright pink under the spray tan and

foundation. She gets up and sets her napkin down by her plate, fake diamonds glittering. "Excuse us," she says to Andrew. She grabs my arm and lifts me from the chair. She's not strong enough to do it for real, but my other option is to go full UFC with her in the middle of the restaurant, so I grab my purse and let her pull me away.

In the bathroom hallway, she turns on me. I back up to the wall, purse clutched tight at my side, my heart pounding in my throat. She flicks her eyes over me, darts them left and right to make sure no one can hear us, and says, "You know we're having money problems."

We've talked about how she's been having a hard time finding modeling work to supplement her catering income. "I mean, yeah, but I've just been using the money I make life-guarding for everything."

"I'm too old to bartend as much as I used to. My modeling work is drying up. Your dad doesn't pay child support. This is not the time to take a moral stand."

"Mom, I'll take more catering jobs with you, every night if you want. But I can't do this."

"You're not understanding. We don't need a hundred bucks here or there. We need fast cash, and we need it now." Her eyes are so intense, I'm crawling with discomfort, but I can't look away. "You're going to do this job, and we're going to use the money to pay the rent for the next six months."

"But I'm not a model! How many times have you told me that? I'm terrible in front of the camera. I hate it. Mom, I hate it." *Hate* isn't a strong enough word. I loathe it, I dread it; it makes me want to dig a hole and bury myself alive.

"It doesn't matter! They'll get body shots. They don't even have to focus on your face."

"Oh God." I want to die. I press my hand to my mouth, my empty stomach roiling. I swallow hard and say, "There has to be another way. Please. I'm begging you."

She studies me with cold blue eyes. "We could pull rent money out of your savings account. You have thousands in there."

I'm shocked, winded. "That's *my* money. From *my* jobs that *I* work. It's for my club fees and suits and travel fees for meets and—and—" Without that money, I can't stay on the club team, and just doing school swim team isn't enough to get the scholarship I need.

She brushes her hair behind her shoulders. She's regal with self-righteousness. "Then do the photo shoot."

I stare at her, emotions pounding inside my head, coming at me from different angles. Betrayal—grief—loneliness. I'm already the only kid on the team who has to pay her own fees and expenses, which I've never minded. We can't all be born wealthy, and it's not my mom's fault my dad has been MIA for the last ten years. But now she wants me to help her pay the rent?

Her face is deadly calm. "We'll talk more later. Right now, I want you to go to the bathroom, fix your face, fix your atti-tude, then come back to the table and be nice to Andrew." She spins and click-clacks out into the restaurant.

I can hear the waiters' muffled voices in the server station around the corner, talking about table numbers and drink orders. Dishes clang and clash in the kitchen at the end of the hallway. The white noise makes me feel invisible, like a ghost haunting the restaurant. I feel that way a lot, like I could scream and no one would hear a thing.

My phone buzzes in my purse. It startles me. With numb, shaking hands, I pull it out.

Liz's name lights up the screen along with the words *You almost done? We're all waiting for you.*

She knows I'm at dinner with my mom. What does she expect me to do? I imagine my mom's anger if I took off. Do I care?

The image of me on a pool deck surrounded by cameras, trotting around obediently in a bikini while my mom and Andrew simper with glee, makes me *want* to piss my mom off.

To Liz, I type, *Come get me.*

CHAPTER THREE

◇◇◇

VERONICA

THE FIRST NIGHT I MET HER WAS THE FIRST TIME I took her photograph.

The living room was crowded and noisy. I was curled up with my back against the wall and my knees to my chest, fidgeting with the aperture ring on my Nikon. The house cat, my new best friend, was sitting in the little cave under my knees. It was Saturday at Ricky's house, and the night had only just begun. The house would be full of drunk almost-seniors by the stroke of midnight. Eventually, I'd probably photograph them piled on top of each other like bodies on a battlefield.

The crowd around the TV roared; someone had done something in the video game that was either good or bad. I raised the camera to my left eye, squinted my right eye shut, and twisted the focusing ring until the backs of the upraised fists resolved into sharp contrast against the white of the TV screen.

Click. An image was forever burned into film. My thumb twisted the film winder, and I lowered the camera.

I don't understand digital photographers. When you're confining photos to negatives and each shot costs money and can't be undone, you're a lot more careful with the pictures you take. I love how my camera makes me commit to every shot.

My phone buzzed in my pocket, and I wrestled it out. It was Nico, calling instead of texting. Weird.

"Hello?"

"Hello, wife." His voice was tinny, like he was on speakerphone.

"Where are you? You were supposed to be done driving your stupid Uber an hour ago. I'm dying of boredom with these peasants." I wedged the phone between my ear and shoulder and lifted the camera to my eye again.

"I have to do an errand."

I sat straight up. "No! You're flaking on me? What kind of errand?"

"I have to pick up those buckets of blood from the butcher before he throws them out."

It took me a few seconds of blinking at my phone, and then I remembered what he was talking about—the blood was for this upcoming installation. "I'm getting ditched so you can drive a bunch of blood around? Wow. This is a new low for me."

He snickered, a sharp sound through the phone. "Do you want to come help? I have to mix it with corn syrup to make it stickier."

"Absolutely not." I heaved a sigh. "Fine. I'll just stay here alone and watch these guys play video games. Maybe I'll take some photos outside or something."

"Jesus, Veronica, enough with the abstracts." He was right. I needed something more interesting for my senior portfolio, and the summer was already half over. All this photographing palm trees wasn't going to get me into a good art school, and my grades were just okay. I needed a truly exceptional portfolio if I didn't want to end up in community college being taught by my mom, who is a ceramics professor at San Diego City College. The idea was cringingly awful.

The front door opened, letting in a cloud of smoke and the pungent smell of cheap weed. A pair of girls in matching Vans traded hugs with mismatched boys.

And then she stepped through the door, and for the first time that night, my hands fell away from my camera.

Which was ironic, because from that night on, I'd be desperate to take her picture.

CHAPTER FOUR

<small>◇◇◇</small>

MICK

IN THE BACK SEAT OF THIS RANDOM GIRL'S CAR, I'M still fuming at my mom, thinking about her threat to take the money from my savings account if I don't do her modeling shoot. How is it my responsibility to pay our rent? I hate her. I really do. I feel hatred for my own mother. My eyes prick with tears, and I stare out at the dark suburbs, blinking hard until they clear.

Liz pokes me hard in the ribs. I whip around. Silently, she mouths, *What's wrong?*

Nothing, I mouth back.

"Oh my gosh, look how cute!" The girl in the passenger's seat turns around to show us a GIF on her phone of a cat falling off a table.

Liz leans forward to watch it and cries, "Awww!"

They look at me. "What?" I ask. Was I supposed to say something?

"O—kay," the girl mutters. She turns around and faces

forward out the windshield. She lifts her phone up and opens the front camera, using it to check her makeup. Over her shoulder, I watch her purse her lips and tilt her head to the side. Her thumb goes for the Capture button; she's taking a selfie. I dive out of the way.

Liz nudges me. "What are you doing? Sit up."

"I don't want my picture taken," I snap, sharper than I mean to.

Liz glares at me, then says to the girl up front, "Hey, did I tell you about this guy who's going to be here tonight? He plays soccer at Bonita. So hot. I think you'd look cute together."

That gets her attention. She whips around, brown hair flying. "Wait, you didn't tell me this! What's his name?"

"Xavier. He's, like, six feet tall and has these gorgeous green eyes . . ."

We pull up to a two-story house that backs up to a hill. Liz and I follow her friends to the door. Pulsing music throbs from behind it, and I wrap my arms around my waist. Liz hisses, "Try to have fun. For once."

"I *am*." The door swings open, and the music roars around us.

It's hot and loud inside the house. The girls we came with get their vape pens out and enter the living room in a cloud. I follow behind, a meet-and-greet smile plastered to my face. My eyes rest on the stairs.

Always the stairs.

They stretch up, reaching to a world I've never known, a world where everyone has their own bathroom, where people have two parents who will wait at the bottom of the staircase on prom night. These are Christmas-morning stairs; first-date stairs; making-a-dramatic-entrance stairs.

A chorus of excitement howls around me. The girls have found their friends, a group of guys, and we're drawn into a vortex of beer and bodies. My fitted T-shirt suddenly feels too tight, the material plastered to my skin. I feel like everyone can see my body. I tug at the neckline, the hem. *Dude, chill. It's just a normal T-shirt.*

I stay close to Liz and survey the room: couples sprawled out on couches; boys laughing in front of the TV; groups on the patio deep in conversation, wreathed in smoke. My gaze lands on a dark-haired girl sitting alone on the floor, petting a tabby cat, her mouth drawn into a disgruntled pout. Doesn't she feel embarrassed? Doesn't she have that pressure in her brain telling her everyone is watching, that she needs to get up and act like a human? I ache with envy, and I wonder if she could be someone to talk to if Liz goes MIA.

Suddenly, the girl's eyes fix on mine. I've been caught staring. *Oh God.* I twist my lips into a grimace-smile. *Sorry,* I think. I force my eyes away from her and onto the pair of boys talking to Liz. Liz is laughing; from what I can hear of their conversation, she knows them from middle school.

I keep my eyes moving, afraid of accidentally staring at anyone again. When I let them roam past the girl with the cat, she waves at me. The pout is gone; her face is full of curiosity. Is she curious about *me?*

I raise my hand just a bit and wiggle my fingertips at her. She motions me forward.

A roar erupts from the crowd around the TV, and I jump, startled. Whatever game they're playing is a bloody one. Someone's avatar is laid out in what looks like a war zone, decapitated. One boy jumps up off the couch, controller in hand, and does a victory dance.

The girl raises a camera from her lap and puts it to her eye. It's old-fashioned, the kind with knobs and dials. I can hear the click from here as she takes the dancing guy's picture.

Cameras everywhere. The world is full of them. I feel weary, like I'm a thousand years old.

The girl lowers the camera and beckons me again, more aggressively this time.

I glance at Liz, but she's still talking to the guys. I steel myself for potential social humiliation and approach. She leans her head back on the wall to look up at me as I arrive in front of her. A curtain of black hair falls away from her face, revealing dark brown eyes with winged eyeliner.

"Hey," she says.

I am tongue-tied. She's beautiful in an artsy, vintage sort of way, a fair-skinned Latina with glossy dark hair and full pink lips. Her jeans look intentionally worn out, like they were bought somewhere expensive. My jeans cost thirteen dollars at Ross. I wonder if she can tell. Her shirt is a V-neck, and I am *not* going to look at her cleavage.

Her eyes flick down to my hands, which I'm wringing so hard they're going numb. "You having a good night so far?" she asks.

I force myself to pull them apart. "Sorry. But do I know you from somewhere . . . ?"

"You don't know me. But I know your friends." She points to the guys Liz is talking to.

"They're not my friends." *I sound like a bitch.* "I mean—I don't know them. My best friend does."

"Oh good. Because they're assholes."

I laugh. "Wow. Okay."

"What? They are."

"You're not, like, worried I'm going to tell them you said that?"

She furrows her brows at me and then calls out, "Lucas. Lucas!" She waves a hand wildly until the guy talking to Liz looks over.

"What?" he yells.

"You know I think you're an asshole, right?" His friends laugh loudly.

"Fuck you, Veronica."

She blows him a kiss and looks at me deadpan. "There you go. He knows."

I'm stuck between awe and embarrassment.

She pats the floor next to her. "Come and meet my new cat friend, Perkins. Help me find things to take pictures of. I'm so bored."

I search for Liz over my shoulder. She catches my eye, waves at me, and returns to her conversation.

I guess that's her giving me permission. I lower myself onto the floor. The cat shoots me a suspicious glare from its little cave beneath her knees.

She smiles at me. "I'm Veronica."

"I'm Mick."

"Like Mick Jagger?"

"It's short for Micaela."

Her smile gives her a pretty dimple in her left cheek. "Can I call you Jagger?"

I can't help but smile back. "Sure."

"Where are you from, Jagger? I'm assuming you don't go to Bonita. I'd have noticed you."

"National City." I wait for her to make a face or a joke, but she just nods like this is normal and interesting.

"What brings you to Bonita? Do you know people here? Besides the assholes?"

"I came with . . ." I try to point out the girls who drove us here, but I've lost them. "I don't know where they went. Some girls Liz met."

She's got her head cocked and is studying me clinically. "You have interesting bone structure. It's unique. Your cheek-bones are exactly even with the bridge of your nose."

Before I can come up with a response to that, she raises the camera. Reflexively, I duck, lifting my hands to cover my face.

She lowers the camera. "Whoa, dude, you act like I pointed a shotgun at you."

My chest feels tight. "I hate having my picture taken."

She pushes the hair out of her eyes. "How much do you want to bet I can take a good photo of you?"

"No, no, no." I push myself off the ground. "I should get back to Liz."

She grabs my hand. "Whoa, whoa, I'm sorry. I didn't realize you hated it *that* much. I won't take your picture, I promise."

I look down at her hand on mine. My nails are short, always

flimsy and dull from the chlorine in the pool. Her hand is elegant, artistic. She moves her knees aside to reveal the cat's head. "Give Perkins a little pet. She's feeling shy tonight. Maybe you have that in common."

I reach out to the tabby. Perkins has decided I'm not a monster and rubs her forehead on my knuckles.

"Petting animals is therapeutic," Veronica says. "They've studied it."

It's true that I feel calmer. I've always wanted a cat. I sneak a look at Veronica. "What kind of camera is that?"

"It's a vintage Nikon. It was my dad's. You want to hold it?" She pulls the strap over her head and hands it to me. I accept it cautiously, and she's right, I kind of do regard it as a weapon. "It's heavier than I expected." I turn it in my hands to study it.

"This is the aperture, the focus . . . This is the shutter, you know, where you take the picture." She points out each part as she names it.

I lift the camera to my eye and look through the tiny window. Inside the rectangle, Liz and the guys are laughing hard about something. Liz's eyes are alive with excitement.

Veronica says, "Go ahead and take a photo."

"Are you sure? It's going to be blurry."

"Can't be worse than the shit I've been wasting my film on all night."

I play with the focus dial, feeling like a professional, and take the picture with a satisfying snap. Veronica shows me how to advance the film with my thumb, which has an interesting clickety sensation.

I like the feeling of control that comes with being on this side of the camera. I should torture Liz for a change, or, even better, my mom. I should take subversive unflattering photos of them, post the pictures on the internet, and say what they always say to me: "I don't know why you're being so *sensitive*."

I hand the camera back to her. "Thanks."

She loops the strap over her neck like she's done it a million times. "You want to walk down to 7-Eleven and get something to eat? This is boring, right?"

I don't know Veronica, but I want to escape from this house. And if I'm being honest, she's different, and cute. I want to talk to her alone.

Liz is drinking a beer and looks happier with me off her hands. Besides, I'm starving.

I smile at Veronica. "Okay. Sure. Why not?"

CHAPTER FIVE

◇◇◇

VERONICA

THE STUCCO FACADES OF THE SPANISH-STYLE HOUSES glimmered in the streetlights. The palm trees tossed in a breeze too high to touch us. The warm air smelled like the desert, a hot summer smell. We walked in silence at first, her hands clenched by her sides. Everything about her felt anxious and tight, like I was making her uncomfortable just by being there.

"So you're sporty," I said, trying to get her talking again. "What do you play?"

She looked surprised. "How do you know that?"

Because you have great shoulder muscles. "I'm psychic."

"Wait, really?"

I shoved her lightly. Yup. Great shoulder muscles. "It's just a vibe, silly. You look sporty, I dunno."

"Well, you're right. I'm a swimmer."

"Cool." Why did I intro with this? There was literally nothing in the world I knew less about than sports. I may as well have asked her about astrophysics.

More silence. My brain decided nervous chatter was the solution. "I'm not a great swimmer. And I won't go in the ocean past my waist."

"Really? Why?"

I hummed the *Jaws* theme song. She looked mystified, so I said, "*Jaws*? Have you never seen that movie?"

"No. I mean, it's really old."

"Dude, it is still so scary. You have to watch it sometime."

We reached the corner, and I pointed left. "The 7-Eleven is down there, by the stoplight."

I held my camera to my chest to keep it from bumping as we walked. She retreated into a moody silence, her brows drawn together. Her shadow flickered tall and short between the streetlights, looming beside us. It was one of those strange highlighted moments you get sometimes, where the whole day—sleeping late, working in my darkroom, wasting hours on Instagram—blends together into one high-speed, blurry memory reel, stopping short at this frozen, hi-res moment. Like a living photograph.

Then it slipped away, and I was just walking down a suburban sidewalk a few paces behind a pretty girl who looked more distressed than the situation warranted.

I reached for her arm and said, "Hey. Stop. Hang on."

She turned to me. "What is it?"

It was the first time I got to see her face straight on, and her features were sharper than I'd imagined. I wanted to put my finger into the groove between her pointy upper lip and her thin, high-bridged nose. Her brows were straight, a natural scowl.

And I forgot what I was going to say. I fumbled for words. "I'm glad you showed up tonight. I'm always alone at those things if my friend Nico doesn't come."

She smiled a little sadly. "I'm always alone too, just tagging along with Liz. It feels so good to be outside. Like we escaped from prison."

She was right; it did feel like that. What was pulling us back to the party, anyway?

Inspiration struck. "What time do you need to be home?"

She shrugged. "My mom doesn't really care. And we're in a fight."

"Perfect. Do you want to go have an adventure?"

"What do you mean?"

"I don't know, maybe go downtown, to the Gaslamp Quarter?"

A little smile crept across her face. "Can we still get a snack first?"

I laughed. "Of course. First food, then adventure."

"Oh thank God. I'm starving." The words tumbled out of her, and for the first time, she didn't look shy or avoid my eyes. The snap of personality crackled, sweet and warm. My hands crept toward my camera, but I held them back. If I wanted a photo, I'd have to earn it.

That was fine with me. I loved a challenge.

* * *

The Uber smelled so strongly of cherry air freshener, I was sure we were going to asphyxiate. I rolled down the window an inch, letting in a hissing snake of wind that ruffled my hair into my eyes. Outside, the freeway flowed past, smooth in a stream of lights. My camera bag nestled tightly against my leg. I always carried it instead of a purse, but I never kept my camera in it. That went around my neck.

"You girls warm enough back there?" the driver, a balding man, asked over the seats.

"We're fine, thanks," I replied. "Are you using Google Maps or Apple Maps or Waze or what?"

He shot me a surprised look in the rearview mirror. "Google Maps."

I pulled up Google Maps and started tracking his route, making sure he wasn't a serial killer taking us somewhere off-grid. Mick was glowering at her phone, thumbs flying across the screen.

"Everything okay, Jagger?"

"Liz is mad that I left." Her thumbs jab-jabbed and she hit Send.

"She doesn't feel unsafe, does she?" I'd thought Liz had plenty of female friends to back her up, but maybe I'd misread the situation.

"Oh, nothing like that." She lifted her eyes from the screen. It lit her face up from the bottom, giving her a spectral look. "I guess she . . . It's complicated. She likes me to be there, but she wants me to be . . . different. More fun. Less shy." She slipped her phone into the small blue purse resting on her lap, and I felt angry with this Liz I didn't even know.

Her purse buzzed. We both snapped our eyes to it. "Do you want to answer it?" I asked.

"I think I'll talk to her tomorrow at swim practice. It's always better to let her cool down."

I remembered my ex, a hot-tempered girl named Brianna who got pissed off every time I stopped shadowing her like a puppy dog. Obviously it didn't last; I'm not an easy person to keep on a leash.

Mick relaxed back into the seat, stretching her legs out in front of her and folding her hands behind her head. I could see the line dividing her abdominal muscles through her T-shirt, which made me dizzy. Oblivious, she said, "Forget about my friend drama. Tell me about you. You go to Bonita, you like to take photos, and you're scared of sharks. What else?"

It was like having the camera suddenly turned on me. I couldn't think of a single thing about myself, not with her freaking ab muscles visible through her freaking shirt. I looked up at the roof and tried to collect myself. What did I like? I had to like something, for God's sake. Inspiration struck. "I like old movies," I cried, relieved. I sounded like a kid who'd figured out the answer to a math problem in class.

"Oh yeah? Any in particular?"

Eyes still on the roof, I said, "My favorite right now is *Pulp Fiction*."

"What's your favorite movie of all time?"

"*Vertigo*," I said without hesitation.

"I've never heard of it."

"I'll show it to you if you want." It was a really premature invitation, and I regretted it instantly. *Earn it*, I reminded myself.

The driver dropped us off unmurdered at the northwest end of the Gaslamp Quarter, a historic section of downtown San Diego full of bars and shops. It's always packed with college students laughing drunkenly and high school kids trying to blend in with them.

On the corner of Fifth and E Street, jammed into a crowd of people waiting for the light, we looked at each other.

"So," I said.

She pressed her lips into a smile. "So."

The light changed, but before we could step into the crosswalk, a herd of middle-aged tourists on Segways whizzed past against traffic.

"That's eight points," I said, already lifting my camera to my eye and capturing the shot. I wasn't sure if it would come out; the lighting was iffy at best.

"What're the points for?" Mick asked.

"I have a rating system for tourist nonsense; it's a scale of one through ten. Groups on Segways are an eight."

"What's a ten?"

"A ten has never yet been achieved." We reached Market Street.

The lighting shone down on her face just right, a golden glow that smoothed her tanned skin into velvet. I almost turned the camera on her, but then I remembered her photo phobia. "Mick, can I ask you something? I'm not trying to be nosy. Just tell me to shut up if you don't want to talk about it."

"Sure."

"What's up with you and pictures?"

She opened and closed her mouth and then said, "My

mom's a model. Like, she's been modeling since she was a teenager."

Interesting.

She took a deep breath that sounded shaky and said, "I think it's like a phobia. It's gotten to the point where when someone points a camera at me, I'm literally afraid." She put a hand to her chest. "Like, I can feel my heart pounding just thinking about it." In a quiet voice, she said, "I can't even go to Disneyland without worrying about those stupid pictures they take on Splash Mountain and Space Mountain."

I wasn't sure what the right response to this was, so I said, "I'm sorry. That really sucks."

"Thanks."

"Do you think . . ." I was afraid to say this, but it was an idea that had been nagging at me. "What if no one ever looked at the photo? Like, what if I took your picture with my camera, but there was no film in it? Maybe that could be a first step. Forget how you look in the pictures, just get used to having the camera on you."

She blinked, hard and fast. "Maybe. I see what you're saying."

My camera still had a few shots left, but what she didn't know wouldn't hurt her. "This roll of film is out. Do you want to try it?"

"For real?"

"Sure." I felt a tiny pinch of guilt. A very, very small pinch.

Her cheeks were red. "You wouldn't mind? What if I had a panic attack? Oh God, what if I cried?"

"I'll just chill out while you hyperventilate. You know how they put someone with a fear of snakes in a room full of snakes? I learned about it in psychology." I racked my brain, and then the words came to me. "Exposure therapy. It's supposed to help."

"You really want to? You don't mind?"

I was *dying* to take her picture. Cool as a cucumber, I said, "I have nothing better to do tonight. I'm all yours."

She took a deep breath. "Okay. Let's do it."

"Yes!" I turned the camera toward her and twisted the focus dial.

"No!" she cried. "Not like that."

"Not with the camera? That's usually how I do it."

"No, I mean, not in front of all these people."

It was Saturday night; the Gaslamp was wall-to-wall flesh. I wasn't sure about the logistics of achieving total privacy, but I am nothing if not stubborn once I've decided to do something. I nodded, decisive. "All right. We'll find a quiet spot to take your fake picture. It's our new mission. We will stop at nothing."

The grin I was starting to like a lot flashed across her face. "Thank you."

I touched the side of her arm lightly, enough to feel the soft, warm skin. *Wait. Is she . . . ?* This did not feel like a straight-girl hug.

And then she pulled away, leaving me with a chest full of air.

I liked her.

We searched the streets, peeking between storefronts, hoping for alleyways, and then the train station emerged in front of us and I knew I had found the right place. I dragged her toward it.

"Are we going into the station?" she asked, keeping up with me easily.

"You'll see."

Inside, the arched, Spanish-tiled walls swooped above us, warm lighting filtering down from the rafters where pigeons snuggled in downy piles. Lost-looking people clustered in front of information windows and ticket machines, and locals sprawled out in the chairs, ignoring the homeless people camped out in neighboring seats.

"See?" I said, gesturing to the beautiful interior. "It's a great spot for photos."

She looked around and said, "There are people everywhere."

We might end up taking these photos in the bathroom. My eyes landed on the flashing time display. The northbound Amtrak Surfliner was due to leave in seven minutes.

"Come on." I took her by the hand and pulled her toward the ticket machines.

"What are you doing?"

"You'll see." I jabbed numbers into the screen and fumbled my credit card out of my wallet.

"Are you buying a ticket?"

"Quiet, woman." I took the tickets from the machine. "Come on!"

"Two tickets?" she cried. "Where are we going?"

"Shhh!" I grabbed her hand and guided her out onto the platform.

She laughed, breathless. "Where are you taking me? Why do I feel like I'm being kidnapped?"

My eyes darted around, and I found track three. Giggling

madly, I pushed her toward the Amtrak train waiting there. *Surfliner* was printed in italicized blue letters along its side.

"Veronica?" she asked. "Help me understand."

"I guarantee you this train will be almost empty at this time of night. It leaves in two minutes. We can get off at the next stop and catch an Uber."

A slow smile crept across her face. "I do like trains."

"All aboard," I said with mock solemnity as the announcer's voice boomed over the loudspeaker, "Last call for northbound Surfliner, track three."

She led the way up the three stairs onto the train, and we jumped inside. I followed her through the rows of seats in the empty carriage.

The train lurched. We stumbled. I almost knocked right into her, but I grabbed on to the back of a seat and planted my feet. The train started forward, taking us north and beyond.

She turned to face me. "You know what?"

"What?"

"I don't want to get off at the next stop. I want to keep going." She almost lost her balance, took a half step back, and steadied herself.

"Oh yeah? Where do you want to go?"

"I don't care. I just don't want tonight to end."

I did a quick check to confirm the train was empty. It was. We were alone. Reckless, dizzy, I reached up and touched her face. I trailed my fingertips across her cheek and along the groove above her upper lip.

She looked frozen with surprise. I pulled my hand away. "Is that not okay? I'll stop."

"Don't." She took my hand and returned it to her cheek. I ran my fingers past her ear, trailing through the golden-tawny strands of hair. My heart pounded hard, out of sync with the rhythm of the train. Her eyes were full of questions. I stepped forward slowly, afraid of falling, giving her time to pull away and run screaming. Instead, she leaned in and brushed her lips against mine.

I couldn't breathe for a moment, and then I kissed her back. I wrapped my arm around her waist, and my camera dug into our chests. Her lips were soft and sweet. I could have kissed her all night, stayed there on that train, past oceans and mountains, never worrying about a destination.

Instead, I pulled back. Her eyes followed me, her hands reaching like I was stealing something from her.

And I did.

I lifted the camera, and I took her picture.

That was it. That was the beginning.

CHAPTER SIX

<><><>

VERONICA

THREE DOTS HUNG IN SPACE. STANDING IN THE middle of my room in the late afternoon sunshine, hopping impatiently from foot to foot, I reread the text I'd sent Mick: *Want to come with me to my friend's art show tonight?*

Should I have waited a few days? Suddenly, I was not sure texting her the very next day after a first kiss was a good idea. Was I being overeager? Pathetic? Pushy?

The dots resolved into a single, glorious word. *Sure.*

"Yes!" I shouted. She wanted to see me again.

I took a deep breath and returned her text. *My friend Nico is picking me up in a little while, and then we can come get you.*

Cool. I'll send you my location.

I had some time, so I headed for the door in the corner of my room. I had the master because my mom knew I needed an en suite bathroom to turn into a darkroom, and because she was a wonderful lady who maybe spoiled me a little, which I encouraged. I opened the door, pushed aside a heavy black curtain, pulled the door shut behind me, and flicked on the wall switch. The room was bathed in a dark, red-orange glow.

I queued up my playlist that had songs from my favorite old movies and returned my phone to my pocket. "Girl . . . dum-dum-dum-dummmmm, you'll be a woman soon . . . ," I sang along with my Bluetooth speaker as I got to work developing last night's roll of film. The red safelight transformed my bathroom-turned-darkroom into a tiny nightclub, and I danced around to the *Pulp Fiction* soundtrack while I waited for the timer to tell me the film could come out of the chemicals.

Loud knocking on the door snapped me out of my loner karaoke session. "Who is it?" I yelled.

"It's me, pretty girl," cooed a familiar voice.

Nico.

"Come in. But be careful with the curtain! I'm developing film."

He slipped in gracefully, first through the door and then through the heavy blackout curtain so no light entered with him. The timer dinged, and I hurried to get my film out of the developer. Nico leaned his tall, fluid frame on the counter at my elbow, arms crossed over the stomach of his Queen T-shirt. "What's up, wife?"

I took a second to wrap an arm around his narrow waist in a half hug. "Just burning pictures, husband."

He kissed my cheek, his chin scratchy. "I finished the chicken. I brought it to show you. I want to see your reaction."

"Oh cool!" I was excited to see this. It was a new 3-D technique he'd been trying to perfect. He'd been very mysterious about it. All I knew was that he was working on a photo-realistic chicken sculpture.

"Come see it." He tried to drag me toward the door.

I pulled my hand away. "Give me a few. I want to finish something. Feel free to grab something to eat if you're hungry."

"Your mom already fed me and gave me a bag of leftovers to take home."

"Good."

Nico had been living on his own for the last two years, since he was seventeen and a half, but my mom never really adjusted to him being an adult and fed him at every opportunity. I liked it, actually. Nico had never had anyone to care for him, not really, and my mom was one of those people with enough love to spread around.

He hummed along to the music as I cut the film into strips and slipped them into a sheet of negative sleeves, aware that he was watching me. He had a way of giving you his undivided attention that made you feel intensely scrutinized. Girls loved it.

I scanned through the rows of negatives, holding them up so I could see them against the red safelight. I really wanted to find that photo of Mick.

There she was, tiny but real, her irises ghostly white in the negative. The focus looked good as far as I could tell, but I wouldn't be sure until I enlarged it. I took the negative strip and clipped it into the secondhand enlarger my mom had bought from a photography professor at the city college. I zoomed in, framing the image until I was happy with the composition. I couldn't believe I'd gotten this much clarity on such a quick, candid shot.

Nico peered over my shoulder. "Hellooooo," he said, eyes on Mick's face, pretty even in negative.

I shoved him off. "Not for you." I gently removed a piece of photo paper from its package and positioned it under the enlarger, then timed the exposure and slipped the paper into the tray of developer fluid. I twisted the dial on the kitchen timer and waited, watching the image materialize. Wow. This was even better than I'd expected. Mick was set against rows of seats that blurred into infinity behind her, adding a beautiful depth of field and a feeling of movement to the image.

The kitchen timer went off with a ding. I used the tongs to pull the paper out of the developer, shake off the drips, and slip it into the fixer. Nico and I leaned in to get a good look as I pulled the photo out of the fixer and slid it into the stop bath.

The photo was incredible. Mick's expression was half shocked, half searching, lips parted, eyes huge. My chest swelled with pride as I realized—I'd kissed her. I'd given her that expression. Me.

"Who is she?" he asked.

"A girl I met yesterday at that party you flaked on. Thanks for working late. Turns out you did me a solid. Oh, actually, I told her she could come with us to your launch party tonight. Do you mind?"

He narrowed his eyes at me. "Actually, I do mind. Do you want to get us in trouble?"

"Why are you so paranoid? There will be hundreds of people there. What's one more?"

"I don't want to go to prison just so you can impress some girl you're trying to—"

"Would you knock it off? You're such a grandma!"

We glared at each other.

He said, "Act like this is some other friend's work. Don't tell her it's me. And don't get any ideas about bringing her to the installs just so you can show off."

"I didn't want to bring her to those anyway—whatever they are." There were four installs in this series, but he liked to tell me about them one at a time. He said the element of surprise made my photos better.

He gave in. "Fine. Now come look at my chicken."

"In a minute." I pulled out another piece of photo paper and started printing a different version of this photo. I wanted less contrast on her face, more on the seats behind her.

Nico became a distant memory as I messed with the photo, first upping the contrast, then dodging and burning. No print was quite right. I heaved a sigh of frustration, clipped this last one to the wire, and started a new one. I was more careful with her eyes this time. I needed one more chance to get it right. I couldn't tell if—

"Veronica. Veronica!"

Nico was standing beside me, a warm palm on my shoulder. "You don't think you have enough? You're usually so stingy with your supplies. And we have to go soon."

I blinked, feeling like I'd just awakened from a nap. I turned and looked at my workstation.

Ten prints were clipped to the line. I didn't remember making ten.

I looked down at the counters, where the trays full of chemicals were usually lined up neatly. Now they were askew, puddles of developer and fixer splashed carelessly across the granite.

I stood in front of the row of photos. Mick's ten sets of lips glimmered, wet and soft-looking in the red safelight.

Nico came to stand next to me. "That one." He pointed to the middle one, the one I'd manipulated with dodging and burning to set her eyes into deeper shadow. It gave her a haunted beauty. She looked otherworldly.

I pulled the print off the line and followed Nico out into my bedroom. I held the photo at arm's length in the soft evening light that streamed through my window.

"Jesus," Nico said. His eyes were fixed hungrily on Mick's face.

"Ew, stop."

"No, not like that! I'm saying Jesus about your skills, girl. Fuck nature photography. You should be doing portraits. Look at this!"

I flushed. Nico was the most talented person I knew, although I'd never have admitted it to his face. "Thanks."

A smile spread across his face. He was reading my mind. "You're welcome."

As I set the photo on my desk, my eyes landed on a large silver object on my bed. "Is that the chicken?"

"Yes!" He leaped to the bed and hefted the object. It was a chicken-sized silver sculpture. He handed it to me and I almost dropped it. It must have weighed twenty pounds at least.

"What is this made out of? Solid steel?" I tried to get a better look without dropping it. It was impressive, definitely photorealistic. I could see every detail of every feather. As I admired the realism, something dawned on me. "Did you cast this using a real chicken, Nico?"

He cackled. "Yup! I got one from a family down the street from the warehouse. They have a little farm in their backyard. The mom showed me how to kill it."

"Oh, gross!" I cried, dropping the thing onto the bed. Now that I knew he'd used a dead chicken, I noticed its pose: limp-necked with toes sort of dangling and eyes half shut.

He gave me a condescending look. "It was much more humane than industrial farming. People all over the world slaughter their own animals. Anyway." He plopped down next to the chicken and picked it up. "I used a new technique to pour in the molten steel, but yeah, I did a plaster cast of the chicken." He grinned at me, waiting to be praised.

"Everything you're saying is the worst thing I have ever heard," I told him. "Like, I'm on the verge of stealing your DNA and sending it to the FBI. What the fuck is actually wrong with you?"

He cracked up, laughing so hard he fell back onto the bed. "I knew you would hate it," he gasped.

"It's disgusting!" I cried, smacking his leg. "You're so creepy!"

"It's just a chicken! You ate chicken with me yesterday."

"That's different from using a dead chicken to create this

serial killer art project! You're like those weirdos who taxi-dermy roadkill!"

He curled into the fetal position, laughing and crying and holding his stomach. I said, "Don't even think about bringing that thing with us tonight. Worst conversation starter ever."

"But, darling, I made it as a gift for you."

"I don't want it! Get it out of here!"

His laughter rose an octave, and he almost fell off the bed rolling around, emitting a loud snorting sound that made me giggle along.

He sat up, wiping his eyes. "Can I take a shower and get ready here?"

"Of course. Go ahead." His living arrangements did not include a shower, so it was my house or the gym.

He grabbed his backpack and let himself out. I picked up the photo of Mick and considered what I was going to do. I had to show it to her. It was too good not to.

She was going to be pissed that I'd taken her photo without telling her. Maybe I could lie and pretend I didn't know there was film in the camera? That didn't feel right.

No. I'd tell her the truth.

I imported the print into my iMac and uploaded it to Photoshop. I killed a few glares in her eyes and upped the highlights on her cheeks and hair. Then I exported the photo to PNG and messaged it to myself.

I opened the photo on my phone and looked at her face.

Wow.

If a photographer saw her, they'd immediately think *high*

fashion. Her sharp cheekbones were prominent, her brows straight and strong. The geometry of her bones set against the softness of her skin and wispy brown-blond hair was breathtaking. She was living, breath art.

I remembered how self-conscious she was. Maybe this photo could be a gift for her, something she could hold on to and refer back to, like an anchor to remind her that she was beautiful.

There was still a chance she'd be mad at me. But I didn't have a choice.

The photo already had its hooks in me.

CHAPTER SEVEN

⋄⋄⋄

MICK

A GRAY SEDAN WITH AN UBER STICKER ON THE windshield pulls up to the curb in front of the public pool. I'm not sure it's Veronica until she rolls down the passenger's side window. Her eyes are hidden behind large cat-eye sunglasses. "Hey, miss. You want a ride?"

"I'm not supposed to take rides from strangers." The words sound flirtatious and bolder than anything I'd normally say.

She grins. "Get in, Jagger."

I let myself into the coconut-scented interior and pull the door shut behind me. Veronica says, "This is Nico. Nico, this is Mick. Don't be weird around her."

Nico is a tall, lanky guy a little older than us. He's handsome, with olive skin and a shock of dark hair that flops over one of his eyes. He turns to look at me, a brief but intense scan that makes my cheeks hot. "Hi, Mick."

"Hi," I reply shyly.

To Veronica, he says, "She's too good for you. I can already tell."

"I will cut your face off."

He hisses out a little mocking laugh, and she smacks his deltoid. The way they are with each other reminds me of siblings.

I busy myself putting on my seat belt, and then I remember my manners. "Thank you for picking me up."

"No problem." He pulls out onto the street.

"What are you doing in La Mesa?" Veronica asks me.

"I just got off work. I lifeguard at a few different public pools."

"Nice," Nico says, and Veronica hits him again.

"So tell me about this art show," I say, to get the conversation off me.

Veronica says, "It's the opening of an exhibit by a group of installation artists. It should be super weird."

"*Eclectic*," Nico corrects her. "Avant-garde. Experimental."

Veronica rolls her eyes at me. "The main artist suffers from delusions of grandeur."

Nico snorts.

"Will it be . . . crowded?" I ask. "Like a party?"

"Yeah, but not like the party we were at. Much more fun."

Oh God. I shouldn't have come. I should have said no. I lace my fingers together and squeeze hard. The street is flying by out the window, headlights and lampposts and neon signs.

"Mick?" Veronica is turned around in her seat, face concerned. "You okay?"

Embarrassment. I force a smile that has to look like a grimace. "I'm fine. Thank you."

"I'm sorry. You hate parties. We can have Nico drop us off somewhere else."

"No you can't, you're taking pictures, remember?" Nico says. He looks at me in the rearview mirror. "You don't like parties, Mick?"

"I'm fine," I protest, my face hot.

"She hates them," Veronica says.

"It's fine, please, honestly," I say, desperate to get them talking about something else.

"I think hating parties is a sign of a healthy aversion to people," Nico muses, eyes on the road again.

"Truth," Veronica agrees. "People are terrible."

"That's why I married you." Nico reaches out and messes with Veronica's hair, and she ducks out from under his hand with a cry of protest.

"Wait," I say. "You're kidding, right? Married?"

Nico turns right onto a dark industrial street; we're east of downtown, in an area I don't know well.

Veronica grins over her shoulder. "No, we actually got married. In Vegas, by an Elvis impersonator, with Marilyn Monroe as my maid of honor, while my mom was out of town. It was magical."

Are they . . . are they a couple? Wait.

Like Nico is reading my mind, he says, "We're platonic. It was just something to do. We had a couple of fake IDs and wanted to do something more interesting with them than get drunk. Carpe diem and all that."

"We did also get drunk, though," Veronica says, and they laugh in unison.

Nico says, "You lost a hundred bucks on the slot machine in, like, five minutes! How is that even possible?"

"They manipulate you!" she cries. "It's like you enter a fugue state!"

I interrupt them. "But wait, did your parents ever find out?"

They glance at each other. "I live on my own," Nico says.

Veronica turns her body so she can sit sideways more comfortably. "I told my mom. I mean, she yelled at me about the dangers of driving to Las Vegas with all the drunk people. But we got married with fake IDs, so it's not legal or anything." She plays with my fingertips absentmindedly. It gives me chills. "I think I want a divorce," she murmurs.

"My heart is broken," Nico says.

"Whatever." To me, Veronica says, "So you're a lifeguard." She gives me a grin and a lecherous eyebrow wiggle. "I want to come watch you guard lives. Can I?"

I can't help but smile back. "You can watch me yell at children for peeing in the pool. I'm lifeguarding for a summer camp event tomorrow."

"Wait. Back up. I'm stuck on the pee in the pool."

"Urine is sterile," Nico says helpfully.

"And there's a *lot* of chlorine," I add, which only etches Veronica's comically exaggerated grimace deeper onto her face.

"We'll be there," Nico says.

"We?" Veronica wheels on him. "God, you're such a—"

"I want to go swimming!"

"Ugh." She folds her arms across her chest.

I laugh. "Nico can come."

"She says I can come," Nico tells Veronica, who replies, "I will smother you in your sleep."

I feel relaxed now, their banter a current on which I'm drifting. I smile out the window, and for once, my reflection looks happy.

And then I remember the fight with my mom, and the smile falls away. When I got home last night, she was asleep, and this morning I left for swim practice while she was still in her room. What am I going to tell her? I have no idea if she really is planning to empty out my savings account to get revenge for my not doing this modeling thing. If so, am I willing to throw all that money away just to make a point?

It's completely dark when we pull into a parking lot across from a giant abandoned warehouse. I hesitate outside the car, not sure what kind of art show or party might be happening in a neighborhood like this. Even the streetlights are scary, flickering like they're about to go out. Somewhere far away, sirens wail, echoing and then dying.

Veronica slams her door and turns to me. She's wearing a tight black tank top, high-waisted jeans, and her camera around her neck. She points across the narrow, poorly lit street to the warehouse. "That's where the show is."

I don't want to sound negative, but . . . "I don't get it. It looks abandoned."

"You'll see."

Nico waves at us. "You coming? Or did you want to stay out here and see if someone comes along to murder you?" To Veronica, he says, "Don't get distracted and forget to take pictures."

"I won't." She shows him her camera, clearly annoyed.

He pulls a bandanna out of his back pocket and ties it across his face, hiding his nose and mouth. Veronica takes my arm and leads me across the street.

I hesitate. She shoots me a questioning look, and I whisper, "Why did he cover his face?"

She smiles, waves it off, and pulls me along without answering. I feel like there's some secret I'm not a part of, and it makes me even more nervous.

Nico knocks on a corrugated metal door that appears to have been rusted shut since before I was born. With great difficulty, it slides partway open, and a large man with long, stringy blond hair peers out. This man also wears a bandanna over the lower part of his face. A shaggy beard pokes out the bottom.

"To the ends of the earth and back," Nico tells him, the words muffled through the bandanna.

These words must be a code, because the door opens all the way, squealing in protest. A wave of electronic music hits me, and the man ushers us in and closes the door behind us with a massive screech. Once we're inside, Nico claps palms with him, a gesture of greeting, and Veronica lifts her camera to take a picture of the interior.

The warehouse has been transformed into a man-made forest, with a cloud of dry ice fog hovering over rolling, mossy earth. Trees are scattered around organically. It's lit with black light, and everyone is a shadowy blue-and-black silhouette. Dance music pounds from unseen speakers.

I stand shocked. I can't believe what I'm seeing. I feel like I've stepped into an alternate dimension.

"It's an urban forest!" Veronica yells over the music. "They stole all of this."

"They *stole* it? The trees? The rocks?"

She nods. Her eyes are wide and excited.

"How do you steal a tree?"

"Developers have been destroying this wildlife sanctuary, just leveling everything, so these artists stole the trees before they were demoed." She slips her hand into mine. It's warm and soft.

"So why are you, like, the designated photographer?"

"Oh." She hesitates. "Nico's a fan of these artists. I said I'd document this for him." I feel like she's hiding something, but we don't know each other well enough for me to dig deeper.

We walk around, Veronica stopping to take photos. Some of the trees have fake flowers and fruit hanging from the branches, larger-than-life apples and lemons and oranges. Hundreds of people mingle around, dancing, smoking, drinking, making out. One group brought picnic blankets and is eating pizza while the music booms all around us.

The trees creep me out. I feel like they're watching me. It's sad, actually, this transplanted nature, these trees dying slowly in this forgotten warehouse. I tell Veronica, "I thought we were going to an art show. Are there sculptures or something in here?"

"It's an installation. The forest *is* the artwork. They do what they call *disruptive installation art*. They're super pretentious about it, but their work is actually really cool. They always do something with vandalism."

"Who is *they*?"

A dark shadow bursts from the tree behind Veronica. Arms reach out and grab her. She screams. A hand claps to her mouth. I jump back, a scream clenched between my teeth. The hand drops from her mouth, and the shadow steps out from behind her. It's Nico, laughing, white teeth gleaming in the black light. "Are you taking pictures? Or are you flirting with your pretty lifeguard?"

"Jesus, you dick, what the hell?" she cries, punching him in the stomach. My heart pounds, and I press a hand to my chest.

He cackles. "You're so easy. It's not even fun." To me, he says, "What do you think, now that you've had a chance to look around?"

Heart still beating ferociously, I say, "Honestly? The trees make me sad."

He cocks his head. "Interesting!" He steps closer to me. "The congressman who's allowing them to destroy this wildlife sanctuary—have you heard of him? Greg Osgood?"

"I don't really follow politics."

"He's a piece of shit. He—"

Veronica interrupts him. "Go away! Unless you want me to take pictures of your face right now."

He covers his face with his hands. From behind them, he says, "Don't forget to get shots of Lily. She's doing a piece on the back wall."

"Fine! Go!" Veronica shoves at him. He gives me one last searching look, like he's trying to read my mind, and then he vanishes into the shadows. "Come on, let's just do this before he comes back," she says.

We walk through the trees into a clearing. The back wall of the warehouse looms above, reminding me how big a space this is. The girl in front of it is dwarfed by the wall she's spray painting. She's wearing jean shorts and a white tank top, and her clothes and skin are streaked with colored paint that glows bright in the black light. Her long dark hair is tied up in a high ponytail, and the lower half of her face is covered in a gas mask, the kind painters wear, with vents on the sides.

She's creating a large mural on the metal wall. It's an ocean scene, with a bridge stretching from an island to a mainland. It looks pixelated, like it's made of dots. I puzzle over that until I see the round stencil in her gloved hands; she's using it to create the entire image with sprayed-on circles in different colors.

One large stretch of wall is unpainted. A projector set up in front of it is flashing stylized words and images onto the metal.

Tomorrow we commence a four-part series, it says, followed by pictures of what must be the wildlife sanctuary, a peaceful-looking stretch of swampland and woods.

Part One: Shame.

The world will know your name and avert its eyes.

An image of a man in his fifties, dressed in a suit and tie, waving to a crowd.

Part Two: Ring of Fire.

The forest will rise up and march against you.

An image of a sweeping grove of eucalyptus trees.

Part Three: Buried Alive.

The earth itself is your judge and jury.

An image of a mud-soaked marsh, the kind that occupies large expanses of land on the coastline north of San Diego.

Part Four: Fishing for People.

The ocean takes back what is hers.

An image of Coronado Island.

A flash of black and white, and the slideshow starts over.

Tomorrow we commence a four-part series . . .

"Whoa," I hear myself say.

Veronica's camera is clicking away. She moves around Lily, getting different angles. Lily notices her and waves. Her eyes crinkle above the mask, and they exchange words I can't hear. Veronica waves me over, and I tear my eyes away from the words and images flashing on the wall to join them.

"This is Mick," Veronica tells the girl. "She loves this piece you're working on."

Lily pulls the mask off and looks me up and down. She's Asian, with high cheekbones and a wide, expressive mouth. "You seem wholesome."

"Oh." I'm not sure how to respond to that.

She says to Veronica, "Play nice with this one," and returns the mask to her face. She resumes painting. I'm hurt. It's like she read the insecurities in my mind and said them out loud.

Veronica returns to me. "I'm sorry. Lily is . . . She's just like that. You okay?"

I nod, not wanting to let on how uncomfortable I feel.

"Want to go sit down?"

"Sure."

We wind back through the forest, away from Lily's painting, and Veronica points to a tree on a little hill. I follow her and sit down on the soft, cool, mossy ground beside her. I ask, "Is this illegal? The whole setup, the installation, the party? The series they're talking about?" I point to the wall, where the images and words continue to rotate, an endless loop.

"Uh, yeah. If these guys ever got caught, they'd do jail time." She lounges beside me. "Are you okay? You want to leave?"

"I'm fine." Trying to forget Lily's words, I reach out and take her hand. "Thanks for inviting me out tonight. I wasn't sure if it was too soon to call you."

She grins. "I was supposed to wait a few days, wasn't I?"

"No." My eyes fix on the warehouse ceiling high above, and I point at it. "They put stars on the ceiling."

She throws her head back to look. Pinpoint constellations glitter across the fake night sky, which is just the inside of the warehouse roof, painted black.

She turns so she's facing me. "I have a confession to make."

"What?"

She laces her fingers through mine and squeezes. "So . . . the train photo."

My face burns remembering it. The feeling of the camera on me, knowing there was no film in it, had been scary but exciting, and there was something edgy and sexy about Veronica studying me through the lens.

"Um . . ." She hesitates, like she doesn't know how to continue.

"What's wrong?"

"So the thing is, there were a few shots left in the camera."

I blink at her. "Like, there was film in it after all?"

She nods slowly.

"Oh God." I sit straight up. Oh no. What did I look like? Panic flies through me, a windstorm. It was so vulnerable, that moment. It's like finding out there are pictures of me taking a shower or something.

She sits up too. "It's fine. It's okay." She puts a hand on my arm.

I yank my arm away. "Did you develop it? Did you see it?" My voice is high and tight.

She nods.

I pull my knees up and rest my forehead on them so she can't see the tears welling up. Just when I felt safe. Just when I let my guard down.

She's close, her face next to mine so she can speak into my ear. "I'm sorry. I know. It was the wrong thing to do. There were only a few shots left on the roll, and I figured I'd just toss them and it'd be no big deal. But—"

Into my knees, I say, "You *knew*? You knew there was film in the camera, and you took the picture anyway?" She lied?

Why are people like this? *Why?*

She slips her phone under my arm into the cave of my knees so I can see it. On the screen is a black-and-white picture. It's a girl, a young woman. It looks vintage, like a still from an old movie. The girl on the screen is looking at the camera with longing, and . . .

She's beautiful. It's me, and in this photo, I'm beautiful.

I take the phone from her and drop my knees, wiping my face. The girl's eyes—my eyes—are searching, full of questions. She wants something. She's *starving* for something.

Veronica snuggles up next to me and rests her chin on my

shoulder so she can look at the photo, too. "I had to develop it, I had to show you. See why?"

The texture of the photo is gritty, better than an Instagram filter. It feels historical, like this is a moment that could exist in any place and time.

"You captured it," I say softly. I'm not sure she can hear me.

She nods, her cheek brushing mine. "This is what you look like. I wanted you to see. Even if it means you hate me now. You're so beautiful. You don't have to hide."

The words unravel me. I turn my face and kiss her. The phone falls onto the grass, and her arms are around me, and we're tangled up, her camera a sharp-edged thing between us. Her hair is between my fingers, and I feel angry and scared and exhilarated and like every nerve in my body has been set on fire. I'm full of wanting—I *need* her, I need her to come closer, closer. I need skin on skin, I need *everything*.

She kisses my cheek. "Let me post it on my photography Instagram," she says.

I pull back. "What?"

"This is the best picture I've ever taken. Please. Let me share it."

I don't want her to do it. My whole body screams, *NO*. But then I remember Lily's scornful *Be careful with this one*, like I'm a little girl who can't keep up. So I say, "Fine. Go ahead. Post it. I don't care."

Like I'm floating outside myself, I watch Veronica post the photo with the caption *Just kissed*.

I watch her hit Share, and I feel that first kiss being torn away from me and flung carelessly into the wide, public world.

She puts the phone in her back pocket. She lifts her camera up and off her neck, sets it aside, and moves forward, pushing me back until she's on top of me. She leans down and kisses me, and the photograph is forgotten. The bass drums pound into my skull. No one can see us, hidden here beneath the dying trees. I'm anonymous and free, existing only in the world of sensation and in the invisible internet sphere in her pocket.

CHAPTER EIGHT

◇◇◇

VERONICA

IN THE PUBLIC POOL'S LOCKER ROOM, I CHECKED MY red lipstick using the mirror next to a kid in a My Little Pony bathing suit getting scolded by her mom. I resisted the urge to take their picture and got my sunscreen out of my beach bag. It was one o'clock, and the sun was waiting to turn me into a sweaty lobster.

I was wearing a fifties-style black bikini with high-waisted bottoms and enough strap action to control my boobs, which always wanted to flop around attracting unwelcome male attention, especially from gross older men who took one look at me and decided I was up for grabs. I finished applying sunscreen, slipped into my vintage silk robe, and shouldered my beach bag. I set my cat-eye sunglasses onto my nose.

I was ready. I was prepared. I took a deep breath. I was *nervous*.

"Come on," I muttered. I flip-flopped through the locker room and out into the blazing-hot afternoon. The pool was pandemonium, kids screaming and splashing and chasing each other around the deck. Pop music played in the background, stuff I didn't recognize but that reminded me of Nickelodeon.

The door to the men's locker room opened, and Nico stepped out. He'd changed from jeans into American-flag-printed swim trunks, a red visor, and a cobalt-blue fanny pack, and he had an entire armful of bright blue and red ring toys, the kind you throw into the pool and retrieve, looped around his wiry arm from wrist to armpit. On the tan skin of his stomach, he'd painted *USA* in block letters.

"What. The hell. Is this?" I demanded as a horde of little boys sprinted between us.

He slid on a pair of drugstore sunglasses that were decorated in stars and stripes. "I'm a red-blooded American man, and I'm here to have some family fun." He pointed to the letters on his stomach. "It's waterproof paint."

A whistle pierced the air. "No running," a voice yelled. The kids ran faster. "No running on the deck!" The lifeguard jogged toward them, blowing the whistle again, and the kids finally obeyed, turning to face the whistle-blower, a girl in a red bathing suit—

It was Mick. She bent down to talk to the boys, hands on knees, her face serious as she pointed to the signs outlining the pool rules.

Christ on the cross. Mick in a bathing suit. What the hell. So much tan. So much muscle. So much skin. Oh my God.

I looked down at myself. I was not prepared at all, actually. Why had I never spent any time developing my abs? This suddenly seemed vitally important.

Mick sent the boys off and straightened up. She spotted me, and her face lit up. "You came," she cried, trotting toward me. Nothing jiggled. Nothing.

I tried to reclaim my confidence. *Come on, Veronica, you're better than this.* I forced a smile onto my face. "Having fun guarding lives?"

She hugged me, a quick hug appropriate for the setting, and pulled back to look me over. "You're so stylish. I feel plain next to you."

I said, "You are *not* plain," which made her blush under the tan, and now my confidence was all the way back.

She turned toward Nico and looked him over. "Wow."

"I'm so sorry about him—" I began.

She gave him a quick side hug. "You're a few weeks late for the Fourth of July."

"Every day is Independence Day in the U S of A." He saluted a pair of moms walking past.

"Mmmmkay." She returned her smile to me, and I noticed it looked a bit forced, divorced from her eyes. "I have a ten-minute break coming up in a little bit. Mind hanging out?"

I squeezed her arm. "Take your time. I know you're working." I glanced at Nico. "I'll keep him in line."

"Feel free to swim," she said, and from the smirk, I was pretty sure she was teasing me.

"I can just spray myself with bleach at home, but thanks," I said, while Nico gave a passing family a Disney princess wave. The mom clutched her toddler closer to her side.

Mick moved to the edge of the pool near two boys playing leapfrog off each other's shoulders.

I pointed at Nico. "You are on my list."

"I'm in a good mood. Tonight is install number one, baby girl." He twirled one of the blue pool rings around his index finger.

"I know, I know." He hadn't shut up about it. I didn't know exactly what he had planned—he always kept me in the dark till the last minute—but it involved the buckets of blood, and he was extremely proud of himself. I couldn't hold it against him; he'd been completely focused on this for months, and I was dying to see these installs he'd been hinting about for so long.

We made our way to the row of lounge chairs surrounding the deep end. I spread my towel on one, between a camp counselor and a mom with a baby. Hand-painted signs declared this to be the YMCA Annual Luau, and there were many parents lounging around with leis strung around their necks. I wondered why Mick didn't have one. She'd have looked cute in a lei.

Nico swam a little, his strokes graceful and clean. I was jealous of his ability to move through any environment with complete comfort. I always felt like I was imitating his self-assurance and never getting it completely right.

Eventually, he settled onto the pool's edge with his feet in the water, throwing rings into the deep end. Instantly, he was surrounded by a group of kids who wanted to play. Over their shrieks of delight, I heard him calling, "Fetch! Fetch, little minions." With un-American flamboyance, he flung the bright little circles into the water.

I pulled out my camera and entertained myself sneaking pictures of Mick sitting on the tall lifeguard tower like royalty, strolling around the edge of the pool, and chatting with exhausted-looking moms about their rowdy children. Occasionally, she cast Nico an amused look, and I was relieved that his antics didn't seem to bother her. Still, after this, he and I were going to have a real talk about proper wingmanning.

The more I watched her, the more I decided something seemed off. There was a heaviness to her mood despite her obvious efforts to be cheerful.

Eventually, a tall, well-muscled guy our age came out of the boys' locker room. He approached the lifeguard tower, and Mick came down to talk to him. They put their heads together about something, and then she waved him off and walked toward me. I sat up straighter and sucked in my stomach as she crossed the deck to my lounge chair.

"Can I sit?" she asked. "I'm on my ten."

"Of course." I pulled my knees up to make room for her.

Mick wrapped an arm around my legs and gave me the tight smile again. "I'm happy you're here. It's nice to see you in daylight."

I peered at her, studying her face.

"What?" she asked.

"Something's wrong."

She looked down at her hand, which gripped my leg a little tighter. "How are you this pale? It's summer in San Diego."

"I'm a vampire, and you're changing the subject."

She sighed and met my eyes. "Just problems with my mom."

"What's going on?"

"We had a massive fight today, again. She wants me to do this modeling thing with her."

"Really?" My eyebrows shot up. "What kind of modeling thing?"

"Please don't tell anyone. It's so embarrassing. It's for this stupid magazine ad for a company called Inner You."

"Inner You?" I repeated, skeptical. "What is that, some kind of feminine hygiene thing?"

Mick snorted a laugh. "No, like, fancy interior design. My mom is supposed to be their ideal housewife. She's, you know, blond and . . ." She gestured to her chest to indicate fake boobs. Wow. Interesting. I would never have pictured Mick having that kind of mom. It sort of made everything make a lot more sense.

Mick said, "So they want a mother-daughter thing. They want me to walk around in a bathing suit—"

"Really? What kind of bathing suit?"

"A bikini," she replied in a small, horrified voice.

I blinked at her. "So they want you, a seventeen-year-old high school student with a fear of being photographed, to get almost naked with your *mom* in front of, like, a million people and then have the photos published in magazines and online."

She nodded. She looked miserable.

"Wow." I didn't know what else to say. First, and most important, I wanted to be the one to take those bikini photos, and I wanted to take them in private. I was willing to bet I could get some *very* interesting bathing suit shots out of Mick if given the opportunity. Second, I wanted to beat up her mom. What kind of mother tried to strong-arm her teenage daughter into getting half naked for some stupid interior design ad? If any adult pressured me to pose for bathing suit pictures, my mom would set their house on fire.

Mick said, "I'm thinking of just doing it. I'm not sure it's worth the fighting. My mom is furious."

"Why can't they hire someone else?"

"She wants the money. Needs it, actually." She looked away, and the expression on her face in profile was, what—ashamed, maybe? She wiped at her cheek with the heel of her hand, avoiding my eyes. She was crying.

Her eyes latched on to something back at the pool. She stiffened and frowned.

"Mick?"

She lifted the whistle to her lips and blew into it hard. She jumped to her feet and broke into a sprint. She took a flying leap and dove in, cutting a razor-sharp line through the bright aquamarine water. I jumped up and ran to the pool's edge, camera bumping my chest. Mick's red suit flashed like a salmon past the kids and parents. She stopped and swirled around a smaller, darker shadow at the bottom of the deep end . . .

"Oh no," I whispered, clapping my hand to my mouth.

It was a kid. At the bottom of the pool.

CHAPTER NINE

✧✧✧

MICK

THE EAR-SHATTERING SHRIEK OF MY WHISTLE. A BLUR of color and light, and then I'm underwater, the hollow weight of silence heavy in my ears.

I didn't think about taking a breath, but my lungs are full of air, and I'm good for at least a minute. I swim past legs and bikini bottoms. I lose no sense of direction; the kid is like a beacon calling me. And here he is, almost touching the bottom of the slope that dips down to the deep end. He's perfectly, horribly still.

I loop an arm around his shoulders and chest. I push off the bottom hard and pull him to the surface.

I burst through into chaos. Parents and kids are screaming. Angel's voice rises above the din, and then his whistle blows. He's in the water, swimming toward me. The kid in my arms is limp. His head flops as I throw him over my shoulder and swim hard for the edge. Angel meets me and gives me a boost, and I toss the kid onto the concrete. I pull myself up and kneel beside him. He's not breathing.

"Fuck!" Angel screams at my elbow. "You want me to—"

"Call 911!" I yell, searching frantically for a pulse and feeling nothing. The little boy's about six years old, with shaggy dark hair. I center my hands on his breastbone, and the song I learned CPR to ("Crazy" by Gnarls Barkley) pops into my head. I start compressions, praying hard with each push.

I remember when, I remember I remember when I lost my mind . . .

"They're on their way!" Angel yells, cell phone in hand. "They want to know if you're doing CPR!"

"What the hell do you think I'm doing?" A crowd has gathered around me—a hollow, staring circle of people. I tilt the boy's head back and pinch his nostrils. I don't have time for that stupid plastic mouthguard that's supposed to protect me from germs. I lower my head and breathe hard into his mouth, three times. Kids nearby are crying.

A woman's voice screams incoherently behind me. It must be his mother. I don't turn around. I resume compressions, hands centered on his chest. Gnarls Barkley starts singing again. *And I hope that you are having the time of your life . . .*

Another whistle blows the moment apart. "Step aside!" It's my manager, Becky, finally out from the office. She shoves me out of the way with her beefy shoulder. She takes over compressions, and it's clear she knows what she's doing.

I stand. I'm trembling all over.

The boy's mom is right at Becky's side. She's a mess, sobbing hysterically, incoherently. I realize I'm crying too, or maybe that's just the way I'm breathing.

Angel is at the side gate, opening it up for the paramedics, a man and a woman. They run fast, all efficiency and blue T-shirts and shoulder bags full of medical equipment. They take over for Becky, asking questions while they work on the boy with obvious expertise. "How long's he been down?" one of them asks.

"Mick!" Becky yells. "How long?"

"Just a few minutes."

The paramedics keep at it. Angel comes to stand next to me. "Get away from me," I tell him.

"Why?" He looks hurt.

"You were supposed to be watching, not flirting with the swim teacher, you dick!" I shove him hard, hard enough to send him stumbling sideways.

"The hell!" he cries.

Becky snaps her head toward us. "Locker room, you two. Now. Wait for the police in there. And clean out your lockers while you're at it."

Angel storms away from me, hot with male rage. The mom and the paramedics are loading the kid onto the stretcher. He's got a breathing tube over his mouth, and they're still doing CPR. I follow Angel and take a left into the women's locker room. As I pass all the people who are now watching, stricken, I'm slammed with a wave of shame and grief. I let the door swing shut behind me, and then I sink down onto a wooden changing bench. My head falls forward into my hands, and I sob so hard I feel like I'm breaking.

I wonder if he's dead, that little boy.

My fault. My fault.

The locker room door opens, and I brace myself to get

screamed at by Becky, but then the person puts an arm around me. Veronica. She sits there quietly, rubbing my back while I cry into my hands.

"He's going to be okay," she says after a minute. Her voice echoes in the empty locker room.

"You don't know that." My voice is muffled in my hands.

"No, really. He was breathing when they left. I'm sure he's going to be fine."

"He was breathing?" I look up and search her eyes. She nods.

"Thank God." I take a deep breath. It feels like I've been holding it this whole time.

"You did so good. I'm honestly in awe of you. If I ever drown, I want you there to save me."

"Stop." I fill to the brim with anger and sadness. It was my fault that kid was in the water. I knew Angel wasn't going to pay close attention. He never does. It's always on me to keep an extra eye on the kids when he's working.

"I won't stop." She pulls me into a tight hug. A flash of realization: No one has ever hugged me like this. Not hard, like they want to squeeze better feelings into me through sheer force. At first I don't know how to react, but then I feel my arms wind around her neck. "Don't go," I hear myself whisper. It's pathetic. We just started dating. She's going to think I'm desperate and sad and—

"Don't worry."

The door swings open and a middle-aged policewoman in uniform walks through it. "Micaela?" she asks.

I pull away from Veronica. "That's me."

"We need you to come down to the police station to give us a statement about what happened. You can call your parents to meet you there." She holds the door open; clearly, I'm supposed to follow her.

Things are bad enough with my mom. No way am I going to call her for this. Veronica says, "I'll go with you if you want."

"Thank you," I breathe, gathering my belongings from my locker. A shiver runs all the way through my body.

CHAPTER TEN

✧✧✧

MICK

THE POLICEWOMAN DROPS US OFF IN FRONT OF Veronica's one-story Spanish-style house, which is on a street not far from where we met. I'm quiet as I follow Veronica up the path to the front door, already feeling nervous about the idea of parents and siblings and trying to make a good impression. "I'm not sure I can do so good meeting your family right now," I tell her as she's unlocking it.

"I know. I won't make you talk too much. You're hungry, though, right?"

I nod miserably. I'm so starving, I have cramps.

"Come on. Let me nurture you with food."

"Are you going to tell your mom about the pool?" Will she think I'm the kind of person who doesn't take lifeguarding seriously enough, someone she doesn't want seeing her daughter?"

"I'll explain everything later, after you leave. She'll understand."

She pulls me into the house and closes the door behind us. We're in a high-ceilinged foyer, the living and dining rooms open in front of us, a hallway that must lead to the bedrooms off to the left. The rooms glow with soft yellow lights, the kind that are embedded in the ceiling. The walls are covered in huge, colorful abstract paintings. Gingerly, I set my gym bag on the tile near the front door, self-conscious about it looking worn out and cheap in the context of this beautiful house.

"Mom, I'm home!" Veronica yells. We wait. Silence. "She's here somewhere. Come on. Kitchen's this way."

I follow her into a kitchen with an island. "This house is really nice," I can't help murmuring.

"Thanks." She tosses her camera bag and beach bag onto the kitchen table, which sits by a window overlooking a rose bed in the backyard. In the landscape lighting, the rosebushes cast skeletal shadows on the gravel path beside them. She starts digging around in the stainless steel fridge. "You want some chicken and rice? Or I could make nachos?"

I hesitate. I look down at my red bathing suit, shorts, and plain black flip-flops. In this kitchen, with put-together Veronica and her red lipstick and these gleaming acres of granite countertops, I understand why my mom is always trying to get me to dress differently. I understand why I should have painted toenails.

Why am I thinking about this? That little boy almost died today. When I was giving my statement to the police, I hadn't wanted to throw Angel under the bus, but I also hadn't known how to avoid saying that he was supposed to be watching the pool. I was on my official break. I wonder if he got arrested.

"Mick?" Veronica asks. "Chicken and rice or nachos?"

I look up from my feet. "Whatever you feel like making. I feel bad putting you to the trouble."

She shuts the fridge and cocks her head, eyes scanning me. "You all right?"

I hesitate. "Maybe I could google it and see if there's a news story, see if the kid is okay."

"No," she says firmly. "I'll google it for you. Promise me you won't."

I nod, relieved.

She pulls her phone out of her purse, and I wait while she searches. "I don't see anything, but I'll keep checking. Okay?"

The back door slides open, and a dark-haired woman steps in. She's very pretty, with Veronica's cheekbones and a taller, narrower frame. Her jeans, T-shirt, and arms are streaked with something white, like paint. She stops in the doorway, looking between us. "Oh, hello."

"Hi, Mom. This is Mick. We're making food."

The woman gives me a smile and a thorough once-over. "Hi, Mick. I'm Claudia."

"Hi," I say, barely audible, and offer her my hand to shake. She bypasses it and gives me a kiss on the cheek. I notice she has both sides of her long hair shaved, which surprises me on a mom.

Veronica's head is back in the fridge. "What are you doing out there? Working?"

Claudia crosses the kitchen and gives Veronica a kiss on the cheek. "I'm all wrapped up in that new piece."

"Ooh, I like that one."

Claudia washes her hands at the sink and returns her attention to me while she dries them on a towel. "You're beautiful, Mick. So fresh and sporty, and Veronica says you swim. Maybe you can get her into the ocean."

"It's a scientific fact that there are sharks," Veronica retorts, head held high. "When they had drones fly over the surfers in Malibu, they saw so many great whites below them. I will show you the footage."

"You're *so* much drama."

My curiosity is burning. I blurt out, "Are you a painter? Or . . ."

She looks down at herself and chuckles. "Oh, Jesus, my clothes are a mess. I'm a sculptor."

"She teaches at the city college," Veronica says with obvious pride. "She does this gorgeous relief sculpture, sort of a Chicanx Kandinsky style. Like postmodern three-dimensional Mexican muralism, but more abstract and geometric."

They're an artist family. That's so cool. I watch them as they shred chicken and cheese for the nachos. They chatter effortlessly, like friends, and I wonder if Veronica has a dad, or another mom, or any other family who lives here with her. At last, while we're seated at the kitchen table, I can't help but ask, "So do you have any brothers or sisters?"

Veronica chomps on a mouthful of chips and guacamole. "I have an older sister. She's getting her MFA at NYU. And my dad lives in Florida. He works in Orlando. Turns out he has a whole second family there, actually."

"Veronica," Claudia says in a warning tone. She'd gotten all the clay off her hands and forearms, but she has a white streak across one tanned cheek.

"What?" Veronica splays her hands defensively. "Am I supposed to keep it a secret or something?" To me, she says, "He moved to Florida to live with the family he likes better, and he left us this house so we'd still be able to 'maintain our lifestyle.' Asshole."

Claudia presses her fingertips to her temples. "I can't take you anywhere. Not even our own kitchen."

Veronica grins at me and wiggles her eyebrows.

After we eat and put the dishes in the dishwasher, Veronica leads me upstairs to her room. It's twice the size of my room. The queen-sized bed is unmade, the black-and-white comforter a tangle at its foot. The walls are painted red and covered in old movie posters. I read the names of the movies out loud. "*Vertigo, The Big Sleep, Dark Passage, Pulp Fiction.* I remember you talking about *Vertigo.* Will you show it to me sometime?"

"Sure, of course."

My eyes land on a large silver thing resting on the desk chair. I squat down to get a closer look. "Is this a sculpture of a chicken?" It's shiny and bright, and when I poke at it, it barely moves. It must be super heavy.

"Oh God." Veronica hurries over. "That's Nico's. Don't look at it. It's an art project."

"He made this? Wow. It's incredibly realistic." I can see each tiny feather, every wrinkle on the legs.

"Hey, um . . . you want to see my darkroom?"

I'm still kind of fascinated by the chicken. "How do people sculpt metal, anyway? It seems like metal would be too hard to use tools on. But then I guess people sculpt marble."

"Come look at my darkroom." She clearly doesn't want to talk about the chicken. Maybe she doesn't like me complimenting Nico. I wonder if she feels competitive with him. She grabs her camera bag, leads me to a door I'd assumed was a closet, and holds it open for me.

I push through the heavy black curtain and peer inside. It's a converted bathroom with counters built over the toilet; the bathtub holds trays and a big machine. She closes the door behind us and flicks on a light switch, which bathes the room in gloomy red-orange light. "This is a safelight. You can't have any phones or anything in here while developing."

I nod. She sighs and tucks my hair behind my ear. "I'm so sorry about today. What can I do? What would make you feel better?"

"I don't know. Distract me. Maybe I could watch you develop some pictures?"

"Good idea." She flips another switch, and a soft yellow light brightens the red into a sunset orange. "This can stay on until I start developing." She pulls out her camera and examines it. "I have five more shots on this roll. Can I take your picture to use up the film? You can watch me throw those negatives away if you want. You can even cut them into a million pieces with your own two hands."

I hesitate. "I don't know."

Camera in hand, she steps forward so our noses are almost touching and kisses me. It's not like at the forest party. She's not as gentle. She pushes me into the door. Her chest is warm and soft against mine, and she runs a hand through my hair, drawing my head back. "Let me take your picture," she says into my neck.

I can't make a sound. She lifts her camera to her eye, focuses, clicks, and lowers it. I lift my hands and press them to her cheeks, looking at her features. She's so pretty, soft where I'm sharp, full where I'm hollow. I pull her toward me and kiss her, and her free hand is on me, running up my chest and over my shoulder and arm. I feel her slip one of my bathing suit straps down off my shoulder.

She steps back and lifts the camera. *Click click.* It's uncomfortable, I hate it, but then she kisses me again, harder this time, and slips the other strap off my shoulder. She's undressing me and photographing it in stages. I almost can't breathe. It's too much, the fear and pleasure all wrapped up together like this. She kisses my collarbone, her hair spilling ticklish down my arm, which makes my head feel woozy. She lifts the camera and clicks. "That's it, I'm out of film."

My breath is coming fast, and I swallow hard to calm it down. I return my bathing suit straps to my shoulders.

She sets the camera aside and is just about to kiss me again when a hard, loud knock just behind my head makes me jump out of my skin.

"Veronica!" calls a male voice, muffled through the door and curtain. "Can I come in?"

Her face twists into a scowl. "Go away, Nico!"

A pause. "But I love you." He launches into an opera riff in fake Italian, his deep baritone almost genuinely operatic. I press a hand to my mouth, about to start laughing, and she rolls her eyes.

"I'm so sorry. Do you mind? I'll get rid of him." She slides the curtain aside and pushes the door open violently, making him stumble backward a few steps. "I seriously hate you."

My eyes squint painfully from the onslaught of light. Something buzzes in the background, a constant *bzz-bzz-bzz*. Nico raises his thick eyebrows when he sees me. "Oh damn. Whoops. Hi, Mick."

"Yeah, cockblocker, whoops indeed," Veronica snaps. "Now go away."

"But wait, I have to show you something."

The buzzing starts up again, and I realize it's coming from my purse. I squeeze past Nico and Veronica, out into the bedroom. I pull my phone out of the side pocket of my purse. Missed call from my mom. Great.

I have a bunch of text notifications, too, dozens of them. What the hell?

Nico is saying to Veronica, "Have you checked your Insta lately?"

"No, why?"

"You should check it."

I have texts from a bunch of people I don't talk to that much, acquaintances from swim team and from school. I have five new messages from Liz. Maybe they're having a party or something? Did I forget someone's birthday?

Veronica and Nico have fallen silent. I look up at them.

Veronica has her phone in her hand. Her other hand is

frozen midair, like she was about to gesture with either excitement or shock but froze halfway through it.

"What is it?" I ask.

Her frozen hand comes down, and she starts scrolling. "Oh my God."

"What?"

Nico is grinning. He has a broad smile and such white teeth. "You should take a look at this."

I set my phone aside and get up. I cross the room and peer at Veronica's phone over her shoulder.

She's looking at the photo of me, the black-and-white one she posted to Instagram.

"I don't get it," I say, but then I see what she's seeing.

The photo has ten thousand likes and hundreds of comments.

"No," I say. My chest feels like someone punched it. *"How?"*

Nico says, "So here's what I think happened. You tagged it with #artistsofinstagram, #photography, #lgbtq, and some other stuff."

"No, we didn't," I protest.

"I did, later," Veronica says.

"What? Why?"

"Just . . . I don't know. Habit, I guess. I always tag my photography stuff. And I . . ." She winces. "I kind of added to the caption."

"Added to it? What does it say?"

Nico reads aloud. *"Just kissed.* And then a line of empty space, and then, *Is it weird to say I feel superstitious that we caught this moment on film? How often do you get to hold the most important moments in life in the palm of your hand? That's photography. #artistsofinstagram #photography #artists #lgbtq #california #summerfun."*

I meet Veronica's eyes. I feel dirty, like our first kiss has been cheapened by the gaze of thousands.

Nico navigates to the Instagram account for *Seventeen* magazine. The photo of me is their most recent post. Nico selects it and shows it to us. "See? Their repost has another ten thousand likes. They tagged you and added some more hashtags. And then it got picked up by a few of those meme-sharing accounts, and a bunch more photography accounts and artist accounts and—" He grins at us. "You're viral, bitches. Internet famous."

"But why?" I cry. "It's just a picture of a girl on a train. I'm not naked, I'm not *doing* anything."

He scrolls through the comments section. "They think you're beautiful. They think it's a photo about first love, about youth and being queer and all kinds of stuff. And look, you're on the front page of recommendations for people following #artistsoninstagram and #photographersofinstagram and #lgbtq."

"No shit," Veronica says through a wide grin.

I snatch the phone from Nico and scroll through the comments on Veronica's post. People are saying things like *Beautiful* and *Haunting* and tagging each other, and leaving follow requests, and talking about who I look like, and asking who I am. I navigate to the meme-sharing account Nico showed me and read comments there. They got a photo of Veronica off her account and posted it along with mine, and the comments are full of guys saying things like, *blah blah TL;DR, I want to watch* and *TAKE YOUR SHIRT OFF AND STFU.*

I drop the phone, numb.

Nico collapses onto the bed in a graceful heap. He looks back and forth between us. Veronica's cheeks are pink, her eyes shining with reflected light from her phone.

"You look like you just won the Miss Universe pageant," he tells her. To me, he says, "And you look like you're about to puke your guts out on the carpet."

Veronica looks up from the phone at me. "You okay?"

I'm so upset, it's hard to form words. "No, I'm not okay. That's our private moment."

"But you said it was okay to post it."

"On *your* account. How was I supposed to know it would get shared like this?"

"How would I have known?"

"Why would you tag it like that if you didn't want a bunch of people to see it?"

She looks back down at her phone. She doesn't have an answer to that. I sink down onto the bed next to Nico. I retrieve my own ancient iPhone, a hand-me-down from my mom, my gut gnawing with the suspicion that all the notifications are connected to this photo. I pull up the messages from Liz.

The first message says *Mick? This is you, right?* accompanied by a screenshot of the picture.

The next message says *Okay, like ten people have sent me this. Why are you all over Instagram? I thought you hated pictures, but now you're like some kind of Instagram model?*

"Oh no," I whisper. It's a nightmare.

Nico says, "And look—you got a huge celebrity retweet." He pulls up Twitter on his phone. Sure enough, it's a famously bisexual pop singer with four million followers. The Instagram photo has been screenshotted, Veronica's Instagram handle still in the frame, and the tweet reads *#LoveIsLove*. I reach out with a tentative finger and scroll down. It has ninety thousand likes. The comments are a disaster, a hodgepodge of support, self-promotion, memes, GIFs, and sexual harassment.

I make a dread-filled whimpering sound. This is uncontainable, uncontrollable. It's a tsunami.

Nico reaches for my hand. "Are you okay?"

Anger wells up in my gut, returning me to the scene of the crime, the moment the photo was taken. The only reason I was that real and raw was because Veronica lied to me and said there was no film in her camera. She knew what she was doing. She *knew*.

I shove my phone into my purse and stand up. "Where are you going?" Veronica asks.

I leave the bedroom. My steps quicken, and I run through the carpeted hallway out into the common area. Veronica's mom is in the living room, reading a book. She says something as I rush past, and I know I'm being rude, but I can't respond. I grab my gym bag and yank open the front door. I run as fast as I can away from that house, away from Veronica, away from the picture. Away, away, away.

CHAPTER ELEVEN

◇◇◇

VERONICA

I JUMPED UP TO FOLLOW HER, BUT NICO PUT HIS hand on my arm. "Don't do that thing you do. Give her space."

I whirled on him and opened my mouth to argue, but he was right. I sat down heavily and shook my head. "I fucked up. She's right. I shouldn't have tagged it."

He sprawled back, head resting on his lanky arms, and looked philosophically up at the ceiling. "You're in way over your head with this one."

I scowled. "What does that mean?"

His eyes left the ceiling and fixed on mine. "You don't even understand what you're dealing with."

"And what would that be?"

He got to his feet in a languid, catlike movement and dug his keys out of his pocket. He pointed to my bedroom door, where Mick had stormed out. "That girl? That's a girl on the edge. Give her a push, and she's going over."

With a flash of guilt, I remembered Mick in the locker

room, sobbing into her hands about the little boy. She'd tried so hard to save him. It wasn't her fault.

I lied to her. I didn't see the kid breathing. I just wanted her to feel better.

No. That wasn't the whole truth. I was afraid to tell her the truth, afraid of her reaction. I felt like it might send her over . . . Over the edge? Was that how I felt?

I *hated* it when Nico was right. And he was *always* right.

At last, I answered him. "You're so condescending. I hate it when you do this know-it-all, big-brother thing. You're barely two years older than me."

He raised an eyebrow at me. "You think I'm wrong?"

"I think you don't know what you're talking about."

Instead of answering, he pulled the door open like he was going to leave. I picked up a shoe from the floor and threw it at his head. I missed, and it hit the door frame. He watched it lazily. "I love it when you throw things at me, but I gotta go. Install starts in an hour."

I had totally forgotten. "Shit. I'll get dressed."

He waved me off. "I don't need you. There will be press galore. They'll take pictures."

"Seriously? This is your big launch. Don't you want pictures of the setup?" All his Tumblr followers would be expecting tons of photos. One of the things they loved about Nico's art was the behind-the-scenes look at the planning and setup.

"I promise you, we got it." He tossed me a smile and let himself out, closing the door behind him gently.

I stared at the closed door.

That's a girl on the edge.

CHAPTER TWELVE

◇◇◇

MICK

I WALK AWAY FROM VERONICA'S HOUSE, DOWN THE hill.

I realize I'm crying. I wipe my face and keep going. The dusk is darker here than where I live; it's more suburban, the houses farther apart, the streetlights more subdued. My gym bag is slung across my chest and bumps against my butt with each step.

That photo Veronica took of me feels like a leaked nude—I'd never show that side of myself to total strangers, but now it's out there for anyone to see. Next up, the Inner You shoot—actual nudes. Why not, right? Soon there will be nothing left of me that hasn't been consumed by strangers on the internet.

I'm the ghost again, screaming, raging, but no one hears me. I feel like I'm being swallowed up by the nighttime ocean, being sucked down into its pitch-black depths, that little boy from the pool drifting mutely beside me. We can be ghosts together, he and I.

My chest feels tight. I push harder, move my legs faster, and I'm almost running now. Maybe my legs think they can outrun the person they're attached to.

My phone starts buzzing again in my purse. I slow down and pull it out with dread. It's a string of texts from Veronica.

Please don't be mad.

I'm sorry.

It's just really exciting for me. None of my pictures have ever gotten any attention. I was starting to think I had no talent.

A few seconds later: *Please come back.*

I stare at it. I feel furious. The anger is blazing, hair-on-fire hot. I shove the phone in my purse and return to walking. My flip-flops slap the pavement.

I make it down to a six-lane street. Cars whoosh past in both directions. Across from me is a mini-mall with a Vons and a Starbucks, cheerily well-lit. I turn left. I don't really know if this is north or south or where I'm heading. It doesn't matter. I don't want to go home. I don't want to go back. This feeling of being untethered is scary. I focus on walking. Walking is something I can control.

A car pulls up on the shoulder just ahead of me. I stop. Some creepy guy, probably, about to harass me. Then I see the Uber sticker on the back window and figure it's just someone getting dropped off.

The driver's door opens and a guy gets out. Nico. With extreme nonchalance, he lopes around to the back of his car and leans against the trunk. "What's up, Jagger?" he calls as I approach.

My eyes fly to the passenger's side window. No Veronica. "What are you doing here?"

"I'm going to work on an art project. Where are *you* going?" He turns to peer in the direction I'm heading. "The equestrian center? Going to steal a horse and go all Medieval Times on these bougie motherfuckers?"

I smile weakly. "I'm just walking."

"You know what?"

"What?"

"I think it's really cool that you don't want to be internet famous. I think it's actually pretty great. I like you, Jagger."

It shocks me into silence. At last, I murmur, "Thanks."

He pushes off the car and steps closer to me. "I bet you're good at keeping secrets. You don't like attention, which is why most people tell secrets in the first place. Well, that and to unburden themselves if they're feeling guilty. What do you think? Are you a good secret keeper?"

I've never thought about this before. I think back on all my friendships, on any fallouts and fights . . . "I guess I am," I reply. "Loyalty is important."

"That's it. I've decided." He grins. "I'm going to tell you my big secret. You ready?"

"I guess . . . ?"

"That forest party we went to? That was mine. I'm the artist. That's my crew."

"Oh." I'm surprised by this, but then I'm really not. "Okay. I won't tell."

"Well, here's the thing. Veronica is mad at me and is refusing to take pictures for me tonight. I have my own camera; would you be willing to do it? The camera isn't like Veronica's; it's point-and-shoot. Just like using your phone."

After a moment of thought, I ask, "What's the art project?"

"It's an install, kind of like a prank. It's fine art disruption." He grips my upper arms. "Say you'll come. You'll love it. It'll get your mind off this Instagram thing. It will just take an hour or two, and then I'll drive you home. Where do you live?"

"National City."

"Nice! I grew up near there, in Chula Vista."

"How did you meet Veronica?" What's he doing out here in the land of Starbucks and immaculate landscaping?

"I was in foster care near here for a minute. Went to Bonita for, like, one semester. I was a junior, she was a freshman. She got moved into advanced photography after wiping the floor with everyone in the ninth grade class. Then I moved to another foster home, and we stayed in touch."

He was in foster care? "I didn't know. I assumed you were from one of these—" I gesture to the houses on the hills.

"Nope. I was a free-lunch kid all the way. You?"

"Yep," I admit.

He holds up a fist, and I bump my own against it. "Now you have to come with me. We're doing an incredible prank on this congressman. He's everything that's wrong with the one percent."

I don't care where he plans to take me; I just want to go somewhere that isn't here and isn't home. So I say, "Okay. Sure, I'll come."

CHAPTER THIRTEEN

✧✧✧

MICK

NICO PARKS AT THE BASE OF A CLIFF ATOP WHICH A golf course overlooks the moonlit ocean. Elegant, looming mansions are scattered through the hills, poking out behind trees where they can take advantage of the view. This is where the truly rich must live.

Nico ducks around the back of his car and starts messing with his license plate. I come to see what he's doing. He's putting a rectangular decal on it, like a fake, stick-on license plate.

"In case anyone calls in my plate number," he explains in a whisper. "This is a private community; they have their own security, so we have to be careful."

"Where are we going?"

He points up the hill. "Congressman Osgood is speaking at a fundraiser dinner tonight. We're doing our install at the mansion."

"If we're walking up there, I better get my sneakers out of my gym bag."

While he gets two bandannas and a black backpack out of the trunk, I put on my socks and Nikes and wonder what I've gotten myself into. He hands me a black zip-up hoodie and tells me to put my hair in a bun. I obey, second-guessing this decision more every minute.

"Here, put this in your pocket," he tells me, handing me a black bandanna. "You'll cover your face with it when we get there. It's to make sure you aren't photographed." He laughs. "Maybe you should just wear this every time you hang out with V."

I return his smile weakly and follow him. He keeps to the shadows, tucked away on the sidewalk as close to bushes and the overhang of trees as possible. Behind us, a white van chugs up the hill, engine protesting the incline. To my surprise, Nico waves as it passes us, and the passenger's side window rolls down to reveal Lily in a T-shirt that matches the slogan on the side of the truck: LA JOLLA CATERING SERVICES.

The bearded man from the forest party leans across Lily and waves from the driver's seat. His hair is tucked into a beanie. "What up?" he drawls in a surfer-bro-dude voice.

"Where's Veronica?" Lily asks, shooting me an unwelcoming look.

"Mick's subbing in tonight," Nico says. "Mick, this is Lily and David."

"What's up?" David says amicably, but Lily snaps, "We've met."

Nico ignores her tone. "I'll see you up there."

Lily narrows her eyes at me, gives Nico a dark look, and

then nods. "Fine." Her window rolls up, and the van resumes its slog uphill.

"Where did you get that catering van?" I ask as we continue walking.

"It's just a plain white refrigeration van that we use for a lot of our jobs. The logo is a magnetic wrap. We swap them out." This doesn't explain where he got the van in the first place, but I'm starting to think it's best not to ask any more questions like that. I recognize the type of van; I've ridden in them with my mom on the way to weddings to do catering jobs. Florists use vans like them, too; the entire storage area is basically a giant fridge.

I'm starting to wonder why Nico trusts me enough to be here, considering they must be doing illegal things. Lily's suspicion seems pretty reasonable. It's not like Veronica and I have been dating for years.

We walk at least a mile through the silent, darkened streets, winding our way up to a giant mansion at the top of the hill. It's white and old-fashioned, with columns and a massive front porch. The whole thing is lit up like a movie set, and the driveway and sidewalk swarm with delivery vehicles, security company cars, and news vans.

Nico avoids the chaos and pulls me around a corner. "You and I are going in through the back."

I don't know what to do but follow him. The sweatshirt feels claustrophobic, trapping my body heat against my skin like a sauna. He leads me around the neighborhood like he knows these streets by heart, stopping a few times to text with Lily and David. At last, he's leading me through someone's side yard, using a gate he apparently opened for this purpose earlier in the day, through a backyard ringed with bushes and succulents, past a darkened pool house and shimmering cobalt-blue pool (these homeowners are out of town, Nico explains), and finally to an eight-foot concrete wall where Nico turns to me, eyes shining with excitement. "Here we are."

He unzips the black backpack and hands me an old-fashioned disposable camera. "You'll be using this. No photos of me, Lily, or David, but otherwise, go ahead and take a picture of anything that seems important, especially the congressman."

My mouth is bone-dry. "Nico, I'm kind of scared."

He puts a strong hand on my shoulder. "I've never been caught. Not once. You can just relax and enjoy."

I'm not sure enjoyment is within reach, but I take a deep breath and try to relax. He's clearly not at all stressed.

I familiarize myself with the disposable camera as he reads a text from Lily. "She's in position, the van is clear, they're unloading. Dinner is almost over, which means we need to get up there and wait for Osgood."

"But what are we doing? Why are we going up onto the roof?"

"You'll see. I want you to be surprised." He wraps an arm around my shoulders and squeezes. "Let's do this, Jagger."

He gives me a boost, and I climb the wall. I jump down onto a pile of dead leaves and Nico lands beside me as quietly as a cat. Between us and the massive, artfully lit house is an acre of grass, an Olympic-sized swimming pool, a tennis court, and an outdoor dining area large enough to host a wedding.

Nico shows me how we're going to get up to the roof: A painter's ladder has been tucked up against the rear patio at the farthest, least conspicuous corner of the house. Beside it rests a large pile of party lights, like someone got pulled away in the middle of stringing them. No one is back here, but through the windows, we can see a dozen workers bustling around in the kitchen.

He hands me a pair of latex gloves. "We have to be careful. No fingerprints. My motto is *leave no trace*." I pull the gloves on, dread spooling inside me, as he does the same.

"Bandanna," he says. We tie them over our faces, and I feel completely ridiculous, like an old-timey cartoon bandit.

Nico has me climb the ladder first so he can hold it steady. The split-level roof is Spanish style, with rounded terra-cotta tiles that look hard to walk on. Nico pulls himself up next to me and leads me carefully along the perimeter to the front of the house, where, tucked between two tiled overhangs, four large white containers sit waiting for us. They look like ten-gallon buckets of paint. Beside them are four black garbage bags full of something fluffy. From here, we can see down onto the front yard, which is bustling with newspeople and valet car parkers and caterers in uniforms that remind me of my mother's. Far beyond the house, glimmering to the horizon, is the dark, oily Pacific.

"Make sure to stay back from the edge," Nico says. "We don't want them to see us."

Nico's phone buzzes, and he reads the text, grinning. "Almost time. Get ready to take some photos."

He has me practice a few shots with the camera, getting pictures of the front yard and the view of the ocean, and then of the buckets and garbage bags. From his backpack, he pulls a small remote and pushes a power button. Down in the front yard, a few spotlights wink on, casting even more light onto the front of the house. No one notices, not in the flurry of reporters and flash photography.

Nico's phone buzzes. "Any minute now," he says. Below, Lily comes into view, looking like a harassed caterer taking a phone call. She stands near one of the spotlights Nico just turned on and gives us a discreet thumbs-up.

Nico gets a screwdriver and pries open the buckets. They're full of a dark, viscous-looking liquid. "What is it?" I whisper.

"Blood and corn syrup."

"Ew."

He moves to the garbage bags and unties the openings. A single white feather flies out of one of the bags, twirling in the breeze around Nico's head.

Above his bandanna, Nico's eyes watch me track the feather. I can tell he's smiling by the way the skin around them crinkles. "This is gonna be epic," he says.

The front door opens below us, and a crowd of people surges out. Lily holds a hand up to Nico. It's the cue he's been waiting for. He tilts the buckets fast—*thumpthumpthump*—and dumps the contents over the roof, down onto the people below. The liquid is sticky and dark, and red like blood. It streaks the front of the mansion and drenches the men below.

Screams. Panicked shouting. The flash of news cameras. The click of my camera.

Nico takes the garbage bags and turns them upside down, releasing huge balls of feathers that tumble to the ground and explode on impact, blanketing the men in white feathers.

He's tarring and feathering them. I can't stop taking pictures.

And then darkness.

All the interior and exterior lighting shuts down at once, leaving us in pitch-black, the front of the house lit only by the news cameras and the spotlights Lily is standing next to. The lights turn into pictures; they aren't spotlights, they're projectors. The front of the white mansion explodes into imagery. As the men stand there, shocked, covered in feathers and blood, scenes of wildlife demolition play out across the front of the house. Trees are silently razed by steamrollers, birds take panicked flight, surrounded by dust and steam and dirt and men in orange vests.

It's silent. Everyone has stopped screaming. The news cameras roll. I take a few more pictures and run out of film.

This is . . . this is . . .

This feels important. This work Nico's doing . . . it *means* something.

"Time to go," Nico says.

We move fast, picking across the tiles to the ladder. He climbs down first, and I follow. As we jump to the ground, two men run toward us from the front of the house. "Stop right there!" They're security guards, dressed in blue uniforms.

"Go!" Nico yells. We sprint to the back fence. He gives me

a boost, and I pull myself over, followed by him. The security guards aren't as fit or as fast as we are, and they're stuck on the other side, trying to drag the twenty-foot ladder over. We sprint along the periphery of the property we'd cut through, heading for the street. We're about to get to the gate when spotlights make us freeze. They're on the other side of the gate. We're trapped in this backyard.

Whoop. A siren—the police are already here. Doors slam. They're getting out. Flashlights flicker. They're coming to search the yard. We're about to get caught.

"Shit," Nico says. "Okay, plan B." He runs to the wall on our right, the one that leads to another mansion's backyard. I follow him; it's only six feet high, and I pull myself over it, toeing off the wall and vaulting over the top. He follows me, and we drop down into a flower bed.

The house is dark, the pool unlit. The water is almost black, only visible because of the moonlight glinting off its surface.

A red-and-blue kaleidoscope shines through the palm trees. Voices boom near the gate.

"The pool!" I whisper. "We can hide under the water."

"We'll ruin the film," Nico protests.

"Would you rather go to jail?"

"Fuck that. I want the pictures." He throws the camera and his backpack into a bank of bushes.

We run toward the pool and slip into the water, making as few waves as possible.

The cool, hollow silence envelops me. I'm safe.

It's a false feeling of safety; this is not the womb, not a

safe haven from the loud outside world, not for long. The ghost of the little boy haunts me, reminding me that the water is a sanctuary only for a minute, only until you need to breathe.

My lungs are protesting inside my chest. We've been under for almost a minute. Nico squeezes my hand, and we surface quietly, our heads exposed just enough to breathe. It's quiet; the searchers have moved on. His wet face is beaming with what looks like excitement and joy.

"Are you having fun?" I whisper angrily.

"Hell, yeah."

"Why do you do all this? You could go to jail."

"Please. They wish they could catch me."

"They might," I argue. "They almost did tonight."

He blinks water out of his eyes. "You have swimming, right? That's your thing?"

"I mean—"

"It saves you. It gives you a future. It's your one thing."

Treading water, I nod. How can he know this about me?

"Well, I have this." He smiles with his eyes and slips back under the water.

I take a deep breath and submerge myself in the darkness. I swim down, brushing the concrete bottom with my fingertips.

I wonder what the other three installations are going to be. I'm afraid and excited. I want to be a part of this.

It's like when Veronica took my picture on the train and in the darkroom—it's fear and exhilaration all tangled together. I loved that feeling of being studied through the lens of her camera. The feeling of having her complete attention was . . . It was like this. It felt wrong, but I'm on fire with longing for her to do it again.

It never occurred to me that fear could be fun.

CHAPTER FOURTEEN

◇◇◇

VERONICA

IT WAS THE MIDDLE OF THE NIGHT, BUT I WASN'T asleep. I was lying on top of the tangled covers, holding my camera in both hands, thinking about my life choices.

Choice one: pressuring Mick into having her picture taken even though I knew she wasn't totally comfortable.

Choice two: lying to Mick, sneakily capturing a picture after promising not to, then developing it.

Choice three: showing it to her, and then putting it on the internet.

Choice four: tagging it so more people would see it, knowing Mick would be upset.

Conclusion: I was an asshole. I was not a god of sex, not a badass photographer extraordinaire. I was just a dick with a camera who did the same thing to girls that guys have been doing through the ages: pressure, push, pull what I wanted out. I was just another misogynist photographer trying to get the model naked.

I dug my phone out of the covers and googled *Congressman Osgood*, curious to see how Nico's installation was going. Front and center were shot after shot of the congressman and a few other men in suits covered in blood and feathers, hands up to shield their faces.

"Ha!" I laughed out loud. Great job, Nico. This congressman had no idea what was about to be unleashed upon him. I texted Nico a single emoji: a smiley face. We were super careful, never texting about anything related to the installs. He'd know what this meant.

I checked his Tumblr page. It was called *I Am the Phantasm* and had a ton of followers. I expected to see images from tonight, taken from media coverage, but I sat up and frowned at the screen. Tonight's post was titled "Shame: The world will know your name and avert its eyes."

The images below were behind-the-scenes shots, pictures from the roof itself. I scrolled down. Here was Nico dumping the blood, face covered by a bandanna. There was a picture of the feather balls bursting onto the congressman's head. The images were captioned, like they always were, with Nico's narration of the artwork.

Tonight, we tarred and feathered Osgood, the focus of this series titled Possession. We'll be exploring what it means to own something living—land, plants, animals, people—and what happens when the possessed rise up against the possessor. Get ready. This series is going to make the news.

I guessed Lily must have taken photos for him. Given the quality, he'd used disposable cameras and developed them at his warehouse. They were grainy and low-grade, but it looked cool. He'd done a good job. I was proud of him. This was so much work, and it required such discipline and planning. I hadn't seen him this committed to something since . . . well, ever.

I left Tumblr and opened Instagram. I had so many notifications. They were uncountable. I navigated to the photo, which now had fifty thousand likes, and I scrolled through the comments.

Beautiful.

Who is this?

A message from someone named Liz: *Is this Mick from National City? It is, right?* I wondered if this was Mick's Liz, who was sending her such mean messages about the photo. I clicked on her profile and realized I knew her. She and I followed each other—I hadn't put two and two together, but she was a friend of a friend, someone from that group of people from the party. She was always posting bikini selfies, showing off her swimmer's body. I'd originally followed her out of an interest in these almost-naked selfies, but now I clicked Unfollow out of loyalty to Mick. I ignored her DM.

This made me feel so good, this attention. I had taken raw material—Mick—and turned it into art. The feeling of power was going to my head like a drug.

A light tapping on the window. It would be Nico, coming to gloat about the success of his install.

I debated pretending to be asleep, but he'd just blow my phone up until I let him in. Grumbling, I swung my legs around and marched to the window. I yanked the curtains apart, opening my mouth to yell at him, but there was Mick.

She was standing in the darkness, face illuminated only by the dim golden light from my window.

She waved up at me.

I was so surprised, I froze into place.

She waved again.

I slid the window up and looked down at her through the screen. "It's you," I said stupidly.

"Can I come in?" Crickets chirped in the background, hidden somewhere in the fragrant flowering bushes that surrounded my house. She was wearing the same outfit—red lifeguard suit under shorts—but her hair was wet like she had gone swimming again, and she wore running shoes instead of flip-flops. The window framed her perfectly, and I wished I could freeze time and take her picture, looking up at me with that pretty, searching expression on her face, her hair tangled and wild.

I shook it off. "I can push the screen out for you to climb in, but would you rather come in through the front? My mom won't mind you being here, but she'll wake up if I open the front door."

"I'd rather climb in than wake up your mom."

I popped the screen out by the corners like I always did for Nico and passed it to her. She set it down on the grass and kicked off her shoes. She stepped back, gripped the window frame, pushed herself up easily, and swung her legs around so she was sitting on the sill facing me. Wait, were her shorts wet?

I reached out to touch the waistband. They were. "Did you go swimming again or something?"

She looked down at herself like she'd forgotten she was soaked. "I ended up going with Nico to his install."

"He took you to that? How? Why?" I had to fight to keep my voice down so my mom wouldn't wake up.

"He saw me walking and offered me a ride, and I ended up tagging along. We hid in someone's swimming pool and almost got arrested."

I blinked at her a few times. What the hell was he up to?

"That sounds right for a night out with Nico," I said at last.

She wrapped her arms around her waist. Her skin was full of goose bumps. I wanted to hug her to warm her up, but I didn't know if she still liked me, if she was here to tell me off or what. Her face looked serious. This was probably bad. I decided the best defense was a good offense.

"Mick, I'm really sorry," I said, in a much more pathetic tone than I was going for. "I'm sorry about the picture. I won't do it again. I'll hide my camera every time you walk into a room." I swallowed. Wow. I was *so* nervous.

She ran a hand down the sleeve of my—*oh my God, I'm wearing a Christmas pajama top*. It had seemed funny earlier, a good way to cheer myself up, wearing Christmas PJs in July, but now I regretted everything.

She lifted her eyes from the little Santas and said, "I'm here because I want you to take my picture."

I was shocked into silence. A rarity.

She said, "I hate the pictures. I hate my face. I hate people *looking* at my face. It makes me want to peel my skin off." Her voice was so intense, it was quivering. "I'm a private person. That moment was supposed to be *ours*."

"I'm so sorry."

She gripped my upper arms hard, her eyes burning into

101

mine. "But I can't stop thinking about the way it felt. In the darkroom, on the train. I want more."

"I don't want to—" I flushed, shy about what I wanted to say. "I don't want to mess things up with us. I like you *so much*. I'd rather have you than a thousand photographs of you. I don't want to make you uncomfortable."

She wrapped her arms around my neck. There was no space between us anymore. Into my ear, she whispered, "I want to be uncomfortable," and then she pulled my face toward hers and kissed me.

Shock waves. I felt like I was floating. This was different. I tried to understand why, and then it hit me. *She* was kissing *me*. The other times, I'd kissed her. This was better.

She pulled back. "Take my picture."

"Mick, no."

She looked around, saw the camera tangled in the duvet, and grabbed it. She returned to me and pushed it into my hand. "Take my picture." She kissed me, one hand slipping up into the back of my hair. Her lips were a little salty, the dampness of her skin infused with an angry heat. Her chest rose and fell with her breath, faster than mine. "Take it," she said, her lips brushing mine. She stepped away from me and sank down onto the edge of the bed. The look on her face was so lost, so completely just for me, that I had to raise the camera to my eye. I had no choice. The picture was already there, framed; all I had to do was reach out and grab it.

Through the lens, I twisted her into focus. Her hands, clutching the duvet at her sides. Her clavicle, sharply shadowed. Her eyes, huge, half child, half old woman, piercing—scary.

Click.

I stepped closer, centered her in the frame, refocused.

Click.

I lowered the camera.

She took it from me. She studied it, turning it over and over in her hands. She was gripping the camera so hard, her fingertips were turning white. I was suddenly worried she might throw it; she was vibrating with suppressed anger. Or fear?

"Be careful," I said. I reached out and tried to take the camera. She fought with me, tugging at it. "Mick, don't break it!" Panic welled up inside me. She wasn't letting go. I pulled it, but she was stronger. "Mick. Stop!" She yanked it away from me, falling back onto the bed. I jumped on next to her, grabbing for the camera. "Mick, don't break it! That was my dad's! Please!"

She let go of the camera and shoved me onto my back. I reached for the camera, but then she was on top of me. She took my hands in hers and pinned them above my head.

The only sound was our breathing.

Her hands loosened on mine like she was going to release me. "I'm sorry," she murmured. She closed her eyes. "I wouldn't have hurt your camera. I just . . ." She shook her head.

"You just what?" I asked, afraid she was about to get up and leave.

She leaned down and kissed me hard, our fingers lacing together. "You think you took those pictures *of* me, but you took them *from* me."

"I'll stop," I promised, light-headed. "I won't take any more pictures."

"No."

She kissed me again, and it was like I had never been kissed before. This was the real Mick, buried under all the shyness and fear. I wanted to tell her, *You're taking things from me, too; we're all taking things from each other,* but then words were lost and so was I.

CHAPTER FIFTEEN

✧✧✧

MICK

I OPEN THE FRONT DOOR STEALTHILY, AFRAID TO wake my mom. It's the dark gray moment before dawn, and the living room is chilly from the window unit next to the front door. This apartment, the eleventh we've lived in, is on the second floor of a courtyard building, and it's old enough not to have central air.

All is quiet. My mom must be asleep. Maybe she won't even notice I was out all night.

Good. I'm starving, and I think there are some Tater Tots in the freezer. I set my purse down and head for the kitchen. I feel woozy with sleep deprivation, excitement, and infatuation. I can't believe I have to swim in a couple of hours. I'm going to be useless. Oh God. Liz is going to be there. Maybe I can sneak in a little late so we don't have time to talk.

"Where have you been?"

I spin, heart pounding. My mom is in the sagging armchair against the window, a sliver of light from the exterior hallway cutting in through the closed blinds. Her legs are folded underneath her, silky pajama shorts leaving her legs bare.

"You scared the crap out of me," I say, a hand to my heart.

"Come here." She reaches for the pack of cigarettes on the side table and slides one out. The gesture is elegant, the Virginia Slim long and slender like her fingers. I walk toward her, my chest full of trepidation. She lights the cigarette with a little pink lighter and pushes the ottoman toward me. "Take a seat." She breathes out a plume of smoke.

I obey, sinking onto the ottoman cautiously. "You're smoking inside the house?"

She shrugs. It makes the left strap of her camisole slip off her tanned shoulder. "You're not going to die of secondhand smoke poisoning in one day."

I wrap my arms around myself, shivering, and keep my eyes on her bright red toenails. My feet are larger than hers, the nails rarely painted. They're the feet of an athlete, not the feet of a pretty girl.

"So I stayed out all night," I say, unable to stand the silence anymore.

"Where were you?"

I decide to tell her the truth. "I went out with a girl I met. I was at her house."

She glares at me as she takes another drag. The cherry of the cigarette lights up orange, which reflects creepily in her eyes. "What are you so afraid of?" she asks at last.

I'm confused. "I'm waiting to see how much trouble I'm in for staying out all night."

She waves that off. "Not now. In general. In life."

It brings back a torrent of memories, times she's tried to get me to climb fences and ride mountain bikes and go zip-lining and I've been too cautious.

"Your dad was like that, you know," she says.

I snap my face up and look at her. "What?" She never talks about Dad.

"He was fearful." She drags deeply on her cigarette.

"Fearful how?"

She rolls her eyes. "Travel. Flying. Heights. He was claustrophobic. He hated parties. People. Crowds. His life was so . . . It was so . . ." She waves her cigarette around, the smoke making lace in the air. "So small. So sad. It was suffocating."

I am stunned. I feel like she punched me. She's never told me any of this.

"Do you want to be like that?" she asks. "Sad, alone, afraid to live your life?"

I try to gather my thoughts. It's not easy; I'm weak with hunger, and my head is swimming with Veronica and this thing she's just thrown at me. When I speak, my voice quivers, and it's not just because of hunger. I'm afraid of her, of the nasty things she might say.

"Mom, I've been thinking. I think it's really messed up that you're threatening to take my savings account. But I'm not stupid. If it's lose my savings or do this photo shoot, fine. I'll do the modeling job with you." My hunger sours and turns into nausea.

She studies me for a long moment. "How big of you," she says at last. "It's going to be really hard for you, then? Being photographed?"

"Well . . . yeah. I mean, you know how I feel about—"

"*Really?*" Her tone is all sarcasm. She puts her cigarette out and grabs her phone off the table. She jabs at it, her movements quick and jerky. "You are full of *shit*, Micaela."

Oh no. Danger.

She flips her phone around to face me. On the screen is the black-and-white photo of me from Instagram. "I called Liz looking for you. She sent me this."

Liz? Liz is texting my mom about Veronica's Instagram?

"Liz wanted to know how I finally convinced you to do modeling," my mom says, and she's vibrating with anger. I am in serious, serious trouble. "I didn't know you modeled either, Micaela. I thought it gave you anxiety. Apparently you just can't model when I need the money to put a roof over our heads!" The last sentence comes out as a roar, so loud it hurts my ears.

"I'm *not modeling*. This girl I'm dating is a photographer. She just took this of me randomly."

She coughs out a bitter laugh. "She, what, staged the perfect shot on an empty train with perfect lighting and took this totally accidental professional picture of you? Are you *kidding* me?" She jumps to her feet, and I flinch. "Don't you think I know the difference between posed and candid? How could you do this to me? All I'm trying to do is put food on the table, and you act like asking you to stand in front of a camera for a few hours is like me sending you off to the coal mines? Poor Micaela, such a rough life, such a tragic martyr." She seizes a book off the table and hurls it at the wall, where it thuds to the carpet.

I jump up off the ottoman and back away from her. "It wasn't like that." I am famished with the need for her to feel what this is like, for her to know me and care. "Besides, Mom, I said I'd do the photo shoot thing. I said yes. You can stop yelling. I said yes!"

"We lost the job!" she screams. "They gave it to someone else!"

There's a silence. Her chest is heaving, her eyes bright with glittering rage.

"What happened?" I ask.

"They had other options. They took one of them."

I don't know what to say. "Mom, I—"

"Get out."

My head spins. "Wait, what?"

"Get out of my house."

She's done this before, twice. Both times I stayed with Liz for a weekend before she'd let me come home. "Fine," I say through a lump in my throat. "I'm glad to have a break from you."

My mom follows me to my room, her anger like a bodyguard behind me. "Better take anything you don't want me to get rid of," she says.

I turn to face her. "Get rid of?"

She's stone cold, arms crossed over her chest. "I can't afford this apartment anymore, can I? So I guess I'll have to move into a smaller place."

She can't kick me out for good. I'm not eighteen. This can't be happening.

"You have ten minutes." She turns her back and walks away.

My throat is hot with the tears I'm holding in. I say, "Mom, where am I supposed to go?"

She stops, turns to face me. "Go wherever you want. You're already doing whatever you want, right? Staying out all night, coming and going as you like, doing jobs if it suits you. Princess Micaela is her own woman. Right? So go be your own woman, then."

I slam my bedroom door and stand with my back to it, panting, tears hot on my cheeks. This isn't fair. It can't be right. It can't be real. You don't just kick your kid out, do you? *Yes*, my brain argues, *people do this*. My mom has been on her own since she was sixteen.

I look around at my room. It's messy, a normal teenager's room, the twin bed unmade, the dresser overflowing. It reminds me that I'm a kid still, older than that little boy I'd held in my arms, but a child nonetheless. His mother had screamed, desperate for him to be okay. Would my mom scream like that for me? The memory makes me want to cling to my mom, to force her arms around me.

But no. That's not a thing.

My chest aching with sadness, I go to my closet and pull my large gym bag down from the top shelf. It's the bag I take to swim meets. I shove sneakers, jeans, shorts, swimsuits, bras, underwear, my brush, anything I can think of inside it, no idea where I'm going. I get my checkbook and the stash of cash from my desk drawer, my diary from my nightstand, and my phone charger. I don't know what else to take. All my childhood stuff is here. Will she really get rid of it? She might be bluffing. Maybe.

I zip the duffel bag and sling it over my shoulder.

I think about the little boy again, about his limp, cold arms flung out on either side of him, of his mom crying. I'm crying, too, remembering. I need him to be okay. *If he's okay, maybe everything else will be, too,* I think irrationally, like this thing that happened to him was bad enough to bind our fates together for life.

I shift the bag to my other shoulder so I can get my phone out of my back pocket. I pull up Google and type in *child drowning YMCA San Diego.*

I wait for results to load, then click on Tools to filter for recent results.

But it's not necessary. There's a new article at the top of the feed.

Child Drowns in San Diego YMCA Pool.

My head swims.

Drowns doesn't mean "dead," I tell myself. I click the link with a shaky index finger.

A six-year-old boy has been pronounced dead after a brief coma following an accidental drowning at a summer camp event, the first line reads.

It might be a different pool. It has to be.

I scan the article and my stomach sinks.

Same pool.

It's the boy. My boy.

He's dead.

I'm on the floor. I don't remember sitting down. My duffel bag is beside me.

"Mick," my mom yells from the kitchen. "Ten minutes are up."

I push myself to my hands and knees, and then to my feet.

I shoulder my duffel bag. I wipe my eyes and nose. I look back to see if I forgot anything.

My whole life is in here.

She's in the kitchen. She doesn't turn around as I walk through the living room. I pause, a hand on the front doorknob. "Don't throw all my stuff away," I say to her back.

She doesn't answer.

"Please." My voice cracks.

Nothing.

I let myself out the front door. The apartment building is rustling with quiet activity. Everyone is getting ready for work—everyone but my mom, because she doesn't believe in working a normal job, because she's "always known she was never destined for a desk."

So this is it, then. No more job. No more best friend. No more Mom. No more home.

Out on the palm-tree-lined street, the morning sun screams in my face, a violent heat. I feel a matching violence simmering inside me, like I'm about to snap and burn the whole sad and stinking world to the ground.

CHAPTER SIXTEEN

◇◇◇

VERONICA

AFTER MICK LEFT, SNEAKING OUT TO CATCH THE Uber I ordered for her in the darkness before dawn, I replayed the last few hours in my head over and over, clutching the sheets to my naked chest. Mick. Mick Mick Mick.

Memories of her slashed through my mind, a slide show.

In the darkroom—*click*. Lifeguarding, turquoise water and red bathing suit—*click*.

The little boy. I wondered what ever happened to him. He had to be fine. Kids didn't just die like that.

I remembered Mick, perched on the edge of this bed. *Click.*

I sat up. No way was I going to be able to go back to sleep, not with this roll of Mick film winding its way around my brain. I needed to develop all those pictures.

I jumped out of bed and threw my pajamas on, hungry to see what the new shots looked like. I spent a few hours in the darkroom, watching her face emerge from the tray of developer again and again.

Here she was, one strap off her shoulder as I'd undressed her. Both straps off—tan lines, Jesus Christ. Eyes hungry, lips moist, staring straight at me with that same look I'd caught so perfectly on the train.

I paused when I got to a shot of her diving into the pool.

Had I really taken this picture? I didn't remember doing that.

I watched the image pull itself into focus through the clear developer fluid. It was Mick in profile, diving into the water. I'd caught her just as her hands were starting to cut through the surface. Her feet and hair were blurry. It was—

The thought was in my brain before I could argue with it.

I'm so glad I took this.

That boy could be dead, I scolded myself.

But I pulled the photo out with my tongs, let the fluid run off it, and clipped it into a place of honor right at the center of my drying line.

At last, I emerged from my darkroom, starving, and grabbed my phone on the way down to the kitchen. I had a string of emoji texts from Nico: a chicken, a heart, a smiley face, another chicken again, a thumbs-up. He was in a great mood, apparently, after the successful install. *See you tonight*, he texted after he was done with emojis, referring to the next install we had planned.

I knew a little more about tonight's install because I was meeting him there. It was going to be badass, a perfect follow-up to yesterday. I wanted to ask him why he'd brought Mick, but I'd do it in person. He had some explaining to do.

My phone buzzed again and again with endless notifications coming from the viral photo of Mick. I was getting tagged all over the place, and that celebrity retweet had a zillion likes and retweets of its own.

Along with the notifications, I had a bunch of DM requests from super-creepy guys (*Are you both girls? Damn, can I watch?*), some DMs from queer teenagers wanting to connect and talk about shared struggles, which made me feel guilty for coming from such a supportive home, DMs from girls wanting to hook up with me (these made me smile a little), models wanting me to take their photograph, and on and on and on. Buried in the chaos was a message from a woman named Carmen Contrera.

Veronica, I'm an editor and scout for PostMod Photography Magazine, based out of Los Angeles. Can you tell me about your process? It looks like you're working analog. Am I right? The photo of Mick was attached to the DM.

Of course I knew *PostMod*. They were a well-respected photography magazine. I checked their account. They had over a million followers.

My fingers shook as I typed the reply.

Wow, thank you for—

No. I deleted it and started again.

Yes, I always do analog. These were shot on Kodak Tri-X 400. I use a Nikon from the 1980s. I'm glad you like them!

I sent this, wincing because "I use a Nikon from the 1980s" sounded incredibly pretentious. I set the phone aside, my heart racing.

My phone vibrated, and I saw with surprise that Carmen from *PostMod* had already answered my DM. I opened it up.

That's exactly what I was hoping to hear. Do you have any interest in participating in an upcoming show? We're running an issue on young talent, and we're donating prints to a fundraising gala with attached silent auction for an environmental nonprofit called Save the Bay. What do you say? Would you donate prints if you got coverage in PostMod?

I read this through five times, and then, with fingers that could barely find the screen, I typed, *I would love to participate.*

Great. Here's my email. Can you send me at least 10 other shots from this series? The gala is this weekend, and I had someone drop out.

I couldn't imagine dropping out of a chance like this. What would make someone flake at the last minute? I typed, *I'd love to take their place. I can't believe anyone would pass up this opportunity.*

She answers, *Me neither. He fell off the face of the earth and stopped answering my emails.*

Wow. What an idiot. *Well, I'd love to do it*, I say. *How did you find me? Did you see the photo on Instagram?*

Yes, the photo was sent to me and I knew right away I had to see more.

Mick.

I didn't know what I was going to tell her. I had a bad feeling she wouldn't react well. She couldn't expect me to pass up something like this. Could she?

I almost called Mick and asked, but I remembered she'd be in swim practice right now. Carmen started up about wanting to meet in person and asked how fast I could produce prints for her to preview, and how many other shots of Mick did I have ready, and I got swept up in excitement.

I'd talk to Mick later. She'd have to understand. This was *PostMod*. This was my future. This was everything.

CHAPTER SEVENTEEN

✧✧✧

MICK

I STAND ON VERONICA'S PORCH FOR A LONG TIME,
the duffel bag strap digging into my shoulder. I'm hot and
sweaty in the late afternoon sun. It took me forever to get here
on the bus.

The inside of me feels . . . shaky.

I stare at her front door.

I don't know what I'm here to ask her for, not really. I know
I can't stay here. We just met. I know that.

I keep imagining that kid's dead weight in my arms.
When I went to the pool this morning for swim practice,
I couldn't even go in. I couldn't bear the idea of smelling
chlorine. I just stood in the parking lot with this stupid,
heavy duffel bag slung over my shoulder, like I am now, and
then left.

The day was a blur. I went to the park. I ate a burrito. I fell
asleep on the bus, went to the end of the line, and had to get
off in some neighborhood I didn't recognize.

So here I am, staring down my first night of not going home and not any closer to a plan than I was this morning.

It's going to be okay, I tell myself. My mom just needs a few days to cool off.

I stare at the pretty wood-and-glass door for another few minutes, and then I back away. I set my duffel bag on the hot front step and sit down next to it.

I shouldn't have come here. I should have other people to turn to. I should have family. I should have another parent. I remember what my mom said to me about my father, and I wonder what other things about him I don't know. She told me once that he'd moved to Arizona, and I've tried to find him, but his name is Michael Young, which is ridiculously common, so I never get anywhere. I do have grandparents, but we barely know each other; my mom doesn't really get along with them. They live in a small town in Michigan.

"Mick?"

I snap my head up. Veronica's mom is standing on the walkway in front of me, car keys in hand, purse slung over her shoulder, wearing a sundress and sandals.

I'm instantly flushed with humiliation. "I am so sorry." I hop up and grab my bag, embarrassed to the core of my being.

She approaches slowly.

"Go ahead. I'm sorry to block your way." I step aside and walk back toward the sidewalk, duffel bag bumping my legs.

"Hey!" She catches up with me. "Hey, hey, hey. Where are you going?"

I don't want to be disrespectful, so I stop, but I can't look at her.

"Are you all right? Did you and Veronica have a fight?"

Suddenly I remember I stormed out right in front of her last night. God, she must think I'm a mess. "No, we didn't. I was just leaving. Thank you." I make a move for the sidewalk.

"Why don't you stay for dinner?"

I turn back toward her, slowly, dread heavy in my gut.

"I was going to make lasagna." She has that X-ray thing I've seen in other moms. It makes me blink hard to keep from crying, and then suddenly, horrifyingly, I am crying. It's happening. There's nothing I can do about it. The tears are just there, spilling down my cheeks. I duck my head and brush them away.

She lets out a low, soft chuckle and puts her arms around my shoulders. "Tell me what's the matter." Her voice is so soothing, so kind, that it just makes me cry harder.

"You don't have to do that," I manage, trying to shrug her arms off me. "You're not my mom. You don't have to worry."

She gives me a light slap on the back of my head and hugs me again. "I'm not your mom, but I'm *a* mom. Now, do you want to tell me what's wrong and why you have that heavy bag with you, or do I need to feed you first?"

She pulls back and peers at me. I've gotten the shoulder of her blouse wet. I shake my head. "You don't have to feed me. It's fine."

She wraps an arm around my waist and pulls me toward the house. "I'm disappointed. Veronica usually likes smart girls. And smart girls don't refuse lasagna."

I can't help but laugh. I wipe my eyes and sniff in a noseful of snot. "Okay. Thank you."

"Good." She leads me to the front door and opens it with her key. "Veronica!" she yells when she gets inside.

Silence.

"She's probably in her darkroom. Come help me in the kitchen. You can toss your things there by the couch." I set down my duffel bag and wash my hands in the sink while she gets stuff out of the fridge. "I saw that photo that's going viral," she says, pulling out Tupperware containers and tossing them onto the granite countertop. "It's a beautiful shot of you. All the photography professors at the city college are talking about it. My girl's got talent." She shoots me a smile. "And a gorgeous model." The photo is the last thing I want to talk about. She pours herself a glass of red wine and offers me some. I decline, shocked at the offer, and she laughs. "You're seventeen, not twelve. You're old enough to drive and have sex, and next year you're allowed to murder people in the military. I think you can handle a little bit of sour grape juice." She pours me a glass of iced tea instead. "So tell me what happened. If not a fight with Veronica, then what?"

I keep my eyes on my glass. "I had an argument with my mom, and she kicked me out."

A frown flickers across her brow. She sets her wine down and says, "She kicked you out? What do you mean?"

"She does that sometimes, when she gets really mad."

A long silence ensues, during which she sips her wine with raised eyebrows.

I say, "I'm sorry. I shouldn't have come here. My best friend kind of dumped me and . . ."

"Why are you apologizing when you didn't do anything

wrong? That's something we teach girls to do—always apologize, never be a burden. You have a right to take up space."

I feel my face go hot. I don't know what to say to something like this.

Veronica plunges into the kitchen like a bolt of lightning, hair falling out of a high bun. "Mom! Finally! I'm out of developer fluid. I've been waiting for you forever so I can take the car—" Her eyes land on me. "Mick! You're here! And you're hanging out with my mom. What is happening?"

"Mick and I ran into each other on the front steps." Claudia pulls Veronica in for a hug and kisses her on the cheek. "Have you been locked in your darkroom all day?"

Veronica kisses her mom back, extricates herself, and comes to drop a casual kiss on my lips, right in front of her mom. "Yes, I've been locked in my darkroom."

"It's a beautiful day—"

"Don't give me shit, Mom," Veronica says sassily, but then she runs and hides behind me as Claudia pulls the hand towel off the stove and twirls it in her hands like she's going to whip Veronica with it. They're both laughing. This is a game. They're having fun with each other. It makes me lonelier than I can ever remember being in my life.

Veronica holds her hands up in a gesture of surrender, but then she steals Claudia's wineglass and takes a deep sip. Claudia shrieks, "You can't do that if you're going to take the car!" and Veronica sets the wine down before the towel can make contact with her butt. I stand back from this, hands gripping the counter, sadness tight in my chest. Eventually, they stop messing around, laughing and a little out of breath, and Veronica steals my iced tea and takes a long swallow.

"You're such a brat," Claudia tells her. "Get your own cup."

Veronica grins at me. *She is kind of a brat*, I think, but in a cute way, like she knows what she is and doesn't really care. I wonder how you get that kind of confidence, and then I look at Claudia and think, *I'd probably be confident too if I had a mom like that backing me up all the time.*

Claudia sips her wine. "So, Mick and her mom had a bit of a fight, and her mom kicked her out."

"What?" Veronica whips her head around to face me. I can tell she wants to ask more, but I shake my head minutely. I'll explain later.

Claudia says, "So, Veronica, if you're comfortable with it, let's have Mick stay with us for a couple days, until her mom cools down and they work things out. Mick, I'll help you call your mom if you think it will help smooth things over."

Instead of making light of it like I expect her to, Veronica brushes my hair behind my ear. "I'm sorry," she says. She gives me a hug so tight she almost lifts me off the ground. "You don't have other family who can talk some sense into her? My grandma would beat my mom's ass if she tried to kick me out."

I feel hot with embarrassment. "Not really. My mom isn't on the best terms with my grandparents. They live far away."

"That's like Dad," Veronica says, and Claudia nods over her wineglass. "His parents are in Mexico City, and he sort of doesn't get along with his family. Or anyone."

"He gets along with his new wife," Claudia says, and Veronica makes an "mmhm" noise.

"I'm going out with Nico tonight," Veronica says to me. "You want to come with us? We're going to get into some trouble. It'll be fun."

"Veronica," her mom snaps.

"A *little* bit of trouble."

Claudia mutters into her glass, "You're going to give me a heart attack."

I smile along, but I'm worried. I'm acting like I know my mom will let me come home in a few days, but I have a gnawing feeling in my gut that this time is different.

Veronica sends me a piercing look when her mom's back is turned. She knows I'm not okay.

Here and now, confronted with her long-lashed brown eyes and memories of last night, I decide not to tell her the boy is dead. I can't bear the idea of those eyes looking at me with blame. Let her think it all worked out okay, that he was breathing, that he's *still breathing*.

I feel like I'm clinging to the edge of a cliff, barely hanging on.

CHAPTER EIGHTEEN

◇◇◇

VERONICA

THE GOLF COURSE WAS ON A BLUFF HIGH OVER THE Pacific, which sparkled orange as the sun sank down to meet it. Its acres of rolling green grass were bordered by a state park full of towering eucalyptus trees and, to the south, a stretch of undeveloped land full of scrubs and native plants. The air was pure ocean; I could taste the salt if I took a breath with my mouth open.

I parallel parked a mile from the golf course on the shoulder of a road that wound through the undeveloped land. The shoulder was speckled with cars, parked there by local beachgoers who took the paths down the cliffs to the white sand beach.

Mick had been quiet all evening, upset about her mom. I felt terrible for her. I couldn't imagine having a mom who would physically kick me out of the house. What would I do if I were in her situation? I was trying to show her that I was there for her in every possible way without being overly clingy, and I was also trying to figure out when to tell her about *Post-Mod* magazine and the gala.

Maybe this installation would cheer her up. She'd seemed really pumped after hanging out with Nico last night. Maybe she liked this kind of art. It made sense; she was an athlete, and installation art was very hands-on, not like spending hours in a darkroom or behind an easel.

I led Mick through the scrubs until we had a view of the coast, then pointed north toward the golf course. "That's where we're going. See that white tent surrounded by grass? By the big building?"

She nodded.

"That's where a big fundraiser party's being held. Congressman Osgood will be speaking here tonight. We're going to surround them with the trees you saw at the forest party and sort of block people in. Like the trees are coming back from the dead to haunt him." I wrapped an arm around her waist, and the ocean breeze blew her hair into my face. Far below us, the Pacific stretched out to the horizon, where the sun hung low in the sky.

In a musing, thoughtful voice, Mick said, "Nico is an interesting guy. What he's doing is—it's really cool if you think about it."

I needed to be honest with her about *PostMod*. The longer I waited, the higher my chances were that she'd be mad at me. "Mick . . ." I hesitated.

"What?"

"I need to tell you something."

She turned, a frown on her face. "What?"

"You know our photo."

She smirked. "I remember it, yeah."

"It's going to be featured in a photography magazine called *PostMod*. It's . . . it's a big deal. For me. Not for you. I doubt anyone you know would see it. And, well, *PostMod* wants a bunch of prints. Of you."

There was a long moment of silence during which her face went completely blank.

"Oh," she said at last.

"That's not all." I swallowed, nervous. "They're going to put the prints in a silent auction at some gala this Saturday. Carmen—the woman in charge of this—wants us to attend the gala and have our picture taken, give a few interviews and stuff."

"Oh," she said again.

"Are you mad?"

"No." It sounded off, though.

I rushed to explain. "I couldn't say no. This might be the difference between getting into Otis and going to city college with my mom. Please say you'll do this for me."

"Of course I will." She turned away from me, her lips pinched together tight.

"Look. I saw how hard my mom had to work to be taken seriously as an artist. It took her *decades*. You don't understand what a . . . a unicorn this opportunity is."

"I said I would do it," she replied, her voice tight.

"Hey." I grabbed her arm. "If you're pissed off, say it. I'm not going to freak out. I can take it."

She looked down at my hand on her arm. Her eyebrows

were drawn together; all her non-smiling expressions landed somewhere between anger and introspection, making her almost impossible to read. At last, she pulled away from me and said, "I don't have a right to be pissed off. I told you to do whatever you wanted with the photos."

"But how do you *feel* about it?" I was begging, desperate for her to let me in.

"You know how I feel," she snapped, unguarded at last. "It feels like shit. I feel like everyone on the internet is seeing me naked. And now I have to go to this gala so people can look at my pictures and look at me in person and ask me, what—what kind of questions?" Her voice had become high and panicky, and she broke off and looked out at the ocean. "I wish I could disappear," she said quietly.

"Mick." The word came out soft and sad.

"Give me your camera."

"Why?" I clutched it protectively.

"Give it to me. I won't hurt it." She held out her hand impatiently.

Reluctantly, I handed it over. She put it to her eye and focused on me.

"You're taking my picture?" I asked, feeling imbalanced.

The camera clicked. She advanced the film and focused the way I'd shown her. "Do you like it?" she asked from behind the lens. "Do you like me looking at you like this?"

"I—" The moment I opened my mouth to answer, the camera clicked. "I wasn't ready," I protested. She was getting faster; she snapped another photo while I was talking. "Mick!" I cried.

She lowered the camera. "Don't like it?"

I wasn't sure what to say.

"That's what I thought." She handed the camera back to me and walked away.

I followed her helplessly. I felt like I was messing things up, like I was on the losing side of an argument I hadn't known was happening. The moment the camera was turned on me, there was a huge shift—the power had swung in a different direction. Was that how being photographed made Mick feel—powerless?

We pushed through the expanse of knee-high brush until we emerged onto the golf course. The white tent was below us, at the base of a half-mile slope of perfectly manicured grass. Beyond it was the golf club, a mansion-looking structure at the end of a long driveway. A stretch of walkway connected the tent to the clubhouse so people could parade back and forth in their fancy shoes. As we watched from above, cars and limousines pulled up in front of the clubhouse, dropping off couples and groups for the event. Even from here, the gowns and cars shone, expensive and sleek. Strains of jazz drifted out of the tent.

A grove of eucalyptus trees marked the border between the golf course and the state park. Nico had asked me to meet him in that grove, where he was apparently hiding the trees he was going to use for the install.

We picked our way down the hill. The sky was huge, the orange sun blinding as it sank closer and closer to the horizon. When we arrived at the grove of trees, I looked around, trying to see Nico, not wanting to call out for him.

Arms wrapped around me and yanked me backward. I cried out and stumbled back, collapsing onto my butt on the grass. Mick screamed and grabbed at me.

A ski-masked face appeared above me, attached to a body dressed in all black. Behind the eyeholes, the eyes were squinty with laughter.

"Nico, you asshole," I cursed. He lifted his ski mask, revealing his usual wide grin.

"You're almost late, wife." He helped me up and aimed his grin at Mick. "Back for more?"

"Yes." Her eyes were gleaming, her cheeks glowing, like she'd come alive at the sight of him. I bristled with jealousy. Nico and I had fought over girls before, but I'd kill him if he tried something with Mick. I filed away a reminder to myself to have an even more extensive talk with him after this.

Nico beckoned us deeper into the trees, out of the breeze, which was picking up and chilling my bare arms. Two black-clad figures were huddled around an open duffel bag, and they were surrounded by dozens of what looked like Christmas trees on wooden X-shaped stands.

"Guys, our photographers are here," Nico said.

I was enveloped in ski mask hugs from David and Lily. They patted Mick, too, obviously remembering her from yesterday's antics. Lily looked annoyed at her presence, which I understood. It was kind of inconsiderate of Nico to allow her in without their approval. But Nico always had to be the boss.

I touched the needles of the tree closest to me. It was dry, almost dead. "Where did you get all these Christmas trees in July?" I asked, getting out my camera.

"We stole them from a Christmas tree farm."

I was zooming in on the tent and admiring its placement, surrounded neatly by trees, when Mick said, "Nico? What's up with those trees around the tent? They look like they're in pots, not rooted in the ground. Are those yours from the warehouse party?"

"Yep! We brought them over this morning."

Her jaw fell open. I understood: The tent was huge, easily large enough to hold a wedding, and there had to be fifty trees circling it.

She asked, "How did you get the truck here without anyone saying anything? How do you just sneakily unload fifty trees when they're in the middle of setting up a party?"

"If I tell you, I'll have to kill you."

I elbowed him. "You're not funny."

"I am, though." To Mick, he said, "We got on the approved vendors list, so we just pulled right up and unloaded them like we belonged here. We're going to fill in the gaps with these," Nico said, pointing to the Christmas trees. "I want a perfect ring around the tent. I want them close enough to touch. We just have to wait for it to be dark and for everyone to be inside. I bet Congressman Osgood gives a speech. Fucker loves to hear himself talk."

I stepped aside, out of the trees, and took some pictures of the setting sun. Nico followed me, asking, "Hey, what's up with *PostMod*? I got your texts earlier."

I shushed him and pulled him aside, glancing nervously back at Mick, who was talking to David. I whispered, "She says she'll do it."

He snorted. "Way to manipulate people into doing what you want."

"Look who's talking," I shot back. "And I didn't manipulate her. I just asked her. Speaking of manipulation, how did you get her to go to your install last night?"

I could feel his scorn. "Please. She needed a ride, and I helped out." Before I could retort, he changed the subject. "Why do you even care about that *PostMod* fine art bullshit? You're such a sellout."

"Just because you didn't go to art school doesn't mean I don't want to."

"She's a sellout," he sang to a tune I could almost place. "She's a phony, phony sellout, yeah . . ."

It hit me. "Is that the 'Car Wash' song from the seventies? You're so random."

"She's workin' as a sellout . . . ," he sang, doing a John Travolta disco dance that he strangely pulled off incredibly well. I had heard his lectures about the gatekeepers of art and culture approximately four thousand times. I was pretty sure he was just bitter after being rejected by the one art school he deigned to apply to.

He stopped dancing, and I said, "Are you done?"

He flicked my forehead with his index finger, spun away, and went to the duffel bag. He pulled two ski masks out of it, handing one to me and tossing one to Mick, and then I spent some time taking pictures of the tent, the sweeping acres of grass, and the crew, dressed in black, huddled together behind the Christmas trees.

The wind picked up speed, dragging strands of hair out

of my bun and lashing them across my cheeks. The grass was an apocalyptic shade of orange; the sun was sinking fast now, hurrying to meet the clean line of the horizon. The wind stampeded past. It whooshed inside my eardrums and up inside my shirt. I felt a tug, and then all my hair exploded out of my bun and around my face. Mick made a hissing noise and tried to pull her hair back.

"Might as well put these on," I said, indicating the ski masks we were holding. We pulled them over our heads.

"You ready?" Nico asked me, his ski mask in place.

"Ready." I lifted my camera to my eye and focused. I had a good angle. These were going to be beautiful shots.

He shouldered a Christmas tree and strode toward the tent, his long legs casting stick-figure shadows behind him. Lily and David followed his lead, and I snapped photos of their all-black silhouettes lugging the trees like goth Santa Clauses. They covered the distance to the tent quickly, set their trees down between the larger warehouse trees, and hurried back. The little pine trees tossed and whipped in the strengthening wind. My camera went *click-click-click*, a metronome.

"I can help them carry trees," Mick said.

"Sure, go ahead."

She lifted a tree easily over her shoulder and trotted down the hill with it, effortlessly athletic. I loved how strong she was.

The ring of trees around the tent was slowly closing, and the sun was sinking fast, the sounds of music and festivities swelling inside the tent. My camera's click was lost in the lupine howling of the wind. Eucalyptus leaves shook loose from the grove, swirling into dusty tornados around us.

Nico set down the last tree, completing the ring. It was almost dark, and his profile glowed at the edges with the golden light from the massive tent. Nico gathered Lily, David, and Mick to him, and then they ran as a team back into the grove and grabbed large items—some kind of jugs, like huge containers of liquid laundry detergent—and returned to the trees.

Nico reached the trees first. He waved at me and pantomimed taking pictures. He wanted to make sure I was photographing this, whatever it was.

Lily and David bent to do something to their jugs. I watched as Nico gave Mick instructions, and she followed suit, pouring clear liquid onto the base of the trees.

I lifted the camera to take their picture, trying to understand. Were they watering the trees? I watched Lily dribble the liquid to the next tree, leaving a trail of it on the grass in between, and then water the base of the tree next to it.

I zoomed in on Nico to get a better look. The jug was big; it must have held at least five gallons. It had a long spout coming out of the pouring end.

Gasoline.

Nico was going to set the ring of trees on fire.

Ring of fire. The title of the install.

His titles were always symbolic; I hadn't thought he'd actually—

I clutched my camera to my chest and ran full speed down the grassy hill. By the time I reached Nico, he was tossing his jug aside and pulling a lighter from his pocket. "Nico, what are you doing?"

Through the holes in the ski mask, his eyes were full of scorn. "Chickening out?"

I gestured toward the wildly tossing trees, to the leafy tornados. "What if the fire spreads to the state park? It's enough to just surround the tent with trees. You made your point!"

He gesticulated angrily. "We don't have time for this. I need you documenting!"

They were done dousing the trees. Mick appeared at my elbow. She had pulled the ski mask up to reveal her face. She lifted her head to look up at the wind.

Lily grabbed two tiki torches from the duffel bag and brought them to Nico. Nico lit the torches, and the flames flaring to life made his eyes terrifying behind the ski mask. I couldn't help it. I lifted the camera and took his picture.

"Good girl," Nico said.

"Fuck you," I yelled over the wind. "What if all those people get trapped in there? What if the tent isn't fire resistant?"

"God, Mom. They don't make tents that aren't fire resistant. Just take the fucking pictures!"

Mick dropped the ski mask on the ground and stepped toward Nico. She looked like she was in a trance. He pulled off his mask and looked down at her, his face like a cat's watching birds through a window.

"Do it," he said.

She reached for the flaming torch, and he gave it to her easily.

"Mick?" I yelled. "Mick, what are you doing?"

I felt like I saw entire novels fly through her eyes; she opened and closed her mouth like she wanted to say something, and then she turned away from me.

She stepped toward the nearest Christmas tree and touched the torch to its trunk.

Flames shot up through the needles in a hot, angry whoosh. The tree exploded with light. At its base, the gasoline ignited, spitting a serpent trail of fire to the next tree. That tree ignited, and then the next, and the next.

She turned to face me, the torch still clasped in her hand. Behind her, trees flamed to life, *whoosh—whoosh—whoosh*.

Her hair flashed and flew around her face. Her eyes were feral, glinting with reflected firelight.

Beside her, Nico murmured, "Awesome."

What I did next—I don't know why I did it. I knew it was incriminating and reckless. But I lifted my camera, framed the shot, and took her picture.

That click of the camera—that was the sound of it all going dark.

CHAPTER NINETEEN

✦✦✦

MICK

THE FLAMES ARE HOT AND WILD. I FEEL POWERFUL. I feel like I control the wind.

This is for you, I think to the dead little boy. *This is for the life you lost.*

A trio of trees bursts into flames at once, spewing a volcano of sparks into the eucalyptus grove, and I can almost feel that boy's whole soul screaming out in rage with mine. We're fire and night; we're fury made flesh.

From inside the tent, someone screams.

Across the clearing, on the other side of the tent, people begin running out of the clubhouse. Panicked cries echo around the peaceful golf course.

"That's our cue," Lily says as Nico pulls the ski mask down to cover his face. My mask is lost somewhere in the ring of trees, probably burning. Suddenly terrified, I toss the torch into the branches of the nearest Christmas tree and run after Lily and Nico into the dark grove, away from the tent, heading south under cover of night. Above us, the eucalyptus branches toss in the heavy wind.

"Where's your truck?" Veronica yells to Nico.

"At the warehouse. Lily drove us here."

A fresh burst of screaming echoes behind us. We turn, and Veronica gasps.

The wind is whipping the Christmas trees, tipping them over, rolling them around the clearing like flaming tumbleweeds, driving them into the eucalyptus grove. As we watch, stricken, three of the burning trees are blown to the base of a tall, papery eucalyptus. The bark catches fire, sending flames up the tall tree faster than I'd imagine possible.

"Give me your camera," Nico says, his voice vibrating with energy.

"No." Veronica's answer is a furious growl.

"Give it."

"No!"

He tries to wrench it away from her. The camera strap wraps around Veronica's throat. Nico pulls harder. She's choking, her eyes panicked.

"Stop!" I scream. I throw myself between them. He shoves me aside hard, and I trip and land on my butt. He yanks the camera off Veronica at last, and she puts her hands to her throat, gasping. He lifts the camera to his eye and messes with the focus, and then I hear the soft *click-click* against the screams of the partygoers.

I turn to look at the tent. People are running toward the fire, away from it, toward the clubhouse and beyond. Far away, sirens wail.

"We have to go!" I yell.

Veronica screams, "Give me my goddamned camera back!"

He's totally unconcerned. He lowers the camera from his eye and examines it. "This roll of film is cashed." He presses a switch, and the back of the camera flips open. He takes the roll of film out, snaps the camera shut, and hands it to her. "I'm only getting started with her. Just wait."

Her faces goes slack, stricken. She looks at me too, like I've morphed into something horrible. She snatches the camera from him, shoves it into the camera bag at her shoulder, turns, and marches away toward the scrubs, back in the direction we'd parked her car.

Nico's eyes are trained on the fire, which is creeping higher and higher into the eucalyptus trees. It moves from one tree to the next, like liquid made light. The air is thick with smoke and wind.

I didn't do this. This can't be real.

I turn away. My legs move faster and faster, and then I'm sprinting through the knee-high shrubs, running to catch up with Veronica.

The night is noisy. On my right, the ocean waves roar at the base of the cliff, the Pacific a dark, glinting carpet stretching to the horizon. On my left, the eucalyptus trees are burning brighter by the moment, the golf course flickering with bonfire light. Sirens scream, closer now. I run faster. "Veronica, wait!" I'm close enough to see the angry set of her shoulders as she picks her way through the succulents.

"Veronica!" I call again, out of breath. I leap over a cactus and grab her arm. "Wait. Stop."

She yanks her arm away. "I can't even look at you."

Red lights flash in front of us, on the street where we left Veronica's car. I think it's a fire truck, driving along the road heading toward the golf course, but then I see it's a pair of police cars. The red light flashes white. It's a searchlight, coming from the roof of the squad car in front, illuminating the cars parked there, and then back, toward the field we're standing in the middle of.

We drop to all fours. The light sweeps over us.

"What do we do?" I ask.

"I don't know. Shit, shit, shit!" Her eyes are wide and full of panic, and I'm sure mine are too.

"They're looking for us," I say.

"No shit, they're looking for us! You started a massive fucking fire! It's going to turn into a wildfire that destroys the whole state park!"

"We should go down to the beach. It's better for us to get caught down there. We can just say we're normal people who went for a walk. There's no good reason for us to be hiding in an empty field, is there?"

Her face is grim. "Okay. Come on, let's find a way down."

The searchlight has swept away, but we stay in a crouch anyway as we scuttle to the edge of the cliff. It's a fifty-foot drop to the beach, a steep incline, and I search until I find a little ravine we can use as a path. I wave Veronica over. "We can get down here."

"Hang on, I don't want to damage my camera." She tucks her camera bag into a little hollow between rocks.

I lead the way down, mapping my steps carefully and holding on to the sides of the ravine. It's not hard, and I'm on the beach in less than a minute. Veronica picks her way down, slower than me. She stumbles at the bottom, creating a cloud of dust. I help her to her feet, and she snatches her hands back from me as soon as she's up.

She glowers at me and stomps through the fluffy dunes toward the water. I follow her to the wet sand. The waves are calm but choppy, the whitecaps blue-gray in the moonlight. If this were any other moment, I'd be struck by the beauty of the dark, lonely beach. To the north, lights twinkle on the cliffs, fancy houses owned by people rich enough to buy the rights to this view for life.

Sirens echo behind us. Up on the cliffs, the searchlights flash white.

I put my hand in hers. "I'm scared. Please don't be mad at me."

She snatches her hand away from me. "You wouldn't have anything to be scared of if you didn't commit felony fucking arson."

The sand flashes white. We look behind us again. The lights are closer now. "Are they driving off-road?" I ask.

"Not in regular police cars," she says doubtfully.

Far down the beach, smaller white lights flicker and flare.

Flashlights. They sweep back and forth, up the soft sand toward the cliff and along the wet sand at the water's edge. It's five people or so, moving in our direction.

"They're searching the beach on foot," she says. "Oh, shit. They're going to see us."

"So they find us. We're just teenagers hanging out at the

beach." I step toward her and wrap my arms around her. She's stiff with anger and stubbornness. "I'm sorry," I say into her hair.

"You smell like a campfire."

"So do you."

We step back from each other, staring with huge eyes. "No, like, you reek," she says. "Someone could smell it on you from just standing near you."

"So do you!"

"Shit!" She clutches the sides of her head. "And, like, forensics. You probably have gasoline residue on you. And I'm sure they can test our skin somehow and match the smoke to the fire."

My mind races. This is like last night with Nico but worse. I wish desperately for the other night, for the pool to hide in.

The pool.

"We have to hide in the water!" I pull her toward the waves. "It's the only place they won't look!"

"No! Mick, no!" She yanks her hand away from me. She looks genuinely frightened. "What about sharks? Or the riptide?"

"Veronica, look at the waves. It's low tide, and they're one foot tall. There are no sharks. We just need to go in deep enough to get our heads underwater for the two minutes it takes them to walk by. Do you want to get caught or not?"

She follows me then, into the waves that chill first our knees, then our thighs. We both gasp as the water gets up under our shirts and tickles our ribs with freezing fingers. The flashlights flicker in my peripheral vision. "Hurry!" I cry. "Get your head under!" I duck and let myself be submerged in the dark, cold, salty waves.

The ocean isn't like a swimming pool. A pool is a clean, controlled place. The ocean is wild and fierce.

I let the current buffer me. My feet are planted on the ocean floor, and I feel calm despite the cold seeping through my skin into my joints and guts. The ocean is in the mood to play nice tonight.

I lift my face from the water. The flashlight people are closer. They're wearing uniforms. Cops. They're shining the lights left, right, up the sand and up the walls of the cliffs.

Veronica's face emerges a few feet to my right. Her teeth are chattering, and she looks miserable, like a drenched cat. The roar of waves in our ears drowns out anything the people in uniforms might be saying.

The flashlights are already past us, heading south back toward the parking lot.

Veronica yelps like she's been stung.

"What happened?" I cry.

She thrashes, reaches into the water, and pulls out a string of kelp. "It touched me."

I can't help but smile. I reach out and find her hand underwater. We're both freezing, shivering, our feet pulled from the sand by the waves and then returned with the swells. Her teeth and lips vibrate in a constant *brrrrrrrrrr*.

This is my fault; if I hadn't started the fire and we'd driven away, leaving Nico and his friends to it, we'd be home by now. We'd be warm and cozy, maybe even in bed together.

Those people with the flashlights are moving south *fast*. They don't look like they're running, but maybe they are.

Or wait. Maybe the current is pulling us north, away from

them. We're in a cove, which means the current is going to be calm in places, but as you get closer to the points, the waves will start going different directions, which is when you have to be careful of rip—

Just as I'm thinking the word *riptide*, my feet are yanked out from under me and I'm sucked down into the dark, ruthless ocean.

CHAPTER TWENTY

◇◇◇

VERONICA

ONE SECOND, SHE WAS TREADING WATER NEXT TO me. The next second, she was gone.

"Mick?" I cried. "Mick!"

Something grabbed my ankle, something strong. I kicked against it.

It seized me. My head went under. It was the ocean itself, pulling me out to sea.

Riptide.

The word snapped inside me, and then I was upside down, crushed under a cold mountain of water.

My lungs were already burning. I couldn't tell what was up and what was down. My head banged on something soft. The seafloor? My fingers raked through soft kelp, and I grabbed for it instinctively, just to have something to hold on to. *I'm going to die*, I realized, the thought blazing neon against the dark, whooshing ocean.

The kelp was fine, silkier than seaweed, and then my fingers slipped and ran over the soft planes of what felt like a face. I screamed, sucked in water—this was Mick. I gripped her hair, animal-desperate. *Dead. We're dead.* I kicked hard, her hair clutched in my fists, kicked toward what I thought must be the surface—

I broke through. The night air was icy. My lungs exploded with breath. The waves flung me forward, dunking me again. I yanked at Mick's hair, kicking like I'd never kicked before. Her head broke through the water. "Mick!" I screamed. I wrapped my arms around her stomach and squeezed, instinctively trying to get the water out of her lungs. She weighed a thousand pounds. I got one good squeeze in, which made her cough-barf out a whole truckload of ocean water, and then my strength gave out and she slipped down, out of my arms.

"No!" I screamed, but I had no more breath; I was at the end of my exertion, and it just came out as a wheeze.

Her head bobbed to the surface. She was awake and blinking, wiping hair and water out of her eyes.

"V-v-v-v-v-eronica," she said, shivering.

I couldn't talk. My head went under. I just needed a break from kicking. I was out of strength.

Her arm wound around my chest. She pulled me to the surface. Over the waves pounding in my ears, I heard her croak, "No! Don't stop kicking!"

I forced my legs to kick. "Keep breathing," Mick panted. "We just have to make it to the breakers and then we can ride a wave in."

I saw now that we had been pulled out past the waves, into water so deep for sure there were great white sharks. For *sure*.

"Oh God," I heard myself say through chattering teeth. "Fucking sharks. Sharks."

"There are no sharks." She pulled me with one arm, swimming with the other. "Help me kick. I'll be your arms." She coughed violently and puked into the seawater.

"S-s-s-s-s-sexy," I rasped.

She tightened her arm around me, and together we kicked, making our way toward the shore, away from the dark pit of sharks. At the wave break, she said, "Do you know how to ride waves? Have you ever been bodysurfing?"

"I'm from San Diego, of course I have," I managed; my jaw felt frozen shut.

"I'm letting you go!" She had to scream this last bit, because the waves were loud and crashing, and then we were swooped up and I scream-choked as the ocean dragged me under. I thought I was doing the whole thing over again, heading back out to sea, but then I got my arms in front of me and my body pointed toward the shore, and I was on my way. The wave spat me out into the knee-high shallows, and I limped and dragged myself to the flat, wet sand, where I flopped forward onto my face. I breathed and breathed. I didn't care about flashlights or police or the freezing cold.

Mick got spat out a ways down the beach. I watched her crawl away from the water, coughing and retching into the sand. At last, she crawled toward me and, when she arrived at my side, she started examining me like a real lifeguard, pressing her ear to my back and taking my pulse.

"You're okay," she panted.

"You're the one who almost drowned." Our voices were both raw, like we'd taken up smoking at birth.

Her sand-smeared face was serious. "I know. You got me out right in time."

"How did that happen? You're a badass swimmer."

"It just somersaulted me really fast, and I got a lungful of water before I could stop it. It can happen to anyone."

I rolled onto my back—I was coated in sand like a sugar cookie—and we lay there side by side, looking up at the sky.

Mick pointed to a cloud, which was lit orange from underneath. "That's smoke."

"Yeah."

"How big do you think the fire is?"

"Big."

"I did that." Her breath came in panicked gasps, and then she said, "That little boy is dead."

"What boy? From the pool?"

She nodded. "Dead. I saw it, there was an article." And then she was sobbing, crying so hard her whole body was shaking. I remembered telling her the boy was breathing. That false hope I'd given her was like poison.

"That kid dying was not your fault," I said.

"The fire was my fault."

"Yes. It was. You did a bad thing, but it's okay. People do bad things."

Tears leaked out of her eyes onto her cheeks, mingling with the other salt water that glistened all over her face. "I shouldn't have suggested we hide in the water. That was another bad thing. We could have both died."

"That was actually a smart idea. They'd have caught us for sure otherwise."

She put her hand on mine and squeezed. "Thank you."

I smiled, soft feelings warming me up a little. "I lifeguarded the lifeguard."

She rested her head on my thigh, almost like she was praying to me. "I'm so sorry," she said into my leg. "Please forgive me. I almost lost you. Like that little boy. I'm so sorry." Her back shook with sobs, violent, and my whole body ached with pity. Maybe that little boy's death had something to do with setting the trees on fire. Like Nico had said, she was a girl on the edge. His words came back to me, click-clicking down my spine: *I'm only getting started with her. Just you wait.* An urge to rescue her swelled inside me, but from what? From Nico, my best friend? He wouldn't do anything except encourage her to do more stupid shit like this fire, and it seemed like she'd learned her lesson. Besides, I did stupid shit with Nico all the time. Who was I to judge?

I placed my hand on the back of her tangled, sea-wet head. She was so many layers. One layer was sweet and shy. The next layer was dark and unpredictable. Under that, a layer of kindness and softness, and under that, a layer of fierce dominance. She *was* the ocean, with its riptides and its soft, clean breeze and its beauty and its chilling, shark-filled depths.

"I could fall in love with you," I realized aloud.

The firelight flickered in the sky like Halloween.

CHAPTER TWENTY-ONE

◇◇◇

MICK

"WHAT DO WE TELL YOUR MOM?" I ASK AS VERONICA pulls into her driveway. My voice is hoarse. It's only ten thirty, but it feels like two o'clock in the morning.

"Just let me take the lead." She puts the car in park and turns toward me. Her hair is stringy from the salt water, and her clothes are rumpled and wet.

"I don't know how you're going to explain this," I protest, indicating our bedraggled appearance.

"You'll see." She pops the trunk, and we go around to get our purses out of it. Thank God we left them in here. We'd have lost our phones to the ocean if we'd had them on us.

I follow her up the walkway to the house. The lights are on; Claudia is clearly still awake. Veronica unlocks the front door, and I follow her, my stomach in knots. If Claudia kicks me out too, I have no idea where I'll go.

"We're home," Veronica calls as I close the door behind me.

"In the family room," her mom calls back.

150

Veronica leads me to the room adjoining the kitchen, where Claudia is curled into an armchair with her laptop, wearing workout clothes. When we enter, her eyebrows shoot up. "What happened to you?"

"We went night swimming." Veronica does a little curtsy with her salt-streaked shirt.

Claudia looks me over skeptically. "In the ocean?"

Veronica nods.

"You?"

Veronica glowers. "Yes, me. I'm not as big a chicken as you think I am."

Claudia looks back and forth between us. "Wow. Well, next time, go during the day. What if something went wrong? Who could help you?"

"Oh God, Mom, we only went in up to, like, here." Veronica puts her hand to her waist. "And then we had a water fight, so now I have fish poop in my hair. The worst thing that's going to happen to me is I'm going to catch a cold, because that shit was freezing."

Claudia returns to her computer, shaking her head. "Go take a shower and change. You look like you just rose from the dead."

"Yes, ma'am, we will go take a shower." Veronica grabs my hand and drags me out of the room.

"Separately!" Claudia calls after us.

"La la la!" Veronica yells, muffling this last command. She pulls me with her toward the stairs. The moment Claudia is out of earshot, she drops the cheerful demeanor and sags with exhaustion.

We're quiet as we take turns showering, her first at my insistence. She returns in a fluffy white bathrobe with her hair wrapped in a towel, looking so delicious and warm that I just stand there staring at her like an idiot. Her words come back to me, the words she threw at me on the beach. *I could fall in love with you*, she'd said.

"What?" she asks, adjusting the towel on her head.

I'm suddenly bashful. When I see her here, in her pretty house, I can't imagine what she's even doing with me. I shoulder my duffel bag and turn away before she guesses what I'm thinking and decides she agrees.

I'm clean and in my own pajamas, old boxers and a ratty Mickey Mouse T-shirt, when I return. The room is empty, but music drifts faintly out of the darkroom.

I get my phone out of my purse and check my messages. Pitiful as I am, I've been texting my mom all day. She's not answering. My texts are a sad string of begging: *You can't just ignore me. I'm your daughter.* And *You can't kick me out.* And *Will you just let me know for sure what's going on?*

No replies.

It's completely possible that she has no intention of letting me come back home. Ever.

I call her. It's late; she'll be mad. I bite my lip as the call connects.

A click. Straight to voicemail. "Hi, you've reached Alana Davis, please leave a message and I'll get back to you!"

"Hi, Mom. Will you just answer me? I know you're mad, but we have to figure this out." I hesitate. "I'm sorry I let you down. I don't mean to be like this." Before I can start crying, I hang up.

I return to texts and scroll through them. And then I realize—the last message I sent my mom that says *Delivered* is from before she kicked me out. Since our fight, none of my texts have *Delivered* under them.

I'm confused.

I google it: *texts not delivered why*. I scroll through results, and it becomes immediately clear. Texts not delivered plus straight to voicemail equals one thing only.

She blocked my number.

I feel weird, kind of like when I was sitting in the locker room after the little boy drowned. I feel like I'm outside my own body.

I sit on the floor.

She's not going to let me come back home.

In my hand, my phone buzzes with a text from Nico.

Did you get home OK?

I stare at it for a minute. The events of the night swirl chaotically around me, dark and strange memories of water and fire and smoke.

I reply, *Yeah. I'm back at Veronica's.*

She's going to freeze me out for a while. Let me know if you want to hang out.

He wants to hang out with me? Without Veronica? I type, *Did you get home okay?*

Yup. I'm tucked up in bed all cozy, listening to the crackhead on the other side of the wall scream at his imaginary best friend.

I wonder where he lives. Obviously not somewhere nice. The thought weirdly cheers me up. I'm not the only one struggling.

Anyway, have a good night. TTYL. He inserts a fire emoji. The fire.

I hesitate, and then I pull up Google.

Is it okay to google stuff about the fire? I want to know if they put it out. Maybe I can just browse news stations.

The moment Google launches, I realize I don't even need to do that. The top Google card based on my location is a headline that reads "Wildfire Rages After Environmental Terrorists Target Local Congressman—Again." There's a photo of bright orange flames and dense gray smoke. It's time-stamped 10:35 P.M.

I click on the story and scan through it. Sure enough, the fire blew through the eucalyptus trees into the nearby canyons. They have it 50 percent contained and have listings of all the roads that are closed. I search for any mention of people getting hurt and find a line that says, *Three of the attendees are being treated for minor injuries.* Nico was right.

I push the Home button. The reflection of my face in the screen makes me look like a frightened spirit.

Growing up in Southern California, you hear about wildfires constantly. Whenever people hear that someone started one on purpose, they look at each other in horror and disgust. What kind of person could do such a thing? What kind of monster would intentionally destroy all those animals' habitats, all that nature?

I'm that kind of monster, apparently. Because Veronica warned us and we ignored her.

The darkroom door opens and Veronica emerges. She's changed into a Powerpuff Girls nightgown and carries a stack of eight-by-ten photographs. I snap my face up, afraid she knows how far the wildfire spread, afraid she doesn't.

"I wanted to show you the pictures that are going in the magazine and to the gala," she says. "I don't want you to feel like you don't have any control over it. You can veto any you really hate."

If my mom's mad now, it's going to be ten times worse when I appear in a magazine. I can't even imagine how pissed she's going to be. It will ruin whatever tiny, leftover chance there is of my going home.

I look down at the prints in Veronica's hands. How can I say no after what I put her through tonight?

I push them away. "I don't need to see them. Just . . . do what you need to do."

"I'm bringing them to LA tomorrow to show Carmen. Are you sure you don't want to approve them?"

I want to set them on fire is what I want to do. I take the photographs out of her hands, set them on the bed, push her backward into the darkroom, and kick the door shut behind me. I'm craving the safe dark cocoon, the feeling of being totally immersed in Veronica's world. It's pitch-black in here. I press her up against the door. The only sound is our breathing. I flip the light switch, and the orange safelight illuminates her face in front of me. It feels secluded and anonymous, like the forest party.

I lean in to kiss her, and then I pause. I whisper, "I'm so sorry about tonight. I'm so, so sorry."

Her dark eyes are liquid with compassion. "I'm worried about you. Be careful."

I want to say I will, but it would be a lie. Something inside me feels like it's been unlocked. As much as I regret setting the fire, I also want to go back to the moment I torched the tree and watch the world go up in flames again and again and again and—

"Mick?" Veronica pats my cheek. "Did you hear me? I—"

I kiss her to make her be quiet, grabbing her nightgown in tight handfuls. She goes soft, her arms winding around my neck, and for once I feel like I'm taking something from people and not the other way around.

* * *

Veronica falls asleep first, and I lie there looking at her profile, deep in thought. She's so pretty, her black hair spread out on the pillow, her face turned away from me so I just see the line of her cheekbone and jaw. She's naked, the sheets tangled around her waist, and I feel suddenly sad. I want to be her almost as much as I want her. I want to be self-assured and beautiful and stable, with a solid foundation to stand on and a raging artistic talent to carry me into a bright and interesting future.

I force my eyes off naked Veronica, flip onto my back, and rest my head in my hands. I look at the ceiling.

I have to swim in five hours. Maybe I'll call in sick. But I just no-showed yesterday; Coach will be furious.

I check my phone again. Nothing from my mom, and I don't think there will be, at least not anytime soon. The reality of my situation is starting to sink in. She's not going to let me come home.

I need to think clearly and consider my options. Obviously,

I could call social services and tell them what's happening. They'll probably put me in a foster home. I've known kids in foster care; you don't grow up poor without having contact with that world. They get moved around a lot. Nico only went to Veronica's high school for a semester. I can't risk that. Swim team is all I've got. And it's scary, thinking about being trapped in some foster home or group home. I've heard horror stories about sexual assault and abuse. There has to be another way. I only have one more year of school. It's only ten months.

I try to look at it from a different angle. What do I need to get me through senior year? I need a place to shower, a place to wash my clothes, food, and a place to sleep. The first three are easy. I shower every day after practice, I can just go to a laundromat when I need to wash clothes, and I can eat two meals a day at school, leaving only one I have to figure out on my own. So I really just need a place to sleep. I wish I had a car. I could sleep in that.

Which gives me an idea. I have money in the bank. I wonder how old you have to be to buy a car. I look it up and scowl at my phone. Eighteen. Of course. And apparently you have to be eighteen to get it registered with the DMV. I still have nine months to go. That's no good.

Veronica's a few months younger than me; I know because she chattered on about horoscopes the other day, analyzing me and her and us. The memory makes me smile a little.

Would I ask her to help me buy a car, even if she were eighteen? If her mom finds out I'm planning to live in a car, she'd call social services for sure. She's a great mom; there's no way she'd let that slide. And the two of them are so close.

I can't talk to Veronica about this. There's no other way.

I hate the idea of keeping something from her. She wouldn't judge me for being homeless, I don't think, but she would get all protective and determined to help, which is a road that leads to foster care.

The solution hits me in a flash—Nico. I wonder if he'd help me out and put my car in his name. He doesn't care about doing things legally, obviously. I think Veronica even mentioned that he drives an Uber using someone else's name because he's not twenty-one.

I don't know. He doesn't seem completely . . . safe.

He had Veronica by the throat, pulling at that camera strap.

I don't think he did that on purpose, though. He was just trying to get it away from her so he could photograph the fire before it was too late.

I rack my brain for other options but come up empty.

I text Nico. *Are you still awake?*

He answers back in four seconds. *Yes. Crackhead is now screaming about his dead mother. Listening to music in my headphones is not helping.*

Can I call you?

Sure.

I slip out of bed, careful, but Veronica doesn't stir. I sneak into the darkroom and close the door behind me.

Nico answers on the first ring. "Jagger," his deep voice purrs.

"How are you?" I keep my voice low, almost a whisper.

"All cool over here. Hang on." He must put the phone to his wall, because I hear faint shouting, clearly the person he's been complaining about. The shouting goes away when he returns the phone to his ear. "So that's my night. How are you? Getting all excited about that gala where you get to be the center of attention?"

"Ughhhh," I groan, having momentarily forgotten.

He chuckles. "That's what I thought. Hey, you were pretty awesome tonight, you know that?"

"Awesome?" I echo with disbelief. "Did you see the news? They haven't even contained the whole fire yet."

"No, no, of course. But you didn't do that on purpose. You stepped out, you took a risk. Sometimes it works out, sometimes it doesn't, but . . . you did it. You know?"

"I guess." I don't actually agree, but I'm going to drop it. "Look, I called to ask you a favor. But I need you not to tell Veronica. Can you do that? Do you ever keep secrets from her?"

"Depends what the secret is."

"It's nothing bad. I just can't have her mom finding out."

"Go on."

"I need to get a car, and I'm not eighteen. I wondered if you could put your name on the paperwork until I turn eighteen next May and then sign it over to me."

A pause. "Your parents won't do it?"

My cheeks feel hot. "It's kind of messed up at home right now."

"Ah." The one syllable is full of understanding. "Where are you staying?"

"Well . . ." I stall out, not sure what to say.

"I got it. Sure, I'll help you out."

"I also need your name on the registration. I can get insurance in my name if you sign off on me driving the car, I researched how to do it already."

I hear a rustling, like he's moving around in bed. "Look. Jagger. I'll do whatever you need. Just tell me what papers you want me to sign, and I got you."

My chest loosens. I wedge the phone against my ear and press my fists to my eyes. "Thanks," I manage to squeak out.

"I'll do it under one condition. Something you can't tell Veronica either."

"Whatever you want. I owe you one."

"I need you to get me into that gala on Saturday."

This is a complete surprise. "Why?"

"Because I'm interested in art."

I hesitate. "Will it get Veronica in trouble?"

"Nope. She won't even know I'm there."

"Okay," I agree, suspecting I'll regret this.

CHAPTER TWENTY-TWO

<><><>

VERONICA

THE GALA WAS BEING HELD AT HUMPHREY'S HALF Moon Inn on Shelter Island, a man-made peninsula with a marina and a beautiful view of the San Diego coastline on one side, the endless Pacific on the other. The hotel itself was a collection of buildings, all covered in dark wood and faux Hawaiian decor, a total tourist trap.

Our Uber was stuck in a long line of arriving cars, most of them limousines and town cars. It gave me a minute to peer out the windows at the fancy people going in through the huge, open front entrance. The sun was setting, reflecting orange and pink off the glass that fronted the hotel's main lobby.

I looked aside at Mick. Her eyes were glued to her hands in her lap, which were clenched together so tight the knuckles were white. "You okay?"

She nodded.

"Upset about something?"

She shook her head, but she looked like she was about to cry.

"Your mom?" I guessed. "Is she being weird or mean now that you're back?" She'd gone home yesterday, but she'd been at swim practice all day today, so I hadn't had a chance to ask how it was going.

She shrugged, brushed at her cheeks with the heels of her hands, and turned her face away from me. I put my hand on her tanned knee. She put a hand on top of mine and squeezed.

"Here you go," the driver said.

Mick climbed out first and trotted around to open my door and help me get out. My dress was vintage and much more complicated than her simple black tank sheath. She helped me up, shut the door behind me, and brushed my skirt off.

"Thank you, darling," I said.

"Just trying to be a gentleman."

"You're doing a great job." Her legs and shoulders in that dress were actually slaying me. I ran a hand through her hair, which was glowing pink in the sunset light.

"What are you looking at?" she asked.

"You're just so pretty. I wish you could see yourself right now." I played with a strand of her neon-pink hair, turning the strands this way and that. I wished I could photograph it, but I knew it wouldn't come out. I realized her expression was dark, her eyes glinting with shards of pink and orange. I released her hair. "Are you okay? Seriously, tell me. How is it with your mom? I feel like we've barely talked the last few days."

"I'm fine. My mom is fine. Everything's fine." A man in

a tuxedo and a woman in a long black dress brushed by us haughtily. We were in the way.

I pulled her off to the side. "Mick, what's going on?"

She sighed and looked down at her toenails; she'd painted them red. "I don't like this. I don't want to ruin it for you, but I hate it."

I studied her averted face. "I'm sorry."

"I know it's not like you asked for this either. It's just working out really well for you."

I frowned, ruffled by the bitterness in those last words. "Well, it might work out well for you, too, if we end up making any money on this."

"I don't need your money."

I put my hands up defensively. "I didn't mean it like that. Just, I keep getting offers from people to pay us if you want to do, like, partnerships on Instagram and stuff."

"I don't want to make money this way. I don't want this." She flung an arm in the direction of the hotel.

Her eyes were gleaming; she was crying. Again. She shook her head fast. "Let's just get this over with," she said, and raked her hands through her hair.

I knew I'd had my head up my ass for the last couple of days—I'd been basically living in my darkroom, and she'd been swimming a lot—but how had I missed that she was this upset? I should have noticed. I'd assumed everything was fine now that she and her mom had reconciled, but maybe it wasn't. Maybe the little boy thing was really haunting her. I wondered if she should see a therapist.

But it wasn't only about her. This event was about my art,

all my years of work and practice, and all she had to do was sit through it for a few hours.

Suddenly, I was angry. "Can you try to be a little more supportive? How do you think it feels that no one noticed my work until I photographed a hot blonde? Do you realize this might be my only chance at this kind of recognition?"

She snapped her eyes onto me. "I hadn't thought of it like that."

We stared at each other—a showdown—and then we both softened.

"Sorry," I said, while she said, "I'm sorry."

I pulled her closer to me. "It's just a few hours. Then you can take me hiking or something as revenge."

She half smiled. "I'm not going to take you hiking." She kissed my cheek, and warmth slid through me. Everything was going to be okay.

Inside the hotel, it was all about high ceilings, geometric lines, and acres of glass looking out on the coastline. A woman in a black suit with a name tag stood waiting to greet us with a bright smile. "Welcome. You're here for the Save the Bay event?"

I nodded. "I'm one of the artists in the silent auction."

"You'll be through that archway." She pointed left. "Along the outdoor corridor, and then to the right in the Grayson Room."

Mick and I followed her instructions. A group of over-dressed, bejeweled people milling around a glass door told us we were in the right place.

Another staff member opened the door for us, and then

we were in what looked like a reception hall converted into a gallery, with temporary white walls erected in a careful maze. A sign advertised the Save the Bay Silent Art Auction, but it was anything but silent. The room was crowded with guests examining the hundreds of paintings, sculptures, and photographs.

Carmen appeared in front of us. "There you are!"

I'd only met her once, at a restaurant in LA where she gave me some feedback on my photos and arranged for me to drop them off here at the hotel. She had full sleeves of colorful tattoos and vintage bangs, a sort of pinup look that was superhot. Tonight she was wearing a fitted white cocktail dress.

"You must be Mick," she said, holding Mick at arm's length and looking her over from head to toe. "You're gorgeous in person. Just wow."

"Thank you," Mick mumbled.

Releasing us, Carmen pointed to where my photos had been hung, in a prominent spot along the left wall. At first, I couldn't see them because they were surrounded by people. More people were crowded in front of them than any other work in the gallery.

The viral Instagram photo was displayed in the very center. I'd blown this one up to twenty-four by twenty-four in a process that pushed my enlarger skills to the max and required my mom to call in favors from the teacher who ran the darkroom on the city college campus. Other photos of Mick were hung on either side, smaller, to highlight this as the centerpiece of the series.

Mick pressed her lips together into a thin line when she saw them. Her eyes flitted from photo to photo, and she took a step back.

Some of these were pictures I hadn't shown her yet, photos of her diving into the pool and stretched out sideways from behind, bare backed, and of her in semidarkness, her eyes closed and mysterious, the rest of her face cast into shadow. People seemed to prefer the portraits where her face was centered in the frame. The darkroom shots with her bathing suit straps falling off her shoulders had people crowded tight around them, as did the one of her sitting on the bed, looking up at me with those haunting child-woman eyes.

To the crowd, Carmen said, "Ladies and gentlemen, here are the artist and the subject of these pieces, if you'd like to ask them any questions."

Hungry eyes turned on us, and then we were surrounded. Diamond-encrusted hands reached out, wanting to touch me and Mick, to feel our skin and grip our hands.

"This reminds me of my first love," one woman told me. "He's dead now, but I'll never forget him. Antonio. We were together for five months, in Mexico."

Another said, "This makes me feel . . . It makes me feel something. Sad, but also, it's so . . . it's so . . . *real.*"

Mick backed away. Her face was blank with panic. "I can't do this."

We were getting separated by the crowd, but I tried to grab her hand. "Mick? You okay?"

"I'm sorry. I can't." She turned and fled. She rushed through the glass doors and then I was alone, surrounded by the crowd. An older man was telling me about the day he proposed. Another woman's eyes were bright with tears.

"Excuse me. Excuse me!" A voice carried over the din around me. "We're with the *San Diego Union-Tribune*. Can we get a shot of the artist? Is that you?" Suddenly, cameras were in my face. "I'm from the *Guardian*," said someone else. "We're with the *Arts Magazine*—"

Carmen's voice lifted over the others. "After interviews, we'll head over to the dinner. Where's Mick?"

"She left. It was too much."

Her face darkened. She clearly didn't like this.

"She's extremely shy," I explained hurriedly. "This is hard for her."

"Fine. Veronica, stand here." She gave directions to the photographers, and I was hurled into the position of subject, pinned by the lenses and the flurry of eyes and flashes. Was this how Mick felt? I tried to smile, to create a flattering angle for the cameras. Someone identified himself as a reporter from the *LA Times*. All these famous publications!

They asked questions between pictures: "How old are you? What school do you go to? Do you know your photo has over a million hits on different accounts? Are you gay? How old is your girlfriend?"

Those questions made me angry. It felt like something they planned to sensationalize so gross old dudes could get off on the idea of pretty teenage girls having sex with each other. "Don't worry about if I'm gay or not," I responded icily. "Ask me about photography."

As the people around me dispersed, I saw that the sky had

grown dark, and the lights from the hotel reflected in the water of the marina and off the sailboats parked right outside. Hotel staff announced it was time for the dinner part of the gala.

Carmen reappeared and pointed to a clear plastic box hanging on the wall at the end of the row of photos. It was full of little white papers. "Silent auction bids." She grinned and gave me a huge hug. "You did a fantastic job. What does this feel like? I can't even imagine experiencing this at your age!"

"I don't know," I answered honestly. I felt like I had spoken more words in the last fifteen minutes than ever before in my life.

"Why don't you head over to the dinner? I'll be down in a few. Take a load off. And congratulations. This is just the beginning for you, Veronica."

I forced a smile. "Will do."

"See you in there!"

I exited through the same door Mick had stormed out of and walked down the long outdoor hallway. The lighting had kicked on, and everything was glowing yellow from the Art Deco fixtures.

I found the banquet hall by the sound of applause. It was decorated like a fancy wedding reception. I scanned the tables carefully for a long minute, examining each seated person.

No Mick. So she left, then. For real.

Dejected, all the joy of the evening gone, I started picking through the tables in search of an empty seat. On the stage, a dignified-looking, grandfatherly man was droning on, listing off names of donors and executives. "And we're very honored to have Congressman Osgood with us tonight." I froze and swiveled to face the stage. "Congressman, you've been a major contributor to our work at Save the Bay, and we'd like to honor you with something special. Come on up."

A slim man with receding brown hair stood up. I knew that toothpaste smile. I knew that wave.

Nico's target.

Onstage, he shook hands with the announcer and thanked the audience. Were they giving him a standing ovation? Why? Bewildered, I looked around me as attendees got to their feet one at a time.

"We know this has been a hard week for you, Congressman," the announcer continued. "And we want to tell you how much we appreciate you. We wouldn't have blamed you for skipping this event, but instead, you continue to further your contributions to Save the Bay, and we can't tell you how much it means." More applause.

Was this a coincidence? Was that possible?

I was here because someone dropped out. They stopped returning Carmen's emails.

Then someone recommended me to her.

I felt cold.

Osgood took the mic and raised it to his lips. "My father used to say," he began, and everyone sat down except for me. "You wouldn't be judged by your actions during good times; you'd be judged by how you responded to hardship. That's why I choose to be here and stand firm. Our causes will continue, and so will I."

Thunderous applause.

"I just hope that you'll remember my—"

Boom.

The ceiling above him collapsed.

An avalanche of leaves and dirt rained down, toppling him and burying him alive. Dirt poured off the stage down onto the front tables. People screamed. A remaining chunk of ceiling was hanging by a thread. As I watched, it vibrated and collapsed, sending another wave of dirt and drywall dust into the room.

Silence.

And then screaming.

I turned and ran for the exit as people jumped to their feet. As I burst through the glass door, they were yelling at each other and trying to dig Osgood out.

Outside, a few hotel workers were running to help, and somewhere someone was shouting, "Call 911!"

"Nico!" I screamed. I was furious, terrified. Had I just watched him kill someone? "Nico!" I yelled again.

Attendees started rushing out onto the walkway with me. I hurried along the perimeter of the banquet hall, searching for any sign of him, my heart pounding in my ears. Ahead, at the back edge of the building facing the marina, something moved along the roofline. I stopped and looked up. "Nico, is that you? Are you up there?"

Something rolled, tumbled, plummeted down from the roof to the paved walkway in front of me, landing with a sickening crunch. I jumped back, breath sucked into my chest.

Up on the roof, a shadow, tall and lean, turned and walked out of sight.

I looked down at the heap on the ground. It was a person slumped into an unnatural ball, dressed all in black, the clothing lit dimly by the walkway's golden lanterns.

"Oh God," I heard myself whisper. I was terrified, hyperventilating. I tried to snap out of it. I knelt down beside the person, unsure if I should roll them over. If they were still alive, maybe I could help. I was afraid to move them and break their spine or something, like you hear about on TV. I found a head of tangled dark hair, and I pushed a few strands aside gently to get a look at their face. The head fell sideways, hair parting, and a pair of dead brown eyes stared straight into mine.

I screamed and jumped back.

It was Lily.

Lily. Dead. Her lips white, her eyes emptier than empty, a mannequin, a corpse, a dead body, dead dead dead.

I could hear myself sobbing, wheezing. My hands were stained with blood. I tried wiping them on my legs. "Oh my God oh my God oh my God," I heard myself chanting.

On the water, a motorboat growled and raced out of the marina, toward the ocean.

A chorus of shrieks at my back—a group of women had seen Lily. "Call 911!" one of them screamed. A woman knelt at my side, doing exactly what I had just done, confirming with unsteady hands that Lily was beyond our help.

Ambulances and police cars screamed in the night. The walls and windows of the hotel and the dark, still water in the marina reflected red light onto the shouting attendees. I couldn't bear the sight of Lily's unblinking eyes. I wanted to close them, but I—

"Miss. Miss!" a man near us was yelling at me. "Get out of the way!" People were running toward us, police officers and EMTs. I got up and backed away from Lily. I watched silently as the EMTs checked her over and the police created a barrier around her. "Step back!" they yelled at the attendees, who were crowding around in increasing numbers. A group of men stood in front of me, blocking my view. On the other side of the building, firefighters and paramedics swarmed into the banquet hall.

Part 3: Buried Alive.

The earth itself is your judge and jury.

Nico's words from the night of the fire popped back into my head: *I'm just getting started.*

"Excuse me?" A middle-aged man in a rumpled brown suit was talking to me. "I'm Detective Salcedo. You found the body of the young lady, correct?"

I nodded.

"Come with me."

CHAPTER TWENTY-THREE

✧✧✧

VERONICA

I WAS IN THE BACK SEAT OF THE DETECTIVE'S
unmarked police car, the grate that separated me from the
front seat contributing to a bone-chilling claustrophobia. I
tried not to look at my red-stained hands and legs, and failed.

I wanted to text Mick, but I was afraid to draw attention to
my phone lest the detective ask to see it. Because the more I
thought about this situation, the more I realized what a huge
amount of trouble I was about to be in.

The detective wanted to do an official interview with
me back at the station. My mom was meeting us there. He
thought I was just a normal witness, someone who had seen a
stranger fall off a roof. And there were questions I was going
to have to answer with either the truth or a lie.

For example: Did I know Lily? The answer was yes. I knew
her. But the next question would be—how did I know her?
We didn't go to school together. She was two years older, not
originally from San Diego. If I admitted to knowing her, I'd

have to tell them how, and the answer to that question really cracked open Pandora's box.

The fire.

If I told them about Nico's art installations, that I was the photographer who took the pictures on his Tumblr account, that would implicate me in felony arson. Right? Because what was I going to tell them—that I hadn't started the fire, that Mick and Nico had done it? I didn't like the idea of throwing either of them under the bus like that.

I couldn't imagine what might have happened on the roof to make Lily fall, but I had to think something went wrong with those bags of dirt or some other piece of the install. But the fact that Nico had left her behind—I'd *never* forgive him for leaving her like that. How could he be so callous?

And then, as the detective pulled the police car into the station, I remembered something that made me go blank with horror.

The photo.

I'd taken that photo of Mick with the torch in her hand. Nico had that roll of film. It was proof that Mick had started the fire. I was on the roll of film too. It tied all three of us to the scene of the fire, the scene of the crime.

A little part of me wondered if the fire meant anything now that Lily was dead. Wasn't this the time to just come clean?

Nico and I had been keeping each other's secrets for years. He was the only person I really trusted. I had to at least talk to him and hear him out before ruining his life and sending him to jail. Because, unlike me, Nico wasn't a minor, and he didn't have parents who would shell out money to defend him.

* * *

Detective Salcedo parked the car. "Here we are," he said cheerfully, checking on me in the rearview mirror. "You doin' okay there, Veronica?"

I nodded, but my whole body was shaking. He must have seen it on my face; he hopped out and came around to open my door. "Let's get you inside and get you a cup of tea. Sound good? I'm sure your mom's waiting for you."

I couldn't ask my mom what to do. She didn't know about Nico's installations; as far as she knew, he was a sculptor and mixed-media artist.

Inside the police station, in a medical-looking room, someone swabbed the blood on my hands and dress and took samples from various parts of my arms and clothing while my mom was deep in conversation with Detective Salcedo.

It had to be only a matter of time until they figured out Nico was the one doing these things to the congressman. Or they'd connect him and Lily somehow. Panic was running through my veins, into my heart and out to my legs. This was so, so bad.

CHAPTER TWENTY-FOUR

◇◇◇

VERONICA

I HAD THE UBER DROP ME OFF IN FRONT OF THE warehouse. It was dark outside, but the air was warm, with a salty ocean breeze ruffling my arm hair. Before he left, the driver rolled down his window to ask me, "Are you sure you want me to leave you here?"

"Yes. I'm fine."

The driver shook his head and drove away, leaving me alone in a decrepit alley under a flickering streetlight.

Keys in hand, I made my way around the warehouse. You'd think it was abandoned, with boarded-up windows and rusty shipping doors that looked like they hadn't been opened in a decade. My approach startled a rat, which had been sniffing the bottom of a dumpster shoved against the warehouse wall. The rat made a squeaking sound and disappeared underneath.

The door had two ancient deadbolts, and I unlocked the

top one; the bottom one was broken. I stepped into a dank, sour-smelling hallway and locked the door behind me.

The factory was owned by a slumlord who rented out the old offices as extreme low-income housing. There was one foul-smelling bathroom down here on the first floor, off this hallway, and all the "apartments" had to share it. There was no shower; Nico showered at my place or the gym, and judging by the appearance of the other inhabitants I'd caught glimpses of, most of them weren't sober enough to bother. The massive warehouse space had been divided with badly constructed barriers, and Nico rented a huge portion of this space to store all the equipment and raw materials for his installations.

This wasn't the first space like this he'd lived in. When he was a senior in high school, he was renting a similar place from a different slumlord in an adjacent warehouse district, and there had been a few other living situations in between. "Putting the starving in starving artist," I used to tease him as he devoured plates of food while my mom looked on pityingly.

My mom was under the impression that Nico rented an apartment in Chula Vista with a few friends. It had taken her a while to be okay with me going to his place, but she'd never have come around if she knew I was hanging out at abandoned warehouses rented out by God knows who.

Music and conversation drifted into the hall from behind the apartment doors. They weren't numbered like apartments would normally be, so people had created their own system for naming their units. One door was painted red and had

REDRUM scrawled in dripping black paint. Another door had been painted blue, and white clouds had been sponged on in the shape of a heart in what seemed like a sad attempt to brighten the darkness. I passed a door covered in yellow caution tape that I usually thought looked cool but now gave me the creeps.

Nico lived on the second floor. I turned left at the top of the cracked concrete stairs and stopped at the door of his unit, which was painted a simple gray. I knocked, using my usual shave-and-a-haircut rhythm. I pressed my ear to the door but couldn't hear anything over the music pounding through the floor below. I knocked again and was halfway through it when the deadbolt disengaged with a click and the door swung inward.

Nico stood in front of me, looking exhausted, his eyes ringed in dark circles, his hair lank and sweaty. "What are you doing here?"

"I'm paranoid about calling you. I'm worried they'll look at my phone records."

He pulled me into the apartment and closed the door behind me. "Where does your mom think you are?"

"Asleep in my bed." The room was as familiar as my own and about the same size. The first thing that always struck me about this place was the neatness. After the dingy, dark hallway with the weed smoke creeping out from everywhere, Nico's room felt spare and clean. It had a single, high window that didn't open; its cracked glass was held together with wire mesh. The walls were painted white, and he had taken the time to paint the concrete floor in a black-and-white checkerboard pattern. A bed was pushed into a corner facing a love seat on the opposite wall. His few clothes were stored in an IKEA wardrobe beside a nightstand chest with a lamp on it that provided the only source of light. A desk against the wall with the window contained a few books, a Bluetooth speaker, and some other art and office supplies. That was it. That was all he owned.

I turned to face him. "What happened to Lily? How *could* you—" Grief rushed through me. "How could you leave her there? How could you do that?"

He sank down onto the love seat. His hands splayed palms up on his knees, and he looked down at them. In slow motion, his hands reached up to his face, and then he crumpled down, head to knees, and did something I'd never seen him do before: He started crying.

I stood above him, watching his back shuddering as he sobbed into his knees. I could see his ribs through his white T-shirt.

My anger evaporated, leaving me deflated. I collapsed onto the love seat next to him. "Tell me what happened. Why did you even go to that gala? And why didn't you tell me?"

He straightened up, wiping brusquely at his face. At last, he looked me in the eyes. "When I realized you were going to be at the same gala I planned to do my install at, I didn't tell you because I wanted you to have deniability."

"So it was a coincidence that we were at the same event on the same night for different reasons? Come on, Nico, how dumb do you think I am?"

He threw his hands up. "And I was worried you would

think I was trying to sabotage you. You get really weird and competitive with me sometimes, V."

"No I don't!"

He shook his head. "Anyway, I thought it would be easier, okay? But the install was riskier than the last rooftop one. I had to store all these sandbags up on the roof in advance. I didn't know if they'd come crashing down before I was ready."

"What happened to Lily?"

He took a deep breath. "We were on the roof. The install went off without a hitch. It worked amazing. Did you see it?"

I nodded. "I was in the audience. I couldn't believe I was watching you kill this congressman. What—"

"I didn't kill him," Nico protested. "He's fine. He's not even in the hospital."

"It looked like—" I took a breath. I was glad Osgood was okay. But still. "You went too far."

"I know," he replied quietly.

"Who was taking pictures?"

"I thought Lily. But she wasn't where she was supposed to be. She was supposed to be planted in the audience photographing, but she had come up onto the roof with us."

"Why?"

"I don't know!" It came out as a shout. He bit his lip. "I don't know," he repeated, quieter. "We finished and were up on the roof, getting ready to leave on the boat we had pulled up in the marina. But— Fuck!" He ran his hands through his hair. "I don't know what happened. David was over by the roof's edge. I heard some shouting. I came to tell David to shut up, that he was making too much noise. He was at the edge, looking down. Lily was there. You found her. I thought she might still be alive, but then you turned her on her back, and I could see that she was dead. So we ran. I mean, what were we supposed to do? If we stayed, we'd all go to jail. We got the hell out of there, and we all went our separate ways, and—" He gestured to his room as though to say he'd been here ever since.

"So you think she fell on accident? David couldn't have pushed her?"

"No way. He wasn't anywhere close to her. No one else was near her. And I don't think she would have jumped. Why would she? It makes no sense. Not there, not then. There's no reason."

I slumped back into the love seat. "She was supposed to be taking pictures?" I asked.

He nodded.

"With what?"

He frowned at me. "What do you mean?"

"With what kind of camera?"

"She was going to use a disposable. But I found it on the roof. She hadn't taken any pictures."

"You found the camera? Just on the roof lying there?"

He looked down at his hands again. "Well, it was in her purse. I took the whole purse."

"You took a dead girl's purse?" My voice rose an octave. "Are you insane? Do you have any idea what that will look like to the cops?"

"I got rid of it! I couldn't let them find evidence!"

"Nico," I breathed. "Holy shit. You have dug yourself a hole."

"I know."

We sat there in silence. He looked so thin and beaten, I couldn't help putting my hand over his and squeezing it.

I turned things over in my mind. "What does David think we should do?" I asked.

"He thinks we should go about normal life and pretend it never happened, stop the installations, and act like we don't know each other. I mean, you and I should still text each other normal stuff, act like normal friends, but the series is dead in the water." He looked hopeless and lost. His art was everything to him.

I wrapped my arm around his waist. I pulled him close to me, and we leaned back into the cushions, looking up at the stained, water-damaged ceiling. "I know your art has gotten you through some really tough times," I began carefully. "I know how much it means to you."

He didn't say anything, but I saw his jaw tighten in profile.

I went on. "I just . . . I know you get so hyper focused. I want to make sure you understand what I'm about to tell you."

He turned his head to look at me. "What?"

"David is right. You need to stop for now. You can start another series when this all calms down," I said. "But he's right. It's enough."

"I know." He put his arm around my shoulders, and we

held each other for a minute. He murmured, "I should have kept a closer eye on her up there. But she's a graffiti artist—*was* a graffiti artist. She was used to being up high, doing pieces on underpasses—this shouldn't have been hard for her."

"I know." He was right; Lily was fine to work on a roof, or dangling from a freeway overpass, or anywhere else she needed to go. She was tough and competent, and it hit me all at once how much I was going to miss her, how badly I wished I'd gotten to know her better.

I felt a little suspicious of how easily he'd given in. I'd expected him to get angry, to yell at me, to get defensive. It wasn't like Nico to be so easily convinced.

We sat like that for a while, arms around each other, lost in thought.

"You should go," he said at last.

"So we're playing dumb. We're pretending to know nothing about the installs. You don't have any evidence lying around anywhere?"

"Nope. Just stuff for sculpture. I'm sure they'll check everyone you know, but all they'll find is a bunch of stuff for metalwork and mixed media."

"What if they get your IP address from when you update your Tumblr?"

He was already shaking his head. "I use a VPN. I'm fine. And I got rid of that laptop just to be safe."

"And the photos themselves? Any film you have lying around? What about the roll from that night at the fire? You didn't publish those pics on your Tumblr. Do you still have it?"

He shook his head and said, "Gone. We've left no trace. What about you? *You* have any film hanging around?"

"No. I always give you the film to develop. You know that."

Again, I was hit with a feeling of suspicion. I couldn't quite picture Nico destroying all traces of his art. It was all he had.

CHAPTER TWENTY-FIVE

◇◇◇

MICK

MY LEGS, BACK, AND SHOULDERS ARE ALL CRAMPING up when Nico pulls the door open. "She's gone," he says.

I stumble out of the IKEA wardrobe and collapse onto the edge of the bed, gulping in big greedy breaths. "I'm not normally claustrophobic, but that took forever."

He sits on the bed next to me, so close our legs are touching. "I didn't want to make her suspicious by rushing her out of here." His eyes are so, so dark. "I'm sorry. I didn't mean to drag you into all this."

After a long moment, I whisper, "I can't believe Lily is dead." He winces like I slapped him, and I rush to apologize. "I'm sorry. She was your friend. I barely knew her."

He shakes his head hard, like he's pushing the whole thing away. "I wish I hadn't asked her to take pictures. If I had just let her do her normal thing, she'd still be alive right now."

"It wasn't your fault," I protest. "How could you have known?"

He stares down at his hands miserably. What he said about

pictures reminds me of the question Veronica asked. "Did you really destroy that film from the night of the fire?"

"Yeah. Of course."

How do you even destroy a canister of film? By burning it? And he'd been so desperate to have it, wrenching it away from Veronica with actual violence. I'm not sure I believe him.

I remember the conversation I heard from inside the closet. When Veronica came in, he switched on a different tone of voice, one that had gotten her to soften and swing from being angry with him to comforting him. It made me wonder how honest he was being with *me*.

"I want to talk to Veronica," I say. "I need to apologize for leaving tonight. I need to come up with an alibi for where I was when everything happened, don't I?"

He shakes his head, his face solemn. "Mick, you need to stay away from this. As far as anyone is concerned, you left and were nowhere near the gala when Lily fell. In a few days, when everything calms down, you can call Veronica. For now, let's focus on getting you a car."

"Okay," I agree, because this does sound like the right way to handle the situation, and because without him, I don't know what I'm going to do. I need that car. I can't risk upsetting him. I feel like I'm walking on a tightrope. If I fall to the left, I'll make Nico angry and be out on the street. If I fall to the right, I'll find myself tangled up in lies to the police and ruining things with Veronica.

"Speaking of calling people, did your phone turn up?" he asks.

I shake my head glumly. "I must have left it in the Uber on

the way to the gala. It's nowhere. And I can't replace it without my mom signing off on it with T-Mobile."

He gives me a sympathetic look. "If you want, I can get you a prepaid phone from the carrier I use. No parents." I'd told him the full story about what was happening with my mom.

"Thank you," I say, grateful and relieved.

"Hey, guess what?"

"What?"

"I have a surprise for you." He stands, pulling me with him, and leads me out of his little apartment, down the dark stairs to the warehouse. He fumbles along a wall and flips a switch.

The now-familiar piles of equipment and boxes light up dimly, illuminated by a row of naked hanging bulbs. Nico's supplies occupy most of the warehouse; the rest is partitioned into smaller cubicles for the other residents. We were in here earlier, loading evidence from the series into a van so Nico could get rid of it, and I'm struck again by how much stuff he has. It makes sense that installation art would need an incredible amount of equipment, but the contrast between the sparsity of his living quarters and the hangar-sized storage area is striking. It's clear that his life is here, not up there.

"Come here. It's this way," he says, weaving past towers of boxes, something that looks like a kiln surrounded by bricks and bags of dry concrete or maybe soil, and a million more boxes, until he stops in front of a poster-sized black-and-white photo tacked to the partition wall that separates us from the next storage area.

It's the picture of me. From the gala.

I gasp. "You stole it?" I don't know how I'm still shocked by him.

He cracks a grin. "No, I outbid the thirty-thousand-dollar offer that was on the table. Of course I stole it."

"Thirty thousand dollars?" I stare at him, dumbfounded.

He cocks his head at me. "You still don't understand what this is, do you? This is just the beginning for this photo. And people know it."

I step closer to the photograph. It's huge, my face so much larger than life.

This black-and-white me is so much more *me* than I am, like I'm a shadow of her and not the other way around.

Nico is at my side. He points to a metal trash can. "I thought you might want to kill it with fire." He offers me a lighter from his pocket, the same black Bic he lit the tiki torches with when we started the wildfire.

I accept it. It's warm in my palm. I say, "It doesn't change anything to destroy this one. It's still online. Besides, Veronica has the negative."

"Sometimes the gesture can be therapeutic." He steps away. "I'm going to work on something. Take your time."

He disappears between stacks of boxes. I step closer, eye to eye with this other version of myself. She looks past me, at the person taking the picture, at Veronica. She's lost and a little frightened, but she's full of adventure. She's me, but better.

I find myself tracing the outlines of her lips with my fingertips, the curve of her arm, the space behind her, the rows of blurry seats.

And then, explosively, I rip her off the wall.

I tear her down the middle. The shiny photo paper protests, a shriek. I ball it up, stiff and unwieldy, shove it into the trash can, and flick the Bic until I get a shaky flame.

I light the edges on fire. It takes a minute to really catch, and her eyes peek out at me from the folds.

Images flash through the flames: the wildfire—the little boy drowning—Veronica pulling me out of the ocean.

Regret fills me. I'm so ashamed of myself for letting that boy drown, for starting the fire, for being here in the first place. As of this morning, the fire has been completely contained. I saw pictures of the destruction: charred hillsides, a burned house, firefighters exhausted and sweaty. I caused that. How can I live with myself?

I know Nico thinks I belong here, that I'm the right person to work on this series with him because of this photo and for other reasons I can't completely understand. Maybe he's grateful to have someone around who understands the kind of family problems he's been through, or maybe he's upset about Lily and is clinging to me out of some grief reaction. I don't know how to extract myself, but I need to. I'm going to put all my energy into figuring out the car situation, and then, as soon as that's done, I'll go make things right with Veronica.

I find Nico back by the kiln thing, crouching on the ground by a small wooden crate. "Hey," I say, approaching. "What are you doing?"

He looks up and grins at me. "Come here, I want to show you my new technique."

I sit next to him and watch as he uses the back end of a hammer to wrench the boards off what turns out to be a shoebox-sized block of white plaster. He hammers away at it, chipping pieces off, until something in the middle becomes visible. It's the size of my hand and vaguely spherical. At last, he brushes the thing off with his big, dusty hands and shows it to me.

It's a flower. A magnolia blossom, I think, each delicate petal rendered in stainless steel, completely photorealistic and heavy in my hands.

I look up at him for an explanation. He's grinning his most excited grin.

"This is for the fifth installation. The last secret piece in the series," he says, his tone conspiratorial.

I'm shocked. "You're continuing the series? Are you serious?"

He crooks an eyebrow. "Of course."

"But what about what you said to Veronica?"

He makes a disbelieving face. "I thought you of all people would understand. You know what this is for me. How can you expect me to stop? Have you given up swimming just because of what happened to that kid?"

"That's different," I protest.

"How?"

It's hard to argue with him when he looks at me like that, so piercing and direct. I look down at the flower, running my fingertip over the perfect petals. "Flowers are the fifth installation?"

"No, not flowers. The *technique*. I'm practicing on flowers. The more delicate the object, the harder it is to cast. I've never seen anyone get this much detail out of a fully bloomed flower." He beams, full of self-satisfaction. "Do you want to know how I did it?"

"Sure."

He takes the flower from me. "So when I made the plaster cast, I made sure there were two holes. One on top—" He turns the flower so I can see a faint imperfection at the top of the blossom. "And one at the bottom." He flips the flower over to show me a similar imperfection. "So now I had a flower encased in solid plaster with a hole at the top and a hole at the bottom. I didn't try to crack the plaster and get the flower out. I poured the molten steel in, displacing everything through the holes in the bottom."

"Wait," I say, trying to put this together. "You poured steel in and, what, like, liquefied or burned the flower and displaced it with the steel?"

"Yes! And when all the biological material had run out, I plugged up the holes and let the metal cool."

I indicate the kiln-oven thing behind him. "Is that what you use to melt the metal?"

"Yup. See those bricks?"

I pick one up. It's heavy and cold, and a dull shade of light gray. "What are you going to use this technique for if not flowers?"

"I can't tell you! It's a surprise. It's going to be *beautiful*." His eyes glow, and he hands me back the flower. "Even prettier than this."

I remember the silver chicken in Veronica's room. Could he have used the same technique on a chicken? Surely not. That would be disgusting, liquefying a chicken.

And yet . . .

Just to confirm, I say, "Veronica and David don't know about this installation."

"I'll get David on board. Don't worry."

I remember the disbelief in Veronica's voice when he told her he destroyed the film from the night of the fire. She's right; look how he refuses to stop doing his art, even with Lily dead and the potential to get in trouble even huger than before. No way did he destroy it. It's around here somewhere.

I have to find it.

He says, "Oh, hey, good news. I made us an appointment to go look at a car for you. That one you found online. The guy can meet us the day after tomorrow."

A flood of relief. So I just have to stick around for one more project and then I'm done.

He turns the flower over and over in his hands. "It's all coming together."

CHAPTER TWENTY-SIX

<small>◇◇◇</small>

VERONICA

IN THE UBER ON MY WAY HOME FROM NICO'S warehouse, I stared out the window at the dark sky and the suburban lights, gnawing on my lower lip.

Something was wrong.

I remembered the things Nico had said about Lily, about the pictures. Everything made sense, but it felt off.

He could have been lying. Even on his best days, he had an open relationship with the truth. But why? About what?

First things first. I needed to tell Mick what had happened, but she was sending me straight to voicemail. Either her phone was off or she was rejecting my calls.

She would be so upset if she saw Lily's death on the news after the horrible week she'd had. I needed to tell her.

Maybe . . .

I started scrolling through my Instagram DMs, searching for that message from Mick's friend Liz.

"Ah!" I cried when I found it. There it was, the message I'd gotten back when the photo first blew up: *Is this Mick from National City? It is, right?*

I typed a reply, trying to come up with something legitimate-sounding. *Liz, are you Mick's friend from swimming? I need to give her a ride in the morning, and her phone is off. Can you give me her address?*

I sent the message and waited impatiently, drumming my fingers on my knees.

"Come on, come on, come on," I whispered. It was one o'clock in the morning. She might be asleep; swim practice was at seven.

My phone buzzed. Sure enough, it was a DM from Liz.

Uh, I'm not, like, giving you her address.

I heaved a sigh of frustration. Well, of course, everyone should be safety-conscious and never give out their address, or their friends' addresses, to people on the internet. But I wished she'd been reckless just for this moment.

I tried to figure out what to say. At last, I typed, *Can you give me her mom's number? I can call and ask for it. Would that be better?*

After a moment, a number popped up on the screen, and I hissed in satisfaction. But would I get Mick in trouble with her mom for calling this late?

I mulled it over, considered it from the police's perspective, and decided it was more legitimate to wake her mom up than to hold this huge news for tomorrow after swim practice.

I dialed the number. It rang once, twice.

"Hello?" a woman said in a high-pitched voice that didn't sound sleepy. In fact, I thought I heard loud room sounds in the background, like she was in a bar or restaurant.

"Hi, this is Veronica. I'm a friend of Mick's."

"Hang on, can't hear you." After a few seconds, the white noise quieted, like she'd stepped outside. "Okay. What did you say?"

"This is Veronica, a friend of Mick's," I repeated.

After a silence, she said, "The girl she's dating? The photographer?"

"Yes!" I was relieved she knew who I was. "I'm sorry to call so late. I'm trying to get ahold of Mick, but her phone is off, and it's really important."

Another silence.

"Hello?" I asked.

"Mick doesn't live with me anymore." Her voice had changed. It was sharp.

I was confused. "I thought she was back home with you. For, like, three days now."

"Well, she's not."

"But then, where is she?"

"Ask her." The line went dead.

The Uber driver pulled up to the curb by my house. I got out, still staring at my phone.

"What the hell?" I breathed.

If she wasn't back home, where had she been staying? Not with Liz, clearly.

I stared dumbly at my phone, like it held the answers. It was full of red notifications on every possible platform. Just to be safe, I checked all of them to no avail. When I opened up my email, I saw one from Carmen time-stamped 11:00 P.M. Subject line: *You've been bumped!*

I opened it. The email read, *You've been bumped . . . to the cover! Congratulations. We go to print in two weeks. And congratulations on the* LA Times *article. —Carmen*

What *LA Times* article?

I opened the attached image, titled *PostModCoverUpdated-SeptemberV3.png.*

Mick stared up at me, hollowed out and haunting, the rows of train seats stretching away behind her. Above her, *PostMod* was printed in white. On the left was a list of articles from inside the magazine, but on the right were the words *Death at the Gala: When Fine Art Turns Dark. Page 32.*

I felt delirious—horrified—elated—racked with guilt. How dare I feel happy? Lily was dead, and Mick was going to be livid about this cover. Where the hell *was* she? I tried to call her again. Straight to voicemail. I left a message. "Mick, it's me. Please call me back. I know you're pissed, but I really need to talk to you. Where are you? Are you okay?"

The next day was Monday. No matter what, Mick would be at swim practice tomorrow morning. Maybe I could catch her there.

In front of me, my house was quiet and cheerful, a safe, clean place. It felt like something from my past.

And then I realized—I hadn't thought of David.

* * *

The driver dropped me off in front of a bar a few doors down from the Whole Foods in Hillcrest, the gay part of town just north of Balboa Park. The bar was a chill, rustic place and hosted open-mic nights for aspiring singer-songwriters and poets. David had been bartending there since he'd turned twenty-one earlier this year, and if we were being honest, for a while before then, too. In a perfect world, Nico would have preferred that none of us knew anything personal about each other. He'd have loved us to maintain a completely anonymous relationship in case any of us ever got caught. But we'd been helping Nico with these installs for two years, and people were going to get to know each other.

I wished I'd known Lily better. I wished her family knew me enough that I would be invited to the funeral.

Her face came back to me, staring blankly up at the sky, sunken, stiff, frozen. I knew I'd never get this out of my head, the image of a person-become-thing. It was horrible, horrifying, much worse than I ever expected death to be. It was different from the little boy at the pool. He'd been unconscious, not dead, not this open-eyed shell of a human being.

I heaved myself out of these morbid thoughts and pulled open the bar's front door. It was quiet and smelled like sour beer. David was at the far end of the bar, drying glasses with a rag. I did a quick sweep, searching for the manager, who always carded everyone, but David was the only person working. That was good.

I slid into the seat beside him and leaned my forearms on the shiny, slightly sticky wood. When he saw me, he froze. "What are you doing here?"

"I called you, and you didn't answer, so I went to your apartment, and now I'm trying here." I checked the time on my phone. "It's almost two. You planning to close the place down?"

Behind the beard, he looked frightened. "You're not old enough to be here. And you shouldn't be anywhere near me."

"I need to talk to you."

"Go talk to Nico about whatever you need."

"I was just at Nico's. I need you to tell me what happened tonight. I think Nico's lying to me, and I don't know why."

"You need to go home," he snapped.

"No."

He glowered at me. A group of nearby guys were watching us. He shot them a look, then leaned in to speak close to my ear. "Please listen to me. Go home. Leave me alone."

"Tell me why Lily was on the roof. Nico said she was in charge of taking pictures. Why would she be all the way on the edge of the roof to do that? There was nothing to photograph up there." I didn't realize until the words were coming out that this was what was gnawing at me.

He heaved a furious sigh and set a glass down hard. "Lily wasn't taking pictures, Veronica."

I frowned. "So then who *was* taking pictures? You?"

"Your girlfriend."

Silence.

"Mick?" I clarified. "No. She left. We had a fight, and she bailed."

He raised his eyebrows and pinched his lips shut. It was an expression of pity, like he was waiting for me to catch up.

"You're serious?" I asked.

"Talk to Nico. Talk to your girlfriend. But leave me out of it." He turned and hurried through the swinging door into the kitchen.

Numb, I stared after him. How was this possible?

She had run out of the gallery. Nico would have been on the roof setting up. Maybe he saw her and asked her to help with the install. But then why hadn't she called me? Why was her phone off? And where had she been sleeping the last few days?

One thing was clear—there was a whole lot I didn't know, and if I was going to lie to the police, I wanted to know the truth.

CHAPTER TWENTY-SEVEN

<><><>

MICK

NICO'S HEADLIGHTS ILLUMINATE AN EMPTY PARKING lot behind a warehouse tucked into a commercial neighborhood. It's five o'clock in the morning, and we barely slept, but he doesn't look as tired as I feel. Plus, I have to be at the pool in two hours, and I was late or absent every day last week. Coach might actually kill me.

I leave my gym bag in the car reluctantly. I'm constantly aware of the stolen roll of film hidden in the side pocket. I feel like any minute, Nico could decide to search my bag and realize what I did.

Nico turns and waits for me to catch up. "You all right?"

I nod.

"You look like shit."

"So do you. Your dark circles have dark circles." It's true. His eyes are feverish behind rings of shadow. You'd think he'd look silly in workout clothes, but he doesn't. Like everything else, they fit him like a second skin.

A car pulls up alongside us, and I recognize David by his beard. He parks and gets out, looking exhausted as he approaches. He's wearing workout clothes too. His eyes are hooded, his face troubled like mine must be. Something is wrong with my being here, like I'm trying to be Lily's replacement.

Nico puts a hand on David's shoulder and one on mine. "This has been a hard few days." His voice is deep, melodic, and sad.

David is bigger than Nico, but he seems diminished by the spiderlike hand on his shoulder. He nods, eyes on the ground.

Nico's voice vibrates with emotion. "It's hard to continue on without Lily. She was the heart and soul of so many of our pieces. Her eye led most of our design decisions. She was ballsy—badass—the embodiment of what street art *is*. That's what killed her; that's what made her run along the edge of the roof. She was *fearless*."

His hand is heavy on me. I don't know anything about art, and even less about Lily, but my heart is stirring with emotion at the words.

He points to the building. "So let's go in there. Let's train. Let's do this the way Lily would have done it."

David looks a little brighter, like the words strengthened his resolve. We follow Nico to the building. There's a glass door along the side, and David holds it open for me. We enter into a reception area, where a sporty-looking blond girl smiles brightly at us. "Hey there! Welcome to Climb! Got a session scheduled?"

It is 5:00 A.M. I picture Veronica's reaction to the extreme cheerfulness of this greeting and miss her so much, it hurts.

"Yeah, it's under Adam Branson," Nico says. By now, I know this is one of the fake IDs he uses.

She looks him up on the computer and awards us another sunny smile. "Great. Go on in."

Nico leads the way through a glass door. We emerge into a cavernous room. Along the walls, fake rocks have been constructed all the way up—practice mountains. Two hippie-looking guys, one with blond dreadlocks, wave at us from the left wall. They're organizing a pile of ropes and clips. When we approach, dreadlocks guy says, "Early birds! Ready to get started? Y'all been climbing before?"

Nico says, "We have," indicating himself and David. "She hasn't, but she's an athlete so she should catch on quick."

"Great!" He looks me over appraisingly. "Swimming?"

I nod.

"You do a lot of dry land workouts during practice?"

I nod again.

"Oh, yeah, you'll be fine. Let's get you set up!" He starts wrapping us in harnesses. When he does mine, he explains what they are. "Step into these; these are for your legs. Here's your belt . . ." He buckles it for me.

Nico is already getting himself hooked up like he's done it a thousand times. David is close behind him.

One more day. We have that appointment with the guy about the car tomorrow. I have to do this one install, pretend I think this is all amazing, and then I'll get my car and insurance, and I'll be free.

* * *

Nico drops me off at the pool at eight, an entire hour late. Coach is going to kill me. I grab my gym bag and run, banging into the locker room. It's empty. I rush to change, ripping my clothes off and shimmying into my Speedo. I pull my hair back into a tight bun, stretch on my swim cap, grab my goggles, shove my gym bag into my locker, and go.

The team is dripping wet and gathered around Coach Morris, who's explaining something with broad hand motions. I slink up, trying to be invisible, but Coach sees me.

"Oh, Mick is here. Lucky us," she says.

I squeeze myself in beside Amber at the back of the group. Cheeks on fire, I say, "I'm so sorry, Coach. My ride dropped me off late."

"What, like, your limo?" Liz snaps. She's at Coach's elbow, holding the clipboard.

"Limo?" I echo.

"You're so important now, right?"

"No. What? Of course not—my friend dropped me off. He was running late. Like I said, I'm so sorry. I'm ready to practice."

"You sure?" Coach's eyes are burning into mine.

I stammer, "I know I've been off my game lately."

"You've been flaking on this team for a week. Maybe if the *LA Times* were here, you would be motivated to treat this more seriously."

Half the team looks amused, and the other half looks freaked out and sympathetic. No one wants to be in the hot seat.

To Coach, I say, "The *LA Times*?"

Beside me, Amber murmurs, "The article? Did you not see it?"

I shake my head.

"We've all been texting you. It was in the Sunday paper."

"I lost my phone."

Coach says, "Why don't you take the day off. Take tomorrow off too. Think about what you want. Clearly this isn't working."

I feel like there's a gaping, growing hole in my chest. I back up, away from the team. Their eyes are like daggers. Liz has a little angry smile blossoming on her lips. I turn and run.

In the locker room, I pull the swim cap off so hard it takes some hair with it. I open my locker and shove the cap in my gym bag. My hand brushes the roll of film, a hard little lump. I pull my shorts on over my bathing suit and step into my flip-flops. I'm crying. It's inside me—Lily, dead—that means something—Veronica's hands on me, the camera—*click*.

The little boy at the pool, cold and clammy.

I press my hands to my face and try to stop the flow of tears. I don't want to see the article Coach was talking about. I can't think about how many other people have seen it. I want to escape, but it's me that's the problem. There's nowhere to go that I won't also be.

I sink down onto the floor next to my gym bag, my back to the lockers, and draw my knees up to my chest. I wrap my arms around them and press my face into the bare, warm skin. My chest is too tight. My ribs are made of steel. I'm dizzy. The floor is rolling beneath me, an earthquake.

In my head, Veronica's voice says, "Sweetie. Sweetie." It's soft, purring—as if she's here with me. There's something so comforting about her. She's the only person who's ever made me feel like all these panicky things are going to be okay, that they're not as big and scary as they seem.

A hand touches my head.

My whole body startles, and I snap my head up.

She's here, sitting on the bench in front of me, leaning down with her hand outstretched.

I can't believe she's real. I feel like I conjured a mirage. I'm still hyperventilating.

"Whoa, you're not okay at all." She slides down onto the floor beside me and wraps an arm around my back.

"I can't breathe," I squeak out in a wheezing whisper.

She squeezes me hard. "Breathe in, one, two, three, not too fast, then out, one, two, three, slow. In again . . ." She keeps counting. I follow the count, sucking air in slowly, then letting it out. After a few minutes of this, my ribs relax and expand.

I let my head fall back against the locker. My whole body is tingly with the aftereffects of the panic attack. Her arm is warm around me.

She says, "Why are you in here and not out there with the team?"

"I was late again, and Coach was mad. She told me to leave. She—" My throat closes. I swallow. "Something about the *LA Times*."

"Oh, shit."

I turn my head and really look at her for the first time. Her hair is in a tangled ponytail, and she has no makeup on. She's wearing an old Beatles T-shirt with cutoff jeans. She looks amazing. I've never been so glad to see anyone.

"Do you know anything about the article?" I ask.

She pulls her phone out of the back pocket of her shorts, and her thumbs fly across the screen. "Carmen mentioned it in an email, but I forgot to look it up. I'm assuming they just wrote something up from that interview they did at the gala." We peer at the screen together as the Google search results load.

There it is, in the *LA Times* Sunday Arts and Culture section. The headline reads "Haunting Portrayal of First Love Precedes Death at Gala." The image accompanying the headline is the viral photo of me, captioned with the words *Just Kissed. Photographer: Veronica Villarreal. Model: Micaela Young.*

"Oh no." My hand is pressed to my lips.

She clicks the link. It pulls up a full-length article accompanied by other images from the gala, including a photo of Veronica standing in front of the wall of photographs, looking composed and brilliant with her red lips and vintage dress. We skim the article, and words pop out at me like bullets: *Hauntingly intense eye contact. Surreal beauty. Artistic integrity— analog process—intentional return to craft—the kinesthetic nature of fine art and true love.*

"Jesus. Christ," Veronica whispers.

"Oh my God," I whimper. This is a disaster.

She lets the phone clatter to the floor and takes my hand in hers. "I'm so sorry. I know you didn't want any of this."

She doesn't even know the half of it. I'm in so deep, with Nico and Lily and the whole rock-climbing bridge thing.

"Come here." She pulls me, trying to get me onto her lap. "Come here and let me hold you. Where have you been?"

"I'll squish you."

"You won't squish me. Come on."

I allow her to collect me into her lap like a child. I bury my face in her shoulder and wind my arms around her neck, and we stay like that for what feels like a long time, until my heart slows and my tears run dry.

My eyes rest on my gym bag.

The film.

I want to give it to her so she can hide it or destroy it. But can I trust her? What if she shows the picture of me setting the fire to the police? Or her mom? Their relationship . . . I don't trust it. It's so close. I can't keep the film, though. I'm not sure how to destroy it; it's not like I can just set a fire right here.

"Okay, now you're squishing me a little," she says.

I back up off her and sit on the cold concrete floor. She keeps my legs, so they're still wrapped around her hips. We're intertwined.

I have to trust her. Don't I?

She's on that roll of film too. She wouldn't want the photos shared any more than I would.

"You've been avoiding me," she says.

"I lost my phone." Sneakily, my hand reaches for the side pocket of my gym bag, behind her where she can't see it. If I can slip it into her purse for her to find later . . .

"But where have you been staying? Your mom says you never went home."

Oh God. She knows. I feel my face flush with embarrassment. "I've been staying with friends. I didn't want to worry you."

"Worry me?"

I feel the blush deepen. "I didn't want you and your mom to get me put in a foster home," I confess.

"I would never," she starts to protest.

"Your mom would."

She shuts her mouth, considers, and says, "Mick . . . why were you still at the gala when Lily died? Why were you with Nico? Did you see what happened to her?"

My fingers have the film pinched between them, but now what? Do I just tell her and hope she—

She says, "I want to believe good things. I want to believe you didn't know Nico was coming that night, that you ran into him in the parking lot or something and got roped into one of his plans, just like you did with the fire. Because you wouldn't hide something like that from me, right? You didn't know he was going to be there?"

I'm fighting a terrible battle in my head. We can have this conversation after I get my car. But tonight, I have to help Nico, and she can't know about that.

My eyes fly down to her purse, resting on the ground beside her. I wrap both arms around her neck, using the gesture to change the film from one hand to the other. Now that it's in my right hand, I slip it into one of her purse's side pockets, the decorative kind no one ever uses. She won't find this for a while, I don't think.

"Mick?"

"I . . . We can't talk about this today. I promise, I'll explain everything soon."

She puts her hands on my shoulders and pushes me away from her so she can look into my eyes. "Mick. Tell me you didn't know he would be there."

A long pause. I can't tell her the truth, but I won't lie to her. Not anymore, not for Nico.

She cocks her head. "I keep remembering what really happened that night of the fire. Nico and I were arguing. You were standing there watching. And then you took the torch from him. *You* set that fire. He didn't make you. He didn't even ask you. You're not this innocent girl. You chose him over me the night of the fire, and again the night of the gala. Do you even understand? I had to get questioned by the cops, I had to lie—you totally screwed me over, Mick. Do you know what it was like to find Lily's dead body and have no idea what was going on and—her dead face—"

She looks like she's going to lose it and start crying. I feel so awful, so full of guilt, I don't know how I'm not sinking into the ground.

"Why?" she pleads quietly. "I thought we were falling in love. Why would you do all of this?"

"We are," I try to say, but she pushes me off and stands up. She turns and heads for the exit. "Where are you going?" I ask.

She stops, a hand on the door that leads out into the sunshine.

"Away from you." She slips outside and is gone.

"Come back," I whisper.

Her question hangs in the air. Why have I been doing all these things? How did I get here?

I'm lost.

CHAPTER TWENTY-EIGHT

◇◇◇

VERONICA

I DIALED NICO'S NUMBER FOR THE HUNDREDTH TIME and hurled my phone across the bed when it went to voice-mail yet again.

I stood in the middle of my room, hands on hips. I was so pissed at Nico, I wanted to go down to his warehouse and set his precious supplies on fire, or at least give him a slap in the face, but when I'd tried to do just that this afternoon, after leaving Mick at the pool, he'd been gone.

He'd recruited Mick to help him with his install at the gala without telling me. They'd been talking and planning together behind my back. Had he been the reason I was invited in the first place? Questions upon unanswered questions cluttered my brain, and I picked up a pillow and screamed into it.

All day, I'd been trapped in this room, trying to figure out what to do. On one hand, I could come clean to the police, turn Nico in, and make up a story that made me look innocent in every way. I could even tell them Mick had something to do with the fire.

I wasn't going to do that. Why I was holding myself to some code of honor when they were clearly backstabbing ass-holes, I had no idea.

I retrieved my phone from the bed and dialed Nico again. Straight to voicemail.

I didn't want to text him anything about this.

Fine. I'd try his warehouse again.

I grabbed my purse, shoved my phone inside it, and threw open my bedroom door. "Mom!" I yelled.

"In the living room!"

I found her in her favorite chair, typing furiously on her laptop with her glasses lopsided on her nose. "You working?"

She smiled ruefully. "Seven thousand student emails."

"Can I take the car? I want to get out of the house for a while, maybe go see Nico."

"Isn't it late? What time is it?"

"It's not even ten yet."

"Oh, okay. Well, be home by midnight."

"Thanks!" I grabbed her keys from her purse and hurried out the front door.

I drove around the back way and pulled into the parking lot across the alley from Nico's warehouse. I put the car in park and was retrieving my purse when a loud crash outside made me jump to attention. I tried to see through the wind-shield, through the flickering streetlights.

I saw movement in the back alley. People were bustling in and out through the sliding freight door. Nico's car was parked so his headlights beamed into the warehouse to provide light. He and David were rushing back and forth to his stolen catering van, loading things into the refrigerated storage area in the back.

There was Mick, exiting the side door, lugging a large duffel bag. She tossed it into the back of the van, and David slammed the doors shut.

"What are you doing?" I whispered. Could they possibly be prepping another install? No way. After what had happened—after his whole tear-filled speech about not being able to do his art anymore? After all the shit David told me?

Nico moved his car into its normal parking spot. They piled into the van, David driving, and backed away from the warehouse.

"Are you fucking kidding me," I muttered, turning the car back on.

I followed them through the seedy warehouse neighborhood toward the freeway. Nico took a right onto the on-ramp for Coronado Bridge.

Coronado Bridge was about a mile long and connected mainland San Diego to Coronado Island, which is mostly a tourist destination. I wondered if Nico was planning something at the big hotel on the island, or if maybe the congressman was there for some reason. And of course, Mick would want to help him. *She's his trusty assistant,* I thought bitterly.

In the middle of the bridge, they slowed down so much, I thought they were going to stop. I had no choice; I had to pass them if I didn't want Nico to know I was following him. In my rearview mirror, the van's headlights swerved right. They were pulling over in the middle of the bridge.

"What are you doing?" I screamed.

Too late to find out now. I'd have to go all the way to the island and turn around. Cursing under my breath, I drove on, the ocean a glimmering, dark carpet hundreds of feet below. The road spat me out on Coronado Island, and I did an illegal U-turn to get back on the bridge.

As I was getting on, the van passed me, heading for the island at full speed. I craned my neck trying to see where they were going. What was he up to? Why had he stopped in the middle of the bridge if the island was his destination?

My phone rang. Maybe Nico had seen me; maybe he was finally calling me back. I grabbed for it, but it was my mom.

I didn't want to get pulled over for talking and driving, so I ignored it. My mom called right back, though, which was weird. I answered the phone as I exited the bridge, back into the warehouse district.

"Mom, I'm driving," I said, putting it on speaker.

"Where are you?" Her voice was urgent.

"I was trying to hang out with Nico, but he wasn't home." True enough.

"Well, get back home. The police are here."

My heart exploded, a horse galloping in my chest. "What do they want? It's, like, eleven o'clock at night."

"Just get your ass home, girl."

This couldn't be good. The layers of lies and secrets were piling up fast now, like dirt being shoveled into a grave.

CHAPTER TWENTY-NINE

◇◇◇

MICK

I STAND ON THE EDGE OF CORONADO BRIDGE, clutching the railing behind me. The harness wraps around me like a vise. The damp, salty wind whips at my ponytail. Earlier, I asked Nico to look up survival rates for falling off this bridge. Answer: zero.

This is the most dangerous thing I've ever done. These could be the last moments of my life.

I wonder if this is how Lily felt before she lost her balance and tumbled off the roof. I wonder if she saw it coming. And that little boy—before he jumped in, did he have any premonition that it might be the last thing he did?

In a strange way, the fear is pulling at me. The water is calling my name. Would it matter if I did fall? My mom doesn't want me. Veronica's face was full of disgust and disappointment when she closed the locker room door behind her. My swim team friends think I'm some kind of . . . I can't let myself remember their faces. The shame it brings is too sharp; it cuts me up on the inside.

When I push those thoughts away, one echo replaces them: my mom's voice saying, *Get out.*

I *want* to jump.

The thought shocks me. I didn't know that was inside me. And at the same time, all these years, all I've ever wanted was to disappear.

Maybe that's why I keep letting Nico talk me into this stuff. Maybe I *want* the worst to happen. Maybe I want to self-destruct.

From behind me, on the other side of the railing, David says, "You ready? You got your headset on? I've got you. Don't worry." I'm outfitted in harnesses and ropes. I just need to rappel down to the top of the column, and the only way to do that is to jump.

My heart is pounding. The water is dark and sinuous. It's beautiful.

I was beautiful too, in the picture Veronica took of me. For one shining second, I was something.

I let go of the bridge and jump.

Free fall, and then my harness catches me with a full-body jerk that knocks the wind out of me. I'm dangling, heart exploding out of my chest while I wait for the rock-climbing gear to fail.

But David has me. He's lowering me down to the top of the column. There's a moment of panicked fumbling, and then I catch the handholds Nico drilled into the column, and I'm clutching the makeshift ladder like a life raft.

In my ear, the headset crackles. Nico's voice says, "You okay, Jagger?" He's on the next column over, a hundred feet closer to Coronado Island.

"This is scary," I squeak.

"You'll get used to it in a second. When I was drilling in these hooks, I was terrified at first, but then it started feeling normal."

I don't believe him. Nothing scares Nico.

My teeth are chattering. "Just tell me what to do. I need to get this over with."

A gust of ocean wind hits me, and my grip on the peg slips. I go bouncing away from the column. I hear myself scream.

"Jagger. Jagger. You're okay. You're attached. You're safe."

To a tiny, skinny rope! I'm dangling, bouncing around in the wind.

"When the wind dies down, you'll swing back to the column, and then you can grab on again," he says, so terrifyingly calm.

He's right, though. The next swing takes me right up to the peg, and I grab it for dear life. I clutch at it, find a spot for my foot on the next one below, and try to let the air out of my chest before I faint.

Another crackle in my ear. "You guys okay down there?" It's David. He's still on the bridge. He's in charge of feeding the net down to us.

"We're good. Just acclimating," Nico replies. "Now, Mick, breathe. Give yourself a moment to get comfortable. You're strapped into your harness safe and sound. People climb mountains this way, thousands of feet up in the air. Graffiti artists everywhere have to do shit like this. You've seen murals in weird places. This is how it's done. You're fine. I promise."

His words are moving through my veins like medicine. "Okay," I say, breathing again. "I'm ready to get started."

"That's my girl!" David hollers, his voice so triumphant that we laugh.

"Go ahead and give us the first section," Nico tells him, and from above, a lacy black curtain drifts down over my head. It's the massive commercial fishing net we've been practicing with. We've been using these same hooks, attached to the walls of Nico's warehouse, testing this technique. It only now occurs to me that we didn't practice with wind. When Nico and I grab hold of the net, it parachutes out between us, pulling me away from the column. I have to clench the hook with all my strength to stay on.

"Damn, that wind is strong," Nico says. "You good, Jagger? Don't forget to clip that net to your harness. It'll leave your hands free for climbing."

We have to climb all the way down to the water with the net attached to us, where we'll clip it to the lowest hooks. After that, we'll climb back up, fastening it to each hook as we go, until the net is secure between the columns, creating a mesh barrier that should be relatively invisible in the dark. Nico's been drilling these hooks in for months, and right now he's like a machine making his way hand over hand down the column toward the water. I have to focus, placing my feet carefully as the wind batters me.

I climb down, searching for the four-inch hooks with unstable, terrified feet and clutching at them with hands that burn even in the rock-climbing gloves. It's scarier the farther down I get, which is counterintuitive. You'd think it'd be reassuring to be closer to the ground. But below me isn't ground; it's water, and I know better than anyone how easy it is to drown. In these circumstances, under a massive bridge with unpredictable currents circulating the columns, the water is more frightening than the fall down to it.

At last, I'm close enough to feel the icy spray on my hands and face. Nico can't see me, not from his column a hundred feet away, but he seems to be pacing me using the tension in the net. "You down here?" he asks in my ear.

"Yes." I'm shivering.

"Let's connect to our lowest hooks."

Beneath my feet, the dark, starving waves slash at the base of the concrete column, their roar drowning out Nico's voice in my ear. There are three more hooks left to descend.

My foot slips; the pegs here are wet. I cry out and grasp for the column, finding a hook just in time. I think I've lost the net. But no. It's clipped to my harness.

I take a couple of deep breaths. "Nico, I can barely hear you, but I'm going to start attaching."

"Okay!" he yells over the roar of the waves. "Me too!"

I unclip the net from my harness and, with shaking hands, find the closest loop. I guide it to the lowest hook and make sure it's secured. I let it go as a test. It holds.

"It's good!" I cry.

Nico's voice is high and happy. "Mine is holding too. Let's get this done!"

I step on the hook I just used and find the next loop in

the net. We make our way up. There are fifty hooks on each column. We get into a rhythm. There's a silence as we hold the wind-blown net in place, as we wrestle it onto the hook, and then as we wait and make sure it holds. There's an "I got it" or an "all right, let's go" and then we climb up and do the next one. This process repeats over and over again for what feels like forever, until my hands are numb inside the gloves and my toes are slabs of ice inside the climbing shoes.

At last, David is only twenty feet above me. "Four more to go!" he hollers into the headset, hurting my ears. "Come on, come on!" He's winding our ropes up as we climb. When I make it to the top, he grabs me by the arms and helps me over the railing. I tumble onto the sidewalk and lie facedown, embracing the solid concrete with more gratitude than I can ever remember feeling.

A blissful realization: I did it. Tomorrow I'll get the car. I'm done helping Nico. I'm free.

Nico is still on the other side. I hear a rattle, like marbles in a jar, and a hissing sound followed by the smell of fresh spray paint. He does this for a while, invisible below us, painting something on the exterior of the bridge. When he returns, David helps him up and over the railing.

"Look," Nico says. His voice is reverent, like he's witnessing a miracle. "Do you see it?"

"See what?" David asks.

"The installation. Look!"

I crawl toward the railing.

The horizon is glimmering, a faint, predawn, silvery glow. No wonder I'm exhausted; we've been here for hours. A fishing boat with lights glowing on its prow is heading for the net. It's the one we were expecting. We're just in time. David joins Nico at the railing. I can't make myself let go long enough to walk over to them.

David cranes his torso forward, looking down under the bridge. "Are we sure this is— Do we feel good about this? What if the boat capsizes or something? Could people get hurt?"

"They could get hurt," Nico answers, unperturbed.

The boat is coming closer. I wonder if it will see the net with its spotlight. Maybe it will. Maybe it will change course before it gets trapped. It does seem like the boat is slowing, actually. Could it be?

"What's happening?" David asks.

"It's changing course." Nico's face pulls into a frown.

"You think they saw the net?"

"No. I think we're unlucky and they're just going between different columns than usual."

"That sucks." A long pause while they watch the boat turn. David asks, "Do you think another boat will come along before it gets light?"

"I don't want to count on it."

"I'm sorry, dude." David casts him a sympathetic look, then returns his attention to the boat.

Nico says, "I'm fishing, right? Maybe I need bait."

"Bait?"

"Yes. Bait."

Nico steps behind David, puts both hands on his back, and pushes him off the bridge.

✦✦✦

CHAPTER THIRTY

VERONICA

MY MOM AND DETECTIVE SALCEDO WERE WAITING for me in the living room, deep in conversation. He was hanging on whatever she was saying with rapt attention. He totally liked her. Ew.

"Uh, hi," I said, entering with great trepidation and setting my purse and keys down on a side table.

Salcedo rose from the easy chair and said, "Veronica! There you are."

My mom rose, too, and kissed me on the cheek. "You want coffee?"

"I guess." I sat down on the edge of the couch cushion.

My mom hurried into the kitchen, and Salcedo sat back down. "Whatcha been up to? Hanging out with your friend Mick?" His tone was suspiciously casual.

Nico always told me a lie sounds more believable when it's close to the truth. He swore anyone could pass a polygraph if they told a version of the truth rather than a straight fabrication. So I said, "No. To be honest, we had a fight at the gala and we're not exactly speaking."

"Again?" my mom asked, returning with a cup of coffee. I accepted it, and she sank onto the couch beside me.

"Don't be judgy." I sipped the coffee. It was sweet and carried the scent of cinnamon. Salcedo had an empty mug at his side, I noticed.

"You don't approve of Mick?" Salcedo asked my mom.

Her eyebrows shot up. "Are you asking me if I'm homophobic?"

"No, no, no. I mean, of their relationship itself."

She relaxed. "Mick is a nice girl. But she has problems."

"Mom!" I cried. Jesus Christ, on a list of things not to say to a cop.

"With her family," she protested. To Salcedo, she said, "Her mother is irresponsible. She kicked her out of her own house with nowhere to go. That's—"

"Mom! Oh my God! Private business!"

"It's illegal," she argued.

"It is illegal," Salcedo agreed. "Did you contact social services? I can get you the number."

"I contacted her mother," my mom said. "We had a little talk."

"*What?*" I was horrified. "How? When? *What?*"

She shrugged, unrepentant. "When Mick was in the shower, I got her mother's number off her phone and called her. We talked about responsibility."

I considered that a bunch of different ways, sifted through the questions that popped up in my head, and finally said, "But Mick's phone is password protected."

She snorted. "Her password is 1287. I watched her unlock it. This isn't my first day as the parent of a teenager."

I stared at her, dumbfounded. Did she know *my* phone password?

Salcedo was looking at my mom with a recognizable brand of male appreciation. He said, "I'm actually here to ask you about Micaela. I haven't been able to locate her, and I thought you could help. She's the only person not accounted for from the charity gala. I spoke with her mother as well, who said she's been staying with friends, but this helps me understand why it seemed like she was being intentionally vague. Have you seen Micaela? Or do you know where she is?"

I think she's doing something weird and potentially illegal on Coronado Island with my former best friend, whom I am going to murder. Instead of that, I said, "I wish I could tell you, but my calls to her are going straight to voicemail." How much was I going to lie to the cops? At what point was it going to be too much?

"Would you be comfortable showing me the texts between you and Mick?"

"What? Wait, seriously?" I looked at my mom. "There's, like, private stuff in there."

To Salcedo, my mom said, "That feels like an intrusion. And with them both being girls, it seems inappropriate. You're a male officer."

He put his hands up apologetically. "Excuse me." But his eyes were cunning, and I felt like he saw more than I wanted him to. "I need you to keep me posted if you hear from her. She's not in trouble, but we are worried. If I didn't know she'd already been at odds with her mother and not staying at home, I'd have a missing persons investigation underway. As it is, I think we'll be launching one in the morning. No one has heard from her since she left swim practice on bad terms this morning, and the girls on her team said she was quite upset. Her mother tried to find her iPhone on iCloud, but it's been powered off. These aren't good signs. Veronica, if you're keeping anything from us, I want you to consider that something may have happened to her. She may not just be ignoring you."

I knew the shock I was feeling must be registering on my face. This was blowing up to bad proportions. Even if I wanted to come clean, I had no idea where to start.

My mom walked Salcedo to the door. I took my coffee to the kitchen and microwaved it. When she returned, she leaned in the doorway with her arms crossed over her chest. "*Is* she a missing person? Tell me the truth, Veronica."

I kept my eyes on the microwave. "I doubt it."

"Do you have any idea where she might be staying?"

The microwave beeped. I pulled the door open and got the cup of coffee out. I sipped it, grateful for the scalding heat and the opportunity to stall.

"Veronica." Her tone was sharp.

"Honestly? That's what I've been trying to figure out. I know she had a fight with her friend Liz on the swim team

225

and they aren't friends anymore, but they could have made up. She could be there. Or with another friend, I don't know."

"She has fights with everyone," my mom muttered.

"Stop it," I snapped, defensive for no reason.

"Everyone persecutes Mick, right? She's always in fights with people, but it's never her fault? Those kinds of people are toxic, Veronica. I know you're young and you want to save everyone, and I'm sure that's coming from your issues with your father leaving, and I don't want to be judgmental, but honey. The people who find themselves always the victim? Those people do the worst things. Because they're so focused on all the bad things being done *to* them, they never stop and think about their own capacity for—for—"

"For what? Evil?" I forced a laugh.

She smiled. "Well, maybe not evil. For being destructive. Does that make sense?"

I remembered Mick starting the fire. Mick dragging me into the ocean. Mick helping Nico at the gala.

It made a lot of sense.

I wondered what else she might be capable of.

Lily's dead face, staring up at me.

Maybe it was time to come clean. I didn't start the fire. I didn't do any of the installations. I was there, I was a witness and probably, legally, an assistant? An accomplice?

I couldn't. I was a lot of things—a pain in the ass, a bitch, a brat—but I was not a snitch.

I went to bed jittery and exhausted. I woke up a dozen times in the darkness, grabbing for my phone, hoping for something, anything.

CHAPTER THIRTY-ONE

◇◇◇

MICK

DAVID SCREAMS ALL THE WAY DOWN TO THE WATER.
My body is skewered with fear. I scream too, a hoarse, raven sound, and then I clap a hand to my mouth, afraid of upsetting Nico.

A crash.

The screams stop.

I can't help opening my eyes. I can't help looking down.

The water is churning where David went in.

The boat, which had seemed to veer away from the bridge, changes course and heads straight for David. They're going to try to rescue him. By the boat's trajectory, it looks like the intent is to pass David and swing around in a U-turn; it's going too fast to stop on a dime.

It steers directly into the net. It pulls hard, stretching the net out to the other side of the bridge. The boat's nose is wrapped in the black mesh. It whirs and chugs, and then it topples sideways into the water.

"Yes!" Nico screams. He sounds like someone watching sports on TV. He turns his face to me. It's bright, glowing in the overhead streetlights. "We did it!"

I feel like I've been submerged in ice water. I can't move my lips, can't make a single word come out of my mouth. Nico starts throwing all our gear over the railing. *Leave no trace*, he always says. Ropes and harnesses and spray cans—they all go down into the water. None will have fingerprints on them; we've worn gloves this whole time. It's a perfect crime.

"But why?" I cry, the words ripping out of my soul.

Oh my God. Lily.

That was no accident.

But *why*?

Run, my brain says.

Before my body can obey, Nico clamps a hand around my wrist, encircling it completely. "Don't worry. I'd never do this to you. You're on a different level. You deserve so much bigger." He pulls me to his side and wraps his free arm around me, my wrist still clamped in his hand. I can feel his heart pounding through his ribs. "I know you're freaking out right now. You're thinking about Lily, you're thinking about David, but what you need to be thinking about is *this*. *Look* at it. Look what we've done." His breath is warm on my ear.

Sirens. On the San Diego side of the bridge.

"That's our cue," Nico says. "Gotta get back to the van. Come on." He takes off sprinting, pulling me with him. He's fast, faster than me. He has my wrist, and the water is roaring far below. I stumble, trying to keep up. He's so fast. Getting away is not an option, not with him dragging me like this and the police closing in from behind.

This is what he does. He paints you into a picture. He turns you into a puppet.

My brain is flying from solution to solution. Wait for him to get in the van and then jump out the door before it starts going quickly. Or make a run for it when he's unlocking the doors. The second his hand is off me, I need to make my break.

When the van is in sight, tucked into a bank of bushes on the Coronado Island side of the bridge, he unlocks it with the remote. He pulls me to the rear cargo doors and opens one without letting me go. "Get in, pretty girl."

I'm horrified, confused. The back is a sealed refrigerator compartment, a small, empty white room. "Into the back? No, I don't—"

He shoves me inside, slamming the door shut behind me. It's so fast, I can't even struggle; I land in a heap on the floor. A muffled *click-click* tells me he's locking the door. I push myself up and try to pull the door open, but the handle won't move.

An overhead light flickers, a tiny ring of fluorescents around the fan mechanism embedded to the ceiling. The van's engine whirs to life, and the fan starts up with a roar of recycled air.

The air coming from the fan is icy cold.

CHAPTER THIRTY-TWO

✧✧✧

VERONICA

WHEN MY EYES SNAPPED OPEN, GRAY DAYLIGHT WAS
seeping in through cracks in the curtains. I grabbed my phone
and went downstairs to make coffee. The house was dark. My
mom was still asleep.

I started the coffeemaker, leaned against the counter, and
opened Google, intending to see if Nico had done something
bad on Coronado Island. Before I could search for anything,
my eyes landed on a San Diego news Google card that read
"Another Deadly Prank: Connection to Death at Gala? Police
Investigating."

There it was. My whole body felt cold.

I opened the article. The picture had to have been taken
within the last half hour, at sunrise, of Coronado Bridge. It
was an aerial shot by helicopter or drone, and it showed a
section of the bridge where a black net had been stretched
between two of the enormous concrete columns. A capsized
fishing boat was tangled in the net, swarmed by smaller Coast

Guard motorboats. On the exterior of the bridge, above the net, *FISHING FOR PEOPLE* was spray painted in fire-engine red.

Nico's words came back to me like he was whispering them in my ear. *Part Four: Fishing for People. The ocean takes back what is hers.*

"Oh, shit," I whispered.

Last year, when Nico had first become interested in environmentally themed installation pieces, he'd floated the concept of disrupting commercial fishing by catching the boats in the nets they used for fish (and sometimes dolphins, whales, and sharks). When he added it as a title to one of the installations in the series, I'd thought it was great. Badass, actually.

I hadn't understood. Not really. I'd never understood how far he'd go.

I scrolled through the article, which detailed exactly what I could already imagine: The net was installed at night, it was black, and a boat drove right into it as it left for its usual predawn fishing excursion. My eyes froze on a paragraph a third of the way down.

"Reports on this are unclear, but it seems that one of the perpetrators of the stunt either fell, jumped, or was pushed off the bridge in order to get the boat to steer in the right direction. The boat, which had changed course to maneuver through the bridge from a different angle, made a sharp left to help this person, at which point it became tangled in the net and capsized. All four crew members and the unknown person who fell from the bridge are dead."

Who fell off the bridge?

God, please let it not be Mick, please God, I prayed, scanning through the article. They didn't have any names listed.

First Lily. Now either Mick or David.

Please don't be Mick.

So was I wishing for it to be David?

I realized I wasn't even considering the possibility that it had been Nico.

Heart pounding, I did a frantic search for *Coronado Bridge* and *fishing for people* and anything else I could think of, but there was only the same information rephrased on twenty different news sites.

I tried googling *Micaela Young*. If it was Mick who'd fallen off the bridge, maybe they'd have something in the news with her listed by name. What I found instead was a whole string of articles that had come out last night from high-profile newspapers like the *LA Times*, the *Guardian*, and every other online magazine in between. Apparently Mick was officially listed as a missing person now. I clicked on the *LA Times* link, my chest shaky and afraid.

"Subject of Celebrated Photograph Missing After Deadly Gala," the headline read.

"Fuck," I heard myself whimper. Oh God. I was in so much trouble.

The police were investigating this blind; their facts were all wrong, and I was the only one who could help them.

The fire didn't matter anymore. This was enough. People were dead. The police needed to know.

I ran upstairs to my mom's room. I knocked on her door. "Mom? Are you up?"

"Veronica?" Her voice was groggy.

I opened the door. "Mom. Can you get up? Something's happening."

* * *

My mom got dressed fast, her face closed down with fury.

"You've known this whole time?" She yanked a pair of jeans on over her underwear. "You knew it was Nico doing all those things and you helped him and you didn't say a goddamn thing?"

I nodded.

"Get dressed. We're going to the police station, we're talking to Salcedo, but then you and I are having a different conversation."

"I know." I left her and went to my room. I threw on a pair of jeans and an old T-shirt. I brushed my hair out, brushed my teeth, and returned to my mom's room.

"Get me a coffee to go," she ordered. "And start the car. Pull up directions to the central police station. I think it's on Imperial." Her voice dripped with disgust.

I went downstairs, tears spilling onto my cheeks. I pushed them aside. I deserved all of it.

I made her coffee, searched for the police station on Google Maps, got her keys out of her purse, and opened the front door.

I stopped.

On the sidewalk in front of our house, a group of people were milling around. When they saw me, they lifted professional-grade cameras to their eyes and started yelling things at me.

"Do you know where Micaela is?"

"How do you feel, with your girlfriend missing?"

"Do you think she's been kidnapped by the same people who attacked Congressman Osgood?"

Their voices swelled up in a chorus, and I stumbled back through the front door. I kicked it shut in front of me. My chest was heaving.

"What's wrong?" My mom was trotting down the stairs.

"There are reporters out there."

"Reporters?" She scowled. She pushed past me and pulled the front door open. They started shouting questions again. She looked back and forth between me and them. "You dug your hole," she told me. She snatched the coffee and keys. "Come on, girl. Out we go."

I followed her, trying to ignore the questions and the clicks of their cameras. In the car, my mom turned the key in the ignition violently and shifted into reverse. "They better get off my property," she muttered. She honked her horn. They still blocked her in. She rolled down her window. "Move your asses!" she yelled, beginning to back up. They stepped aside, and she rocketed out of the driveway.

The drive through the bright, clean summer morning to the police station was silent. I wondered if Mick was dead. Bright sun and death. Palm trees and fear.

She parked in the police station lot, and I followed her inside. She found someone at a desk and said, "I'm looking for Detective Salcedo. He knows us."

We were told to wait, and I contemplated the toes of my checkered Vans while she seethed.

Salcedo only kept us waiting a few minutes. He trotted out from a back hallway and said, "Claudia, Veronica. What can I do for you?"

His face was unshaven, and it occurred to me that he must not have slept much. My mom said, "Can we speak with you? Veronica's just told me some things I think you need to hear."

He led us past desks and people waiting in line, into a small room with a table and a couple of chairs. He shut the door behind us and sat in a chair, gesturing that we should sit across from him. "How can I help you?"

My mom waved her hand at me. "Go on, then. Tell him what you told me."

I looked down at my hands in my lap. "I know more about the whole thing than I told you."

"Aha!" To my mom, he said, "Teenagers." To me, he said, "Go ahead, honey."

I scowled at the *honey*. "My best friend, Nico. He's—" I felt like such a traitor despite everything. "He's the guy who's been doing all the stuff to the congressman. He's an artist. He does what he calls disruptive installation art. Kind of like a fine art Banksy. It was his crew that did the install—that did the thing at the gala. And it was his crew last night that did the *Fishing for People*. Lily works with him. She's a street artist. He has two other people with him." I looked up at him, and then at my mom. I hadn't told her this yet. "One of the people with him is named David. And the other one is Mick."

"Are you kidding me?" my mom cried. "They're searching for her, thinking she's a missing person, and this whole time she's with *Nico*?"

"Mom, stop, let me finish. One of them died last night; I saw it on the news. They were on Coronado Bridge doing another install. I need to know if that person is Mick. Please," I begged Salcedo.

Salcedo sat back in his chair and crossed his arms over his chest. "What's Nico's full name?"

"Nico Varalica." I spelled it for him. "I think Nico might be short for Nicolas. Obviously."

"Is that Italian?"

"No, I think his family is Croatian. I've never met them. They're not close."

"Age?"

"Nineteen."

"You know for a fact that Mick has been hanging out with your friend Nico since the gala?"

I nodded.

"How do you know?"

"I followed them," I mumbled.

"You did what?" my mom shrieked. "When?"

"Yesterday, when I had your car."

Her rage was mounting. I could count down the seconds until she started yelling at me. Three, two, one—

Salcedo cut her off. "Sorry, Claudia. I'll let you have her back when we're done. Veronica, the person who fell or was pushed off the bridge was not Mick. It was a young man. Do you know who that could have been? We don't have any ID."

"Oh my God," I breathed, the relief flooding my body like a drug. I put my face in my hands. "It was David, then."

"Or Nico," my mom said.

"It wasn't Nico," I told her.

"How do you know?"

"I just know."

Salcedo interrupted. "It was a tall Caucasian man with blond hair and a beard."

"David," I confirmed, disgusted with myself for the relief I felt. How was David's life worth less than hers? He was a sweet guy, straightforward, kind, gentle.

But then . . . what was Mick's role in all this? With Nico? Was she with him willingly, or had he, like, made her help him? The idea of him forcing her to help was appealing. I hadn't considered it before now.

Salcedo leaned forward across the table, his face molded into a reassuring expression. "You said you followed them yesterday. Tell me more about that."

"I followed them from Nico's warehouse to Coronado Bridge. My mom called me to come home, so I left, and that's when I saw you."

"Do you have the address of the warehouse?"

I pulled it up on my Uber history and showed it to him. He typed it into his phone. I said, "If you're going there, I should go with you. It's complicated; there's a weird side door that's always locked, and the people who live there aren't exactly the kind that will be helpful to police. I have a key."

"We can't break in, even if you have a key," he cautioned. "Someone has to let us inside."

"That's fine. They know me."

He considered for a moment, then stood. "Let's go."

My mom stood too. He looked back and forth between us

and said, "I'm going to ask you a favor, Claudia. Can I take Veronica without you?"

My mom frowned. "Why?"

"Honestly? Because I want to ask her some more questions in the car, and I want to make sure she's not filtering out stuff she doesn't want her mom knowing about."

My mom seemed to consider that.

"It's informal, off the record, and as a witness only."

My mom nodded. To me she said, "Don't try and protect Nico or Mick. Just tell Salcedo whatever he needs to know."

He excused himself to talk to some other cops and arrange backup.

"I feel like I don't even know you," she said.

CHAPTER THIRTY-THREE

✧✧✧

MICK

NICO TAKES A HARD LEFT TURN, SENDING ME SPRAWL-ing across the floor onto a pile of cardboard. The refrigerated compartment gets colder and colder as the vent spews torna-dos of freezing air down onto me.

There has to be a failsafe, some sort of mechanism to keep people from getting locked in here. I've seen those in walk-in coolers in restaurants I've worked in, a little white button you can press. I search the door, the walls, but there's nothing like that. I'm shivering so hard my teeth are chattering.

The van slows, bumping along an uneven surface, and then stops. I press my ear to the door, straining to hear what's going on. Faintly, I catch the familiar sound of the creaky warehouse door rolling up.

The van moves forward again, and then I feel him put on the parking brake and hear the rolling metal slide down.

We're inside.

I can figure this out. I can make a plan. I'm strong and fast.

The second he opens that door, I have to launch out, attack his face, make a run for it. I know the layout of this warehouse. It's a maze of boxes and equipment, and beyond that is the front hallway with the exit out onto the alley. It will just take me a minute to reach the exit, and then I'll sprint onto the street and get help from the first person I see. He'll expect me to be timid and afraid. He's probably getting me cold on purpose to weaken me so it'll be easier to . . .

To do what?

A million stories about girls getting raped and murdered fly through my brain. He wouldn't, would he? If he wanted to do those things to me, he could have attacked me in my sleep while I was crashing on his couch.

And then his voice drifts in, faint above the roar of the fan. "How you doin' in there, gorgeous?"

I can't breathe. My chest is tight. My heart is an earthquake. I'm dying to be out of here, but at the same time, I'm praying, *Don't open it, don't open it.*

The fan drones on and on, and now my entire insides are shivering. It's getting colder in here by the minute. It's way colder than a refrigerator; it's as cold as a freezer.

Oh my God.

He's not going to take me out of the van to kill me. This is it. This is him killing me. He's freezing me to death. This isn't a refrigerator van; it's a *freezer* van.

Why? *Why?*

It doesn't matter why. I have to get out. Panic and claustrophobia swoop through me. My hands are numb; my face feels like I've been injected with Novocain.

I have to think. I have to be a lot smarter than I have been. I have to get Nico to open the door.

What can I use to bargain with him? Do I have anything he wants?

No, nothing. There's nothing I have, nothing I know—

That's not true, actually.

It's a revelation: the roll of film. He doesn't know I gave it to Veronica.

I'm thinking fast, playing a mental game of chess. It's a bad idea. Nico seems like he'd be great at chess. But here goes.

I press my hands to the door. "Nico? Can you hear me?"

"I can hear you, pretty girl," is his muffled reply.

"Are you punishing me for what I did? I'm so sorry. I didn't think you'd find out."

Silence.

I pretend to start crying. "I'm sorry!" I scream. "I'm sorry I'm sorry I'm sorry! What more do I have to do? I'm sure the police won't find it. If you let me out, I can try to fix it!"

That should get him nice and curious. He's still quiet. I call, "I can probably get it back. I bet I can. If you just give me a chance, I'll get it back for you. Please."

"Get what back?" His voice is low and close. He's just on the other side.

I almost jump up and down. It's working! I take a deep breath and say, "Wait, what?"

"Get what back, Mick?"

God, his voice is scary. My heart is pounding, my body shivering with cold sweat. I say, "I'm so confused. If that's not what you're mad at me about, why would you lock me in here?"

"Get what back?"

"Wait, what?" *Open the door.*

His voice rises, loud against my ear. "What do you need to get back, Mick?"

I pretend to dissolve into incoherent sobbing. "Please," I blubber. "I can't. It's so cold. Please, I'll get it back. Please just let me out. Please, Nico, please . . ." I try to sound hysterical.

He roars with frustration and pounds the door with his fists. I jump back away from it. I hear him rattling the knob, keys jangling. I have one second to prepare. My heart stops beating. My muscles coil, ready to spring. Fight or flight.

The door swings open. His furious face is just below eye level. "What did you do—" he begins, but I round off and kick him in the face. He stumbles backward. I leap out of the van and sprint into the maze of boxes.

CHAPTER THIRTY-FOUR

✦✦✦

VERONICA

SALCEDO LET ME SIT IN THE FRONT SEAT ON THE WAY to Nico's warehouse. He acted like this was a huge honor, him allowing me to sit next to him unhandcuffed. "You have major trust issues," I muttered, buckling my seat belt, and he chuckled as he pulled out of the parking lot.

"Hazard of the trade. So, Veronica. How close are you with Nico? Is he your boyfriend?"

I wrinkled my nose at his profile. "No. But seriously? That's what you thought I wouldn't tell you in front of my mom?"

"It seemed like the easiest question to start with." He glanced in the rearview mirror, checking on the squad car that followed us.

I said, "Well, skip to the harder ones."

"The harder questions, like whether you know if your friend Nico killed this Lily?"

I inhaled sharply. "Of course not!"

"Lily didn't die in the fall," Salcedo said casually, turning right onto the freeway ramp. "She was murdered."

I stared at his profile. "Define *murdered*."

"Do you know what it means to garrote someone?"

"No."

"It's like strangling someone with wire. She was dead before she hit the ground."

The image was so visual and visceral, Lily getting strangled with wire, that I thought I was going to throw up. I put a hand to my mouth.

Getting strangled. Passive voice. As if it was something happening to her. No, it was done by someone.

Like he was reading my mind, Salcedo asked, "Do you think your friend Nico could kill someone this way?"

"No. Jesus Christ, no!" My mind was like a hurricane. Lily, dead like that. David, dead from the fall. Mick, with Nico now. The urgency I felt to get to her and make sure she was safe had tripled. I kept my eyes on the windshield. "Get off at the next exit," I said after a few minutes. "Turn right. Then left. There. It's that warehouse on the corner."

He braked in front of the boarded-up, rusty-looking building. Another squad car pulled up next to us. Salcedo parked where I told him and followed me to the side door while the uniformed police waited in their car. I pounded on the door. "Hello?" I called.

Silence. I pressed my ear to the door.

"Go ahead and try your key," Salcedo said.

I got my keys out of my purse and could barely get the correct one into the lock.

It didn't turn.

I pulled the key out and examined it.

"Something wrong?" Salcedo asked.

I handed it to him. "Maybe I'm just too shaky."

He tried it. "You sure you got the right key?"

"Positive."

To be safe, he tried the other keys on my key chain as well. Nothing worked.

Nico had changed the locks.

I considered. "Maybe we can get in through the warehouse doors. If someone's in there, they might answer if I knock."

I trotted back to the sliding doors and started banging on the nearest one. "Hello, hello, hello," I yelled.

Silence. Nothing.

Salcedo was right behind me. "No luck?"

"No. Dammit." I kicked the door. "Open up! Hello!"

I stepped back, frustrated.

Then I noticed—the door wasn't locked. The usual padlock was there, but it hung loose and open. I cried out and pounced on it. Salcedo said, "Whoa, hang on, we don't have a warrant."

"Mick might be in there!"

"I don't see or hear any threats. There's no cause." His phone rang in his pocket. It was loud and sounded like an alarm clock. He held a finger up to me and put the phone to his ear. "Hello? Yes. Yes." He beckoned to me, indicating that I should follow him back to his car. I started to obey, and then I slowed. I turned around to face the warehouse.

Fuck it.

I attacked the door, grabbed the handle, and heaved it up

as hard as I could. It rolled up with a deafening clang. Salcedo hollered at me. I sprinted into the warehouse, heading for the door that led to the hallway and the apartments.

I stopped.

Nico's section of the warehouse was empty. Its concrete floor gleamed clean.

Leave no trace.

I ran toward the stairs. "Veronica! Stop!" Salcedo yelled behind me. I ignored him. I swerved through the other tenants' piles of old furniture and boxes and lumps of fabric. I burst through the mess and hurled myself into the hallway and up the stairs, Salcedo hot on my heels. I flew around the corner at the top of the stairs and ran to Nico's door. It was slightly ajar.

I pushed it open.

The room was empty. The checkered floor shone, spotlessly clean like the warehouse floor. It smelled like bleach and lemon cleaning fluid.

Salcedo exploded into the room behind me.

On the floor in the center of the room lay a single item, reflecting the dim yellow light from the hallway.

Another chicken sculpture. Silver in death, limp, its feathers glistening.

"Veronica, we have to go," Salcedo said, taking my arm.

"Why did he leave the chicken?"

"I don't want to arrest you, Veronica, but I will."

"You don't know him. This means something. Everything means something."

"I didn't want to tell you this until you had a chance to check out this warehouse, but . . ."

"What?" I spun to look up at him.

"I looked Nico up in all our databases. He isn't a real person."

It took me a few seconds to process those words. "Explain," I demanded at last.

"You said his name was Nico Varalica, right?"

"Yeah, so?"

"Honey, *varalica* means 'trickster' in Croatian. There's no one named Nico Varalica. It's not a name. It's a trick."

I was stunned.

"Do you have any letters, emails from him?"

"I mean, we text and call each other all the time."

"We checked his number. It's a burner phone. What about pictures? Do you have any photos of him?"

Nico didn't have social media except his Tumblr account, and he always wore a mask or a bandanna during his installs. I didn't think I'd ever taken a photo of his face, actually.

"No," I said. I looked at the empty room, the checkered floor. The chicken's death, immortalized in steel. His art, his true obsession, the only thing he really loved.

I never knew him. Not at all.

And then I remembered something. I remembered the photograph I'd taken of Mick setting the fire. I'd been so consumed with worry about Mick and me that I'd forgotten something huge.

Nico was in that picture too. Without his mask on.

CHAPTER THIRTY-FIVE

✦✦✦

MICK

THE WAREHOUSE IS EVEN MORE CLUTTERED THAN I
remember. I'm disoriented, the piles of boxes blocking my
view of the rest of the room. I head toward the hallway. I have
to get out onto the street.

"Mick!" Nico screams from the van, the sound vibrating
with rage.

It's so blissfully warm in here, I feel myself slowing down.
No. I have to push forward. Faster.

I hit a wall. It knocks the wind out of me.

There's not supposed to be a wall here. This is supposed to
lead to the stairwell.

I look up and around. The warehouse is smaller than I
remember.

Oh no.

This isn't the same warehouse.

I have to keep moving. The rumbling of the van's engine is
covering up any noise I'm making. I catch a whiff of fresh air.

He has a door open somewhere. That makes sense; he can't run the van in a closed warehouse without dying of carbon monoxide poisoning.

A plan forms. I'll search the perimeter until I find the door.

I squeeze past more boxes, an old golf cart, a set of garden tools, some rusty-looking rock-climbing gear, an old piano, a random assortment of traffic cones and road signs. Ahead of me, the large metal oven-kiln thing sits surrounded by bags of plaster.

The van goes silent. He turned it off.

A loud rolling-clanking sound fills the warehouse, and the light dims to a glowing amber.

He shut the door.

My heart is pounding inside my ribs.

"Mick," Nico calls from the other side of the warehouse. "Tell me what you did."

Oh God oh God oh God.

Crouched down, I hurry past the oven-kiln. Next to the bags of plaster sits a coffin-sized wooden box surrounded by the loose boards from which it's clearly been constructed. I'm continuing on my way when something catches my eye, something large and silver lying on the floor.

It's a pig. A bright silver sculpture of a pig.

I touch it with one finger. It looks like it's sleeping.

He, what, liquefied this pig the way he showed me with the flower? That is horrifying, disgusting, terrifying.

The coffin box. It's bigger than the pig.

What—

"You found it."

Nico is leaning on a stack of boxes, watching me.

I jump, scream, and turn to run. There's nowhere to go. He leaps forward and catches me by the arm. I fight, scratching and hitting him, but he whips my arm behind my back in a quick, fluid motion and raises it, hard. My shoulder feels like it's going to dislocate. I scream in pain and fall to my knees. He throws me down on the ground next to the coffin box. I hit my head on the concrete, and the breath is knocked out of me. I lie there beside the box, stunned, pain flowing through my shoulder and head.

His deep voice is smooth and calm. "Check it out. It's the perfect size. I knew exactly how tall you were the day I met you. Five foot five and a half. It's that artist's eye." He scrutinizes me. "You're just perfect. I couldn't have asked for anyone better. You know when I first knew? At the pool. It was the first day of the series, and I knew you were supposed to be a part of it. Something about how hard you worked to save that kid. It was pointless; he'd been under way too long. But you were going to die trying."

I roll onto my back, ready to make a break for it. He steps on my chest, crushing me. I can't breathe.

The boy.

It feels like it's come full circle somehow. I squeeze a breath out of my lungs and can barely suck in another one. Am I going to die like he did? Struggling to breathe? I feel tears slip out of my eyes into my hair.

Nico leans down to study me, which relieves some of the pressure. "Are you crying about the kid?" he asks, like he's fascinated.

I can't help it; a sob escapes. "It was my fault," I whisper.

He half laughs, incredulous. "No, it wasn't. I made that kid go under. I told him to dive too deep on purpose."

What?

He shrugs. "I was bored. I wanted to see you lifeguard someone."

Something buzzes. His phone. He stands, and his foot grinds down on my chest again. I struggle, try to slip air in.

He flips through something. Texts? The phone case is bright turquoise. *My* phone case is turquoise.

It's my phone he's holding. It was never lost. He stole it.

"Shit," he curses. He puts my phone in his pocket. "I know what you did."

He squats down next to me and puts a strong hand to my throat, thumb wrapping around my jaw. My head spins. His shadowy eyes are calculating, running over my face and shoulders. "You're a living, breathing piece of art," he murmurs. The room goes dark around the edges. The darkness takes my eyesight, and the last words I hear are, "Everyone's favorite little *thing*."

CHAPTER THIRTY-SIX

✦✦✦

VERONICA

MY MOM PULLED INTO THE DRIVEWAY AND TURNED off the car. It was bright, the hot summer sun roasting me through the windshield even with the air-conditioning going full blast.

"Mom, I'm sorry," I said.

She turned to me. "It's not that you've made these mistakes. You're a teenager. That's normal. It's all this lying. How long have you and Nico been doing these things? It's—"

"I know it's wrong. I know it's bad. I should never have lied to you like that. But it's, like—some things you just don't tell your mom. You know?"

She looked so hurt, so betrayed.

"I love you," I said. "I tell you almost everything."

She reached for me and hugged me fiercely. We were separated by the console and gearshift, but we hugged as tight as we could. "I'm so glad you're okay," she whispered into my shoulder.

Someone tapped on the window. It was the reporters. They were in our driveway. My mom pulled away from me. "Goddamn reporters—" She opened her door, jumped out, and slammed it behind her. I could hear her yelling at them through the windows.

I grabbed my purse, got my phone out, and checked it for the millionth time for anything from Mick. I texted her even though I knew her phone must be off. *I'm worried about you.* My finger hovered over the letters. *Please let me know you're okay.* Send.

Next, I composed a text to Nico. *Will you just tell me if Mick is okay?*

And suddenly, I was crying. I couldn't stand this. How could Nico have been a completely different person all this time? He was my best friend. Could he have killed Lily like that, so horribly? Had he pushed David?

My mom opened my door. "Come on, honey." She'd beaten back the reporters. She grabbed my purse from my lap and leaned forward to help me out. The purse came partway open, and I grabbed it to keep everything from spilling out.

Something was in the side pocket, something small and round. I peeked inside. It was a roll of film.

My mom ushered me out of the car, into the house. While walking, I extricated the film from its little black canister and examined it. It was color film—Kodak Ultramax 400. I tried to remember when I'd last used color film. It was strange that a roll of film would have ended up in my purse. I didn't even use this purse much; I'd put all my stuff in it for the gala and hadn't switched back to my camera bag since.

In the house, my mom said, "I need to stop by work for a while. You okay here alone for a few hours?"

"I'm fine, I'm going to work in the darkroom."

"Oh." She turned and faced me. "The police searched your room and darkroom while you were with Salcedo."

"What?" I cried.

She put her hands up defensively. "I didn't let them search your private things. They were looking for pictures and film and stuff related to Nico. They did take your computer in case there was evidence on there."

"I never uploaded any of my Nico pictures to my computer."

She shrugged, not really sympathetic. I felt violated by this, but how could I be surprised? The look on her face told me she'd yell at me if I said anything, so I headed up the stairs, still turning the film over and over in my hands. I had been pretty sure this purse was empty when I put my stuff in it for the gala, but I supposed I might not have checked the side pocket. This could be years old.

Could it, though? Had I ever used color film before I started shooting for Nico?

My darkroom was messy, the trays of chemicals moved around, my supplies obviously ransacked. I straightened them angrily, flipped on the safelight, and got my chemicals ready. With shaking hands, I extracted the film from its casing and spooled it into the developer.

I set the timer and waited. My phone was silent in my pocket. I hadn't expected Nico or Mick to return my messages, but I couldn't help but hope.

She has to be okay. She has to.

The timer dinged. I rinsed the film off, cut it into strips, and held one up to the safelight to get a quick look.

It looked like nature shots. Trees, ocean? Boring.

I clipped them up to dry, turned on the light, and started cleaning up. As I wiped the counter, I glanced up at the negatives. Something caught my eye, and I stopped. Some of the later shots had people in them.

I set the paper towels aside and pulled that strip down. I held it up to the light.

"Oh, shit!" I cried.

It was the film from the fire. In the shots, Mick and Nico, faces covered in ski masks, were carrying Christmas trees down to the tent. Frantic, I grabbed my magnifying glass and searched through the negatives.

There it was. The shot of Mick setting the fire.

In the negative, her hair was black, the fire dark behind her. On the right, Nico was wearing his best I-told-you-so expression. He was looking straight at the camera.

How had these gotten in my purse?

And then I remembered.

Mick.

The locker room.

I'd seen her doing something to my purse. I thought she was just fiddling with it. It had left my mind as quickly as I'd noticed it.

I grabbed my phone from my pocket and texted her.

Mick Mick Mick OMG I found the film you put in my bag. Mick please, call me. I'm going to take this to the police. Please call me.

After a minute, three dots appeared by her name.

I cried out with relief and triumph. She was alive. She was okay. God, I'd been so worried. I was going to give her so much shit when I saw her.

Finally, a response. *Sorry I've been MIA. I'm so glad you found them. I'm with my swim team. I was just going to call an Uber to come see you. Wait for me, and we can go to the police together. I have to tell them stuff too.*

I had to sit down. I was so relieved, I was actually sobbing. I could barely answer her. *You scared me so bad. I'm going to be mad at you for such a long time. Where's Nico?*

Three dots, and then: *I don't know where Nico is. I haven't seen him since yesterday.*

Hurriedly, I type, *Mick, he's dangerous. Do not hang out with him. Don't even answer his calls. They think he killed Lily and David. The police are searching for him.*

Oh my God.

I know, I answer frantically.

Her answer comes quickly. *I've been out of control. I think all the stuff with my mom really messed with me. I have so much to tell you. Can you forgive me?*

I wiped tears off my cheeks and typed, *Maybe. Probably.*

I'll text you when I'm on my way. Maybe an hour or so. Make sure to bring the prints and the negatives for the police.

Perfect, okay, good call.

I pressed the phone to my chest. Mick was okay.

I pushed myself up and got to work. I wanted to make sure I got good, clear prints to show Salcedo. I worked as fast as I could, snapping negative after negative into the enlarger, burning images onto photo paper, and sending them through the chemicals in a sort of timed photographic ballet. I kept my eye on the clock.

In forty-five minutes, I managed to get a good number of the photos printed, all the interesting ones, anyway. I took a moment to look at the eight-by-ten print of Mick, torch in hand, flames billowing around behind her. The way the light struck her, golden-orange and red like hell, she looked like an angel of death. It was a glorious shot. She was made to be photographed by me. I was made to photograph her.

I said a little prayer before putting the prints and negatives in a manila envelope: *God, please don't let us go to jail.* I stuffed the envelope into my purse just as a text from Mick came in.

The Uber is going to pick you up before me, in like 5 minutes. A white Subaru Outback. Driver's named Jorge.

I was so eager to see her. I couldn't wait.

I felt awful suddenly. David and Lily were dead. Nico was a murderer. And here I was, excited to see my girlfriend? I was such an asshole.

No. This was good. I was helping the cops. We were figuring this out.

I got my keys and let myself out the front door. The reporters started yelling at me immediately, and I groaned. I'd forgotten about them. I was about to go back inside when a white Subaru pulled up at the bottom of my driveway. I pushed past the reporters, who were yelling things like, "Do you think Micaela is dead?"

I opened the back door to the Subaru.

"Veronica?" the driver asked in a hoarse old-man voice.

"Yep." I hopped in and pulled the door shut behind me. The driver pulled away from the curb and the doors locked all at once, an automatic feature that made me nervous every time. He smelled strongly of cologne and had a thick black beard, a fedora, and a beer belly that protruded against the steering wheel. "Please put on your seat belt, miss."

I hurried to obey, but the seat belt felt stiff as I pulled it out of the seat. I was hesitant, not interested in getting trapped by some messed-up seat belt.

I pressed the release button on the seat belt, just making sure it felt normal, but it didn't push in at all. Weird. I tried pressing the release button on the seat next to me, but same thing.

He said, "Seat belt on, miss?" The tone of his voice carried a certain patriarchal bossiness that made me feel oppositional.

I pulled it around myself but didn't buckle it. "Yeah. All buckled up." I opened up iMessages and sent a text to Mick: *Just got picked up. On my way. Where are you? I want to map it.*

I waited for her to answer while I watched the streets go by. I hated it when Uber drivers wore this much cologne. He turned right onto the freeway heading east and accelerated to the speed limit. If he was heading for National City, we were going the wrong way. I opened Google Maps on my phone. Sure enough, we were on the 8 heading east.

I checked my phone. No answer from Mick.

"Excuse me, where are we headed?" I asked the driver. "My friend ordered the Uber. Where are we picking her up?" His face was turned slightly away from me. He hit the gas harder. We were up to eighty now.

"Excuse me," I repeated, starting to get scared. "Where are we going?"

Quick as a snake, he reached back and grabbed my phone out of my hands. I cried out. He laughed. He took off his fedora and beard and looked back at me, a grin stretched across his face.

Nico.

In his normal voice, he said, "How did you not recognize me? Honestly, Veronica."

I was frozen, my entire body stone-still.

He pulled a pillow out from under his shirt and tossed it aside. "Frankly, I'm offended."

"Nico, what are you doing?" My voice was low and scared.

"I'm taking you on another road trip."

Desperate, I jiggled the door handle. Child locked. I jammed at the window controls. Also child locked. Tinted windows. No one would see me if I waved, and no one would hear me if I screamed.

The seat belt. It was a trap. If I had buckled it, I'd be completely stuck.

I said a prayer of thanks for my suspicious and difficult personality, and I made sure the seat belt buckle was hidden under my butt, so that he couldn't see that I wasn't buckled.

So that was my one advantage, then, that I could attack him from the back seat without him thinking I could.

I checked the speedometer. We were going eighty-five miles per hour. There was no way I was going to attack Nico and cause an accident at this speed.

"Think about it," he mused. "Don't you know me well

enough by now to see through a simple disguise? You need to check your narcissism, girl."

"You're such an asshole."

"*You're* such an asshole. You use people. You used me. You use everyone. You are an entitled, spoiled little bitch."

I was stunned, hurt, drowning in confusion. "Where's Mick?"

"Back at the warehouse. We have plans after this."

This sounded ominous. "Is she okay?"

He didn't answer.

"Where are we going? This isn't the way to your warehouse."

His eyes flickered up to the mirror again. "East."

"No shit."

He cackled. "The best things in life are surprises, wife."

I inventoried my options: Try to choke him from behind. I discarded that immediately. Gouge his eyes out with my nails. That wouldn't work at eighty-five miles an hour, but maybe if we slowed down.

"So are you going to murder me?" I asked.

"Of course not, darling."

"Like you didn't kill Lily? Or David?"

He shrugged. How had I not recognized the familiar squareness of his shoulders?

"So you have an envelope in your purse," he said. "What's in it, wife?"

I clutched the purse.

In the mirror, his eyes were smiling. "Just kidding. I know what's in it."

CHAPTER THIRTY-SEVEN

✧✧✧

MICK

I'M SPLAYED OUT ON THE COLD FLOOR OF THE VAN, my head pillowed on the pile of cardboard. My chest aches where Nico stepped on it, and my shoulder hurts every time I breathe. I'm lying directly beneath the fan, which is mounted into the ceiling. I watch its blades spinning inside the casing, the cold wind freezing my face and bare arms. I wish I had some way to jam it, to stop those blades from spinning. I can't think with this awful whirring-freezing wind.

I hear myself whimper with despair. I don't want to die in here. Veronica is out there. Nico is doing who knows what to her.

I pull one of the pieces of cardboard over my head, trying to create shelter. It's a tiny bit warmer and quieter, but it's no solution.

But the cardboard—the fan. It gives me an idea.

I stand. My shoulder protests and my head swims.

I rip a long, narrow strip from the cardboard and poke it up into the fan. It catches, snatched violently from my fingers. It rattles and whirs inside the fan, which chokes momentarily like a garbage disposal with a spoon in it.

Encouraged, I rip another piece off the box and shove it up into the fan. The fan sucks it in. I get another strip and then another. The fan shrieks, grinds, and chunk-chunk-chunks to a stop.

"Ahhh!" I cry out, triumphant.

A couple things occur to me at once.

First: Without the fan blowing in air, I'm going to suffocate eventually.

Second: I'm still stuck inside this stupid fucking van.

It hits me: The vent must suck air in from the outside. When they installed it, they must have cut a hole in the ceiling of the van. I wonder if I can pull the refrigeration unit out. I wonder how big the hole is and if I'd fit through it.

I imagine it has to be attached to the ceiling with screws, but the metal of the unit itself looks pretty flimsy.

I jump up, grabbing for the vents. I slip and fall the first time. I get up, ignoring the pain in my shoulders and chest, and jump again. This time I catch on to the vent and hold tight. This isn't so different from working out, right? I swing back and forth, trying to loosen the unit from the ceiling. I imagine I'm on the rings in elementary school, or the monkey bars. I swing and swing. I feel the unit creak.

I lose my grip and fall, crashing to the cold white floor. I'm winded, and I take a minute to catch my breath.

I push myself to my knees. I try to talk myself up the way Coach would. I try to hear her voice telling me, *You can do this. How long have you been swimming? Is today the day it becomes too much?* I think about all the hours spent running bleachers, climbing out of the pool again and again and again.

I jump, grab the vents. They're sharp. I feel wetness—the metal is cutting into my fingers. It doesn't matter. I adjust my grip and swing, swing, pull, disrupting it as much as I can. It creaks, and I'm moving it! I feel it loosening in the brackets.

I crash to the floor, the unit with me. My fingers are stuck in the vent slats, and I pry them from the crevices. They're covered in cuts, the blood sticky and scary to look at.

The hole in the ceiling is at least a foot in diameter, but something is on the other side, blocking it. Maybe the refrigeration unit has two sides to it?

I grab one of the pieces of cardboard and roll it into a cylinder, smearing it with my blood. I poke it up through the hole in the ceiling. It encounters something metallic and wobbly. I jab harder. The cardboard cylinder breaks through. Something goes clattering. I track its progress down the roof and off the side of the van, and I hear a faint crash as it hits the concrete ground. Through the hole, I see a visible patch of dim light.

I wait for Nico to yell, for the van's door to open. I hold my breath.

Without the fan blowing tornados of air around, it is dead silent.

I remember him texting with Veronica on my phone. He must have left. He must be doing something bad to her.

I have to hurry. I have to get help.

I jump up and grab the edges of the hole in the ceiling. I slip right down; my hands are slick with blood. Quick, I yank off my shoes, shed my socks, and use them as gloves. With my shoes back on my bare feet, I jump up and catch the edges of the hole.

CHAPTER THIRTY-EIGHT

◇◇◇

VERONICA

WE'RE FAR OUTSIDE THE CITY NOW, IN THE BRUSH and hills that form a buffer between the suburbs and the desert. I watch it fly past, an endless, undulating series of rocks and bushes and cacti. The sky is huge, an eye-watering powder blue, even through the tinted windows. I'm waiting for him to slow, waiting for my chance to strike.

"I used to be jealous of you," Nico says out of nowhere. His face is calm, eyes flicking back and forth between the road and his mirror, keeping a close eye on me.

"What were you jealous of?"

He shrugs. "Your house. Your mom. You have everything, you know that? I used to think you were this interesting Great Gatsby sort of person. Someone who was really free and different."

"Okay . . ."

"But you're not." He makes eye contact in the mirror for a moment. "You're not even really an artist. Everything you want is safe and boring. You want to fall in love, you want a successful career. You have a picket-fence life, and that's all you want."

"What's wrong with falling in love and being successful?"

"Mick is interesting. She's unpredictable, she's different. You're show. She's substance."

I'm winded, shocked, hurt. "Fuck you," I say at last.

He snorts. "Original."

I hate him so, so much. "How did I never see this in you? How did I never know you? How could you pretend to be one thing and be something completely different?"

His eyes flick onto mine in the mirror. "I never pretended to be anything I wasn't. You're just really self-involved, V."

"*I'm* self-involved? You *garroted* your friend because, why? Because she wasn't interesting anymore? Because you felt like it?"

"The series I'm doing next is different; I can't leave anybody behind who knows me. I need a fresh start."

"That's so . . . ruthless."

He glances at me in the mirror. "Come on. You steamroll over everyone. People are just furniture to you. You think Mick wants to be in your pictures?"

"She said she did."

"Bullshit. She told you what you obviously wanted to hear, because she *does* feel empathy and she *isn't* a selfish asshole."

It hurts because he's right. What kind of person is best friends with a murderous psychopath and has no idea? I'm like those wives of serial killers who wear the dead girls' jewelry and know their husbands are monsters on some level but don't care, don't believe.

We're fully in the desert now, far outside the city. The road has gotten narrower, one lane in each direction. We're slowing down. My heart palpitates madly in my chest. There's a turn coming up, a smaller road leading off to the right. He puts the brakes on and takes the turn. The desert goes on forever in all directions, an endless landscape where anyone could disappear.

I check the speedometer over Nico's shoulder. We're going forty miles per hour. This is it.

I lunge forward. I grab his head from behind and dig my index fingers into the squishiness of his eyes.

He grunt-screams and twists the wheel. I dig harder, nails gouging his eye sockets. The car spins out, whips around, hits the embankment. He's trying to get ahold of the steering wheel while we spin. I scratch at his face, hoping I'm drawing blood, hoping I'm blinding him. The car catches on a hill, half rolls, gets stuck on a rock with a scraping squeal, and shudders to a stop.

No time to waste.

I grab my purse and jump forward, over the front seat, trying to escape out the front door since the rear doors are child locked. Nico grabs at me, catches my ankle. I kick him in the face. I unlock the door and fling it open. The air outside is hot like an oven. I plunge out of the car, which is tangled with a guardrail. I can run either way on the road, or I can run out into the desert.

I choose desert.

I run.

Behind me, I can hear him laughing.

I run harder. I'm wearing slip-on Vans, and I'm making bad time on the rocky terrain that bites at my ankles and legs. I head for what looks like a line of hills. Maybe I can hide on the other side. I run uphill, my chest burning, cursing my lack of cardiovascular fitness. Mick would never have this hard of a—

I vault to the top of the hill and push my legs harder, intending to sprint down the other side.

I'm on the edge of a cliff.

It's too late. My feet hit air where ground should be.

I fall down the cliff head over heels. I can't scream, can't think. I feel impacts—rocks hitting my head, my back, my butt, my ankles. A whir of motion.

And then stillness.

Darkness.

I drift.

Eventually I drift into wakefulness. Into pain.

Hot sky. Blue.

Birds.

Whizzing above me. Wings leaving trails like fireworks.

Above, on the edge of the cliff, a slender silhouette. He's watching me die.

More birds. So loud. So many.

Pain.

First Lily. Then David. Now me. We all fall down.

I never thought much about birds, but now I think—I'd love to be one. Imagine the freedom of movement. They're living in three dimensions while the rest of us are pinned flat to the earth.

Maybe I'm safe in this moment. Maybe there's something

to be said for just holding still and appreciating the simple beauty of birds in a blue sky.

The thought makes me feel close to Mick. She sees all the simple, important things.

I close my eyes.

CHAPTER THIRTY-NINE

◇◇◇

MICK

I PULL MYSELF UP ONTO THE ROOF OF THE VAN AND
squirm-wriggle out until I'm heaving, panting, and crying on
the smooth metal surface. My sides burn from scraping the
rough-cut hole.

I did it.

I check my hands. They're swollen and bloody. I climb
down the windshield to the hood, then jump to the floor.

The small, crowded warehouse is lit by a single lightbulb in
the ceiling. It occurs to me now that the rolling door is probably locked. I was so focused on getting out of the van, I didn't
even consider how to escape the warehouse itself.

I'm filled with dread as I bend down to grab the rolling
door's handle. I say a silent prayer and pull.

It doesn't move. It's locked.

Of course.

I back away from it, checking the perimeter for doors and
windows, pushing through boxes, past the kiln thing, past the

pig, around in a large rectangle. Nothing. I pass the kiln a second time and pause next to the coffin box.

I remember the things he said, and I wonder if he was planning to bury me in this box. Was this how he was going to get rid of my body after he'd frozen me to death?

I look at the pig. Something about it sets off little internal alarm bells. *Look at me*, it seems to cry. *I'm important.*

And then I know.

The coffin, just my size. It's surrounded by discarded wood; he built this himself, in exactly my size.

The refrigerated van.

He wants to freeze me and then make a sculpture out of me. The pig was a rehearsal. He wanted to practice on something large, human-sized.

I'm the fifth piece. *I am the finale.*

I have to get out of here. *Now.*

Clang.

A series of clatters at the front of the warehouse, and then the sliding door starts rolling up. Daylight floods in, stinging my eyes.

He's back.

I look around for something to defend myself with. I'm sure the warehouse is full of stuff, but it's all in boxes, and I don't have time to start digging around hoping for an ax. As blinding daylight floods the warehouse, I grab one of the boards from the stack next to the coffin box. My hands scream in pain when I grip the rough surface.

He pulls the door down, locks it, and steps through the warehouse toward the van. He starts unlocking the back door.

What's he planning to do? Will he strangle me first with his bare hands? Or maybe he's hoping I'm already frozen to death.

An image strikes me, as real as the board clutched in my aching, stinging hands: me, dead, cast in bright silver steel. Would he strip me down? Where would he put me—in some public place for me to be gawked at and photographed, naked and dead?

Rage.

He killed that kid for no reason. Out of *boredom*.

I run at him from behind, heft the two-by-four, and swing it like a bat. It whacks him brutally on the back of the head. He topples away from the van, smashing into the concrete and rolling over onto his back. A trickle of blood streams from his hair. His eyes are closed, face slack, arms splayed out beside him.

I poke at him with the board. My hands are shaking so bad, the entire board vibrates.

His eyes flutter open. My heart stops. I raise the board, ready to hit him again.

His gaze flickers over me weakly, eyes scanning me from head to toe.

He smiles faintly. "Awesome," he whispers, and closes his eyes. His head falls to the side.

I lower the board.

My whole body feels like it's being blown by wind, like I'm back on the bridge, like I just jumped and am rappelling through empty space. I kneel down beside him and feel his chest.

He's breathing.

What do I do?

Where is Veronica?

My phone. He has it.

I dig through his pockets, keeping the ring of keys I find. There are two phones in the left one and another in the right. I recognize the turquoise case as mine and the black-and-gold case as Veronica's. The third one must be his.

One eye on him in case he wakes up, I open up my text messages to see what he was doing earlier. I find the last exchange with Veronica and read it fast. There's the text she sent that must have triggered his reaction to me—*I know what you did*—and his response, that he was sorry and that he'd have an Uber pick her up in an hour. A white Subaru?

I fumble with the keys and find one that fits the padlock on the sliding warehouse door. I heave the door up. Outside sits a white Subaru.

He has her phone. I know what that means.

I return to Nico's limp shape and scream, a wordless sound of fury, reach back, and slap him across the face, so hard the cuts on my hand explode into burning and his head rocks to the side. Blood trails along his lips in a little river from his nose. I notice the skin around his eyes is scratched, and he has a bruise on his forehead. I might have given him the forehead bruise when I hit him, but I didn't scratch at his eyes.

Veronica is feisty. If he attacked her, she'd fight back. If he strangled her, hands tight around her neck like they'd been on mine, she'd scratch his face.

Oh God. Oh God, oh God, I'm going to be sick.

He was gone for hours. He could have been anywhere. How can I even begin looking for her?

Maps. If he used navigation, I can see where he went.

With bloody, sticky, shaking hands, I try to unlock his phone. It's password protected. I grab his limp right hand and press the thumb against the Home button. The screen opens up, and I see Apple and Google Maps. Before the phone can close and lock again, I go to Settings and disable the password protection.

In Apple Maps, I find nothing. But in Google Maps, I find a list of saved places. The most recent search he did was for a lonely freeway intersection, seventy miles east in the desert.

Oh no.

I can't just leave him here to escape, but I'm not calling the cops and losing hours trying to explain things and taking this phone to the station and having them come here and search the warehouse and—

I have to go to this desert place now and try to find Veronica.

She's going to be dead.

No. Maybe not. No.

I'm in denial. I know it.

Doesn't matter. I'm going.

I attack Nico's Converses, pulling the shoelaces out. I use one shoelace to tie his wrists tightly together in front of him and another to bind his ankles. I want to hit him with the board, over and over again. If I find Veronica dead, I might come back here and do just that. I could kill him. It's in me; I can feel it.

I keep all three phones and his keys. I padlock the warehouse door behind me and turn toward the Subaru.

The front is damaged, like it's been in an accident. Half of the bumper is actually missing, along with a large chunk out of the tire well, and what's left is brutally scraped up. I squat down to examine the dents and scrapes. They're brown, caked with dirt and pebbles.

It's clearly drivable, since he managed to get it here. I stumble inside, adjust the seat, and use Nico's phone to map me to the location he'd pinned. It's roasting hot in here, but I can't stop shivering. I feel like I'll never be warm again.

I start the car. My hands are so unsteady, I almost can't get the key in. As I drive to the freeway, I consider calling Claudia. But then I think I might be about to find Veronica's body. Again, I consider calling the police.

I call no one.

I leave San Diego behind, traveling until I'm surrounded by dry, rocky hills covered in brush and cacti. According to Nico's map, I'm supposed to turn right ahead, on a road that leads into the desert. I slow to take the turn. The map says to turn right at what looks more like a trail than a street.

This is somewhere you go to bury a body.

Something ahead catches my attention: a few pieces of white, scattered along the right shoulder. I pull over and get out.

Black tire tracks are scrawled on the cracked asphalt onto the opposite shoulder and then in a circle, like someone spun out. I approach the pieces of white. They're the Subaru's missing bumper and tire well, still caught on the large rock that claimed it.

So he had an accident here. And he just left this evidence and drove away?

I mean, I guess the car isn't his; it's probably stolen. So he wouldn't care.

So if he had the accident, he'd want to get rid of Veronica's body immediately. He'd have gotten her out and brought her somewhere nearby, done it quickly before someone came along and offered to help. I survey the area, trying to imagine where he'd have gone.

On one side of the street, the hills are steep, cragged, and rocky. I can't imagine him carrying her over that.

To the other side, a wide, flat expanse rolls gently up to a hill. It's a flat enough surface to carry someone across.

He left me alive in the van. Maybe he did the same with her, neglected to strangle her all the way. If he was in a hurry, he might have dug a very shallow grave. Or he might not have dug a grave at all.

I lock the Subaru and pocket the keys. I walk into the desert.

The brush and cacti stretch out around me in an endless, rocky expanse. The ground is rough, and even in my running shoes, I can barely keep my footing. Ahead is the small range of hills. Maybe I could aim for that and get a better vantage point. I pick my way across the rugged landscape. It's burning hot, my skin frying in the sun, and the air is alive with the singing of birds.

At the top of the hill, I come to a screeching halt. An unexpected, steep drop plummets down to a deep ravine. I look back the way I came. There's the Subaru, small and lonely. In the distance, a series of wind turbines rotate creepily.

I can't imagine him rock climbing down into the ravine

while holding her. He's strong, but he's not Superman. Unless he just threw her down there. God, please, no.

I peer into the shadows of the ravine. The ground is far away, hidden by the rock protrusions in the cliff. I pace the edge, eyes on—

I see her.

Splayed out on her back at the bottom, one arm bent at an unnatural angle. Pale skin. Dark hair.

"No!" I hear myself scream.

I stumble back. I fall on my butt.

I'm sobbing. I can't. This can't.

With hands that shake so hard they almost don't function as hands anymore, I get out Nico's phone and I dial 911.

"Please have service, please have service," I whisper.

"Nine-one-one, what is your emergency?"

My voice is unrecognizable, rough and broken. "I'm in the desert and my friend Veronica fell off a cliff. I need you to send an ambulance, fire department, everything."

The connection crackles, and the voice changes, sharpens. "Do you know where you are, miss?"

"I took the 8 east from San Diego and turned left onto a street called McCain Valley, then turned right on a tiny road near the wind farm. Can you find that?"

She repeats it back to me.

"You'll see a white Subaru parked on the shoulder of the road. That's where I am."

"We'll send a team out. They should be there in half an hour. Please stay on the road so they can see you and you can lead them to her. What is your name, miss?"

"Mick. Micaela Young. But half an hour? What if she's alive down there? They need to get here sooner!"

"It takes time to deploy a search and rescue team. I promise, they'll be there soon. Do you have water for yourself? You need to stay hydrated."

"No! I'm going to try to go down and help her! The car is on the road right behind me. They just need to turn right at the car and head for the hill."

"Miss, do not try to go down there. You'll hurt yourself and delay her medical treatment. Do you understand?"

"Fuck you." I hang up the phone, shove it in my pocket, and start looking for a way down. At last, I decide on what looks like a mini-ravine, where I can get my feet and hands into a crack in the earth that runs all the way down to the bottom.

I try to remember what I learned at the climbing gym, always moving one limb at a time, never placing a foot before having a steady grip. Slow and steady, the instructor had told us.

My foot slips, and one of the rocks I'm holding on to disengages from the cliff. Rocks go tumble-bouncing down. My right hand and foot flail, and I panic, but then I catch a new handhold and take some deep breaths.

I did this on the bridge. I was panicking, but I did it. Coach's voice echoes in my memory. *Is today the day it's too much? Is this the thing that defeats you?*

"No!" I roar. I find a new hold and keep going. Foot, hand, foot, hand. Left, right, left, right. My hands are past pain, my heart past pounding. I'm empty, void of anything but concentration.

And then I'm there—it's done. My foot finds the ground, and I fall to my knees. For a moment, I can't move. My limbs are limp and useless.

I push myself to my feet. I stumble upright and run toward where I remember seeing her.

There she is, tangled and bent, her head fallen softly to the side, lips parted, eyes closed, skin red from sunburn.

I reach out and touch her neck, searching for a pulse. She's warm, but it's a hundred and ten degrees out here; that means nothing.

I feel a pulse!

There's blood on the dirt around her head. "Oh God," I hear myself say. I check her head, feeling up inside the back of her hair. My hands come away bloody. I find a large cut just behind her left ear.

I need a bandage, something to put pressure on the wound.

My shirt. I whip it off and fold it into a long, narrow rectangle. Afraid to move her neck, I slip it under her head and wrap it around tight.

What else can I do?

I feel for her pulse again. Super fast. That's not good.

Her eyes open halfway.

"Veronica!" I put a hand on her cheek. "You're really hurt. Please don't move. Paramedics are on their way."

Her brows draw together. She swallows, the sound dry. A low, weak moan pulls from her throat.

"You're in pain?"

She nods, just a hair, and then winces.

"Can you tell me what hurts? Don't move."

She moves her lips for a minute before the words come out. "Arm," she whispers.

"It's broken. But they can fix that. What else?"

"Head."

"You have a cut and probably a concussion. Anything else?"

"Everything."

"Can you feel your legs?"

She frowns. "My hip. Something."

I laugh. I realize I'm crying. I'm so happy she's alive. "Can you move your toes? Your feet?"

I watch as her checkered Vans wiggle around, and then she screech-moans. "Owwww."

"Leg?"

"Ankle. Leg. Side."

"Ankle and leg is okay," I say. "There's nothing that can happen to an ankle or a leg that can't be fixed."

"Side."

I pull her shirt up to look. Her ribs look buckled, and a dark blue bruise stretches from her armpit to her hip. It reminds me of an injury I saw on a reality show, where someone got kicked by a horse. She has broken ribs, and she's bleeding internally.

I pull my phone out of my pocket and call 911. When the operator picks up, I say, "I'm waiting for paramedics off a road called McCain Valley, my friend fell off a cliff. When will they be here?"

"What's your name?"

"Micaela Young."

"One moment."

The operator from before takes the line. "Mick?"

"I found her," I say, breathless. "I mean, I got down to her. She's alive. But she's hurt really bad. She has internal bleeding, broken ribs, broken arm and leg, a head injury, and I don't know what else. She can move her feet, so her spine probably isn't broken, but I'm still not moving her."

"Mick, I'm glad you're okay, but I wish you hadn't gone down there."

"Well, it's too late now."

"Search and rescue are on their way. Keep your phone on. We'll call you if we have a hard time finding you."

We hang up, and I return my attention to Veronica, who's watching me with a spaced-out, half-awake expression on her face. I tell her, "They're on their way. Hang on. Pain meds coming your way soon."

"Drugs are good," she whispers.

I'm sobbing. "I thought I'd find your body out here. I can't believe Nico let you live."

"He thought I was dead." She smiles faintly and closes her eyes.

"Don't get sleepy!" I pat her cheek. "Keep those eyes open."

She seems to drag them open. Instead of looking at me, she looks up at the sky. "I never noticed birds before," she whispers.

I look up. Sure enough, sparrows are flitting around above us, going on with their sparrow business.

"Oh," she gasps. Her eyes open wide, and she clutches at me with her working hand. "The envelope. The pictures."

"What pictures?" Is she delirious?

She points around in circles, at the rocks and bushes. "Find. Hide. The envelope. The pictures."

CHAPTER FORTY

<><><>

MICK

THE PARAMEDICS TAKE ANOTHER ENTIRE HOUR TO arrive. It's the longest hour of my life, longer than being trapped in the van. I keep my fingers to Veronica's neck, feeling her pulse get quicker, slower, quicker, slower. She finally passes out, leaving me alone in the heat, surrounded by birdsong and the smell of blood and dust.

I keep my eyes up, glued to the top of the cliff. *Come on, come on, come on*, I pray inside my head.

When they peek their heads over the cliff, I stand up and scream. "Down here! *Here!*" I wave my arms around maniacally.

They wave back, and one of them screams, "We'll be right down!"

"Hurry!"

They unspool a rope ladder. With impressive speed and efficiency, two uniformed, backpack-laden paramedics descend. Another pair lowers a stretcher from the top of the cliff. They run toward me, and I give them a breathless rundown of

Veronica's condition. The woman, a deeply tanned blonde with crow's-feet and strong-looking hands, gives Veronica a quick examination. "She moved her feet? You're sure?"

"Yes. While she was awake, I asked her to move them. I haven't moved her back or neck at all except to bandage the head wound. It was bleeding like crazy."

She raises her eyebrows to me while her partner, a young man, examines Veronica's broken arm. "How did you know to do all that?"

"I'm a lifeguard. We're trained for things."

"Not this trained."

"I don't know, I just wanted her to be okay!"

I watch them tape Veronica's arm across her chest and strap her onto the mobile stretcher. I hold my breath as they get her up the cliff. It's incredible. They're so clean, so quick. I could watch them work all day.

I want to do this, I realize. This job they have. This is the job I want.

I grab the phones out of the Subaru and ride in the back of the ambulance with Veronica and the female paramedic. As we whoop our way to the hospital, I say, "I'm worried about internal bleeding from the broken ribs."

"Me too, honey." She's busy with her stethoscope. "How did she fall?"

I stare at her for a long moment, and then I say, "I didn't see." I get Veronica's phone out. "Let me use her thumb so I can unlock her phone and call her mom."

She steps aside, and I use Veronica's uninjured hand gently. I pull Claudia's number up out of the contacts. It's listed under

Mama Kitten, and I have to take some deep breaths before dialing.

"Veronica?" Claudia's voice is worried.

"Claudia, it's Mick."

Silence for two seconds, and then, "Where's Veronica?"

"She's here. She's hurt. Nico tried to kill her. But we're in the ambulance now, heading to the hospital."

Silence for one second, and then, "Oh my God. She's okay?"

"She's not okay, but she's alive. I left Nico back at his warehouse. I hit him and ran to help Veronica. Can you help me figure out what to do?" I sound like a little girl, and it's only now that I realize how lost I feel. I hear myself start crying.

"What's wrong with Veronica?"

"I think he pushed her off a—" I'm not going to say cliff. "Off a big hill. She has some broken bones, and she hit her head. But she was talking, she was coherent."

She makes a few choked noises, and then she says, "What hospital are you going to?"

"I don't know. Hang on. What hospital are we going to?" I ask the paramedic, who's looking at me with huge eyes.

"Scripps in Eastlake, off the 125," she replies.

I pass the name of the hospital along. Claudia says, "I'm going to meet you there, and I'll call the detective so you can give him your statement. Keep her phone on you."

The phone goes dead.

I put my face in my hands.

The paramedic says, "It sounds like we need to call the police."

"They're going to meet us there."

"Even so."

It takes a thousand years to get to the hospital. They rush Veronica to the back, leaving me in the waiting area. I feel naked in my sports bra. I ask the nurse behind the counter if she can give me a shirt, and she says she'll do it, but it never comes.

At last, Claudia bursts in followed by a middle-aged man with close-cropped black hair in business clothes. I stand and wave them down, and then behind them, a man slips in with a big, professional-looking camera. He raises it and takes my picture. I'm so confused, I just stare at him like an idiot. The man with Claudia follows my eyes, swings around, and then pushes the photographer forcefully out of the ER. He slams the door shut on the guy.

Claudia goes straight to the counter. "Veronica Villarreal. She's my daughter, and you're going to tell me where she is right now."

The woman at the counter pulls her aside, and the man turns his attention on me. "I'm Detective Salcedo. We've been looking for you, Micaela."

I nod, numb. I wrap my arms around myself.

"Are you cold?"

"They're supposed to be getting me a shirt. I used mine to bandage Veronica's head."

He marches to the counter and shows them his badge. "This teenage girl is standing here in her bra. Get her a god-damn shirt right now."

A woman goes scurrying and comes back with a blue scrub shirt. He brings it to me. "I'm sorry. Here you go. You're very scraped up, though. Have you seen a doctor?"

"I'm okay." I pull the shirt over my head, wincing. My hands hurt so much.

He takes one of my hands and looks at it. "What happened here?"

"Nico. He tried to kill both of us." I tell him about the warehouse and describe my trip out to the desert to help Veronica. More cops show up. A female detective takes me into a treatment room and photographs all my scrapes and cuts, and then a nurse stitches up the deeper cuts in my hands.

When she's done, she tells me to go back to the waiting room. Instead, I scope out the treatment areas. On my third try, I find Claudia. She's sitting on a chair against a wall, crying.

Oh no. "Is Veronica—is she—"

She beckons me toward her. "She's in surgery. For the ribs and the ankle and the arm. She's going to have pins in her ankle. And a plate in her arm."

There's an empty chair next to her. I sink down into it.

"I loved him like a son," she whispers.

I wrap an arm around her shoulders. "You couldn't have known."

She puts her arm around my waist. It feels warm and safe. "Where's your mama?" she asks.

"I didn't call her."

"You should."

I don't say anything.

"Do it now."

"After we find out about Veronica."

She nods. "So I think I owe you an apology."

"For what?"

"The paramedics told me you climbed down a cliff to give her first aid. That they told you not to climb down there and you ignored them. Cussed at them, actually." She gives me a smile with one side of her mouth.

"Well, they were being stupid. What was I going to do, just sit there while she—"

"If you'd been climbing down the cliff to help anyone else, I'd agree with them. But that was my baby down there." She wraps both arms around me and gives me a hard squeeze.

I hug her back, and it feels so good to be held, I stay like that for a long time.

CHAPTER FORTY-ONE

◇◇◇

MICK

CLAUDIA SAYS, "SHE'S GOING TO WAKE UP SOON."

I nod.

We sit there staring at Veronica. She's surrounded by machines, an IV and finger monitor attached to her good hand. Her head is wrapped in gauze, her right arm and leg in white plaster casts. It's not going to be an easy few months, with her entire right side out of commission. She won't be able to use crutches or push herself in a wheelchair.

"They said there was no reason she wouldn't wake up," Claudia says.

I nod.

"She's just wiped out from the anesthetic and the surgery, and her body is tired," she goes on. "It needs to recuperate."

"Did they shave her head?" I whisper, like she can hear me.

"Just around the cut. Her hair should cover it."

"That's good."

A figure appears at the door. We look up with half interest;

nurses and doctors and police have been in and out for hours. But the person standing there is wearing yoga pants and a V-neck exercise shirt that shows off her boobs. Her blond hair is coiffed, her French manicure shining, but her face is pink like she's been crying.

"Mom?" I say, confused.

Claudia snaps to attention. "Oh, hello, I'm Claudia. We spoke on the phone."

"You *called* her?"

My mom stays in the doorway. "You're okay?" she asks me.

"I'm fine."

"Claudia made it sound like you were hurt."

"Just my hands. But they're fine. Just cut."

She nods. "Good. Fine. Okay." She hovers in the doorway, pats the door frame awkwardly, and then turns and walks away.

Claudia makes a shocked noise.

"It's fine," I say. "There's no point. She's—"

"Absolutely not." She gets up and storms out after my mom.

"Hey," comes a faint voice from the bed. Veronica's eyes are open. She clears her throat and licks her lips.

I jump up and rush toward her. "You're awake! Are you thirsty?" I have a glass of water on the bedside table waiting for her to wake up. I bring it to her lips with a straw. She takes a few thirsty gulps. I say, "Your right arm, leg, and ribs are broken, but you're going to be okay. How are you feeling? Are you in pain?" I search for parts of her body I can touch. I find her good hand and grab it.

"I'm pissed." Her voice is rough.

"Why are you pissed?"

"You put a shirt on. And such an ugly shirt, too."

I laugh and start crying. It's such a Veronica thing to say. It means she remembers the cliff, that her brain can't be messed up that bad. I bring her good hand to my face and cry into it, everything that's happened crashing down on me: Lily, David, Nico telling me I was everyone's pretty little thing, my mom, being trapped in the van . . .

She whispers, "Where's Nico?"

I hesitate. I don't want to upset her, but I'm not going to lie to her. "He was going to kill me, Veronica. I hit him with a board and left him at his warehouse, then came to find you. I think he might be dead. We're waiting for the police to tell us for sure."

She closes her eyes, clearly in pain.

"I'm so sorry," I murmur. "For everything."

"Me too. I should have seen it in him."

I rest my forehead to hers. She's alive. We're both alive.

She pats the sheet beside her. "Come on. Climb up here. Snuggle next to my good side."

I kick my shoes off and, as carefully as I can, stretch out next to her with my head resting on the pillow beside hers. She turns a little, hissing in pain.

"Don't make yourself uncomfortable," I protest.

"Quiet. Come closer."

I bury my face into the crook of her neck, and she sighs. "Tell me they didn't shave my head."

"It's the first thing I asked. No. They didn't. Just a little bit underneath where no one will see."

"Good girl."

I run my hand down her good arm and lace my fingers through hers. I pull the hand to my lips and kiss it. I'm so full of gratitude, I can't stand it.

"Mick?"

"Yeah?"

"The pictures. They're in an envelope—"

"Don't worry about it. I took care of them."

"You didn't give them to the police?"

"No. I . . . didn't think we should. I wanted to talk to you first."

"That was the only picture of Nico."

We meet each other's eyes, sharing the same worry. If we show them the picture of Nico and prove he was linked to the fire, we'll also prove our own guilt as accomplices.

"No one knows they exist except us," she whispers. "They already know he's guilty of killing Lily and David. They don't need proof of the fire too."

I nod slowly. It's a pact we're making here.

"Okay," I say.

"Okay."

She's quiet for a long moment. I think she might be falling asleep, but then she says, "He killed Lily before he pushed her."

I prop myself up on my elbow and look down at her. "Wait, what?"

She nods, winces. "He strangled her with a wire or something. Horrible."

"Oh God," I say. "And I helped him after that. I'm so stupid."

She pulls me down to rest my head on her shoulder again. "We were all stupid. But, Mick. Why were you helping him?"

I swallow. I don't want to tell her this. "I never went home like I told you. My mom kicked me out for good. I didn't have anywhere to sleep. I asked Nico if he'd help me get a car so I could live in it. That's why I was helping him. And in the meantime, he was letting me stay with him."

She processes this for a long moment. "You wanted to live in a car?"

"I didn't know what else to do. I still don't."

"You could have stayed with me. Why would you go to *him*?" Her fragile voice is so hurt, I feel horrible.

"I was scared your mom would call social services and send me to a foster home."

"I would have helped you. I wouldn't tell my mom. Do you know how much I covered for you? Even when I wasn't sure what happened to Lily."

Carefully, I wrap my arm around her waist and pull myself as close to her as I can. "I'm so sorry."

"I'm sorry too." She pauses, like she's almost too tired to talk anymore. "The pictures. I just did what I wanted."

"I don't care about the pictures." The thought is so petty in context. "Lie still. You need to rest." I pat her cheek.

My thoughts are all at once overtaken with worry. The problem with not having anywhere to live hasn't gone away.

Once this hospital visit is over, I'm out on the street. No car, no home. Can I get a motel room if I'm underage? Maybe in a really seedy area. And I don't have that much money saved up, not enough to, like, live in a motel now.

"What are you thinking about?" Veronica whispers.

I steel myself and tell her the truth. "Trying to figure out where to go after this."

"Why don't you worry later. Let's try to sleep now. Okay?" She's comforting me. She's got a body full of broken bones, and she's trying to make me feel better.

I can't speak. I kiss her carefully, without putting any weight on her, and lie so she can rest her head on my shoulder. Her breathing deepens. And there, squished in the hospital bed, we fall asleep.

I wake up to whispering.

Claudia is leaning over Veronica's other side, faces pressed together, and they're whispering in each other's ears. Claudia pulls back. A tear drips from her nose onto Veronica's cheek, and she wipes it off.

Carefully, I push myself up. "I'm so sorry. I passed out. I'll leave you two alone."

She stands. "Mick, come outside with me. Veronica, the nurse told me she needs to change your catheter."

"Jesus Christ, Mom. You couldn't have waited until Mick was out of the room? Are you trying to make sure I never get laid again? Is that my punishment?"

Claudia kisses Veronica's forehead. "My little angel."

I get off Veronica's bed with a minimum of jostling and follow Claudia into the hallway, rubbing my eyes. It has to be midnight. I'm dying to know what happened with Nico. Why are the police taking so long?

"So, I talked to your mom." She's peering at me with something like pity. "She seems . . . unstable."

I shrug. I look down at the floor.

"Does she have a drug problem?"

I blink at her. I'd never considered this. "I . . . don't think so. I don't know." I don't know that much about my mom, I realize. When I look at Claudia and Veronica, I see how not close my mom and I are. We're separate, living parallel lives, not entangled in any meaningful ways. Single moms are supposed to be close with their kids. That's how it usually works. Somehow this realization lights up the same pain as when I almost lost Veronica. Is it grief? It feels like losing something huge, something that was never quite mine to begin with.

She touches my shoulder. "I told her you'd be staying with me for a while. If you like. Through senior year."

I snap my head up. "What?"

"I know Bonita has a very good swim team. I can help you deal with the transfer. If you're interested."

I feel winded, like she punched me. "Don't say this if you don't mean it."

She steps forward and folds me into a hug. "You deserve a chance," she says into my ear. "This is me paying you back."

I can't help it. I'm crying *again*. "Okay," I squeak.

She pulls back. "Yeah?"

I nod, wiping my eyes. I feel like a little girl.

"You have college plans?"

"Actually, I . . . This might sound stupid. I've been dreaming of going to college somewhere far away, and I've already been scouted for a school in New Hampshire. But I think I want to be a paramedic, or an EMT or whatever. Or maybe work for the Coast Guard. You know those search and rescue people? I realized when I saw them get Veronica. That's what I want to do."

"That doesn't sound stupid. I can totally see you doing that. The paramedics were very impressed with you." She keeps an arm around my waist, and we head back into the room. "We'll have to look into what kind of school you go to for that," she says.

It's so kind, her offering to help me figure that out. My mom never did anything like that.

As soon as we cross the threshold, Veronica points to the nurse tidying up the counter and says, "She did terrible things to me while you were gone."

Claudia says, "I need to tell both of you something. It's about Nico. I have news from the police."

I sit on the edge of Veronica's bed. We've stopped breathing. I don't know what Veronica is hoping for: Nico dead? Nico in the hospital, recovering so he can go to jail?

Claudia says, "So, Mick, the police went to the warehouse. And, honey. He wasn't there."

I try to understand this. It makes no sense.

"There was no van. They found the pig, the box, the plaster, the air-conditioner unit you said you'd torn off the roof, the other things you described. But no van, no Nico."

"Oh, shit," I whisper. I lean back against the wall.

"They saw blood on the floor, the two-by-four, and even the shoelaces you described tying him up with. There were tire tracks that matched the description of the van you provided. But Nico is gone."

"Gone," Veronica repeats. Her eyes are huge.

I say, "That's bad. He could come back. He could get us."

There's a long silence. At last, Claudia says, "We have an alarm system."

"He probably knows the code," Veronica replies.

"I'll change it."

My brain flies from thing to thing. "He could get us at school. Whenever we're alone. He's so smart. You don't understand—"

"They're not going to let him do that."

I don't believe her.

CHAPTER FORTY-TWO

✧✧✧

NICO

IT'S BEEN SIX WEEKS SINCE I'VE SEEN YOU. I WON-der if you miss me. From what I can see, you're doing well, you and Veronica. You're playing house. You feel safe. That's nice.

I've been keeping quiet, but it's a frenzied quiet. Art is like that: months of planning, all for one glorious moment of creation.

Homeless people and children can go absolutely anywhere. Did you ever think about that? And they're always carrying luggage: backpacks, shopping carts, duffel bags, sleeping bags.

If I were to wander into the Department of Water and Power's server room with a backpack containing a bomb with a timer on it, I'd be immediately arrested. If a nine-year-old girl did it, she'd get sympathetic cooing. "Oh, sweetie, are you lost on a field trip? Let me help you find your class." And the nice man who gave her the backpack to leave in the control room would give her *twenty* dollars.

If I walked into Universal Studios carrying a backpack full of bombs and fireworks, would I get escorted peacefully out? No. But send a first grader in. She could take the backpack to a service alley, leave it, and a few minutes later, a whole amusement park full of people would be traumatized for life, thinking there was an active shooter about to take them all out. And there you go—a ton of cops deployed, resources scattered, the city brought to its knees—total chaos.

And homeless people? Forget about it. If you were to send a homeless person into Grand Central Market in downtown LA with a stroller full of fireworks, would people ask to search the stroller? No. They'd avoid eye contact. They'd hide from the smell of stale urine. Want to know how much you'd have to pay a homeless guy to set off fireworks in a crowded place?

Fifty bucks.

CHAPTER FORTY-THREE

◇◇◇

MICK

THE BLACK-AND-WHITE PICTURE STARES AT ME OUT of my phone. It's so familiar now, my eyes half-starved, the rows of seats stretching off behind me, my lips parted, having just been kissed.

"Famous First Love Series Goes on the Road," the headline reads, followed by the tour schedule for Veronica's photos. They're making their way across the country, doing the gallery circuit. She has a manager for the tour, an agent, the whole thing. I don't bother to read the rest of the article, which I can tell just says the same thing they all say, talking about death in an enthusiastic way, like Nico killing off his friends one by one is a selling point.

I close the article. I'm sitting on the queen-sized bed in the room that used to be Veronica's older sister's but which is now mine for the year. Claudia let me paint the walls any color I wanted so that it would feel like home, something so nice it almost hurt. I picked light blue. It makes me feel like I'm outside.

A small, guilty part of me misses my apartment. This house is so big and airy, I don't think it could ever feel like home.

And I miss my mom. If I'm being honest.

Why doesn't she want to be a part of my life? It feels like a death, having to face her lack of interest in me once and for all.

My new therapist says these feelings are natural, and that I should try reaching out to her when I feel ready. Sometimes I go to the Sunbrella website and look at pictures of her lounging by pools, a model for a lifestyle that will never be hers. As soon as I see her face, anger takes over and I shove all thoughts of her aside. She doesn't get to come into this new life I'm building and poison it, too.

I open up my photos. I feel like I'm sneaking something.

I've been taking pictures.

There are shots of the pool, bright turquoise with the sun rising in the sky above it. I took this because I love the feeling of getting to the pool first, with only the birds to keep me company.

There are shots of the beach, from when I went alone at Veronica's insistence while she was in the hospital because I needed to get outside. It was the middle of the day, bright and sunny, and at first I'd been a little afraid to go in the water. After a lifetime of being told how weird and wrong it is to want to do things alone, I felt like everyone was looking at me.

But then I remembered everything I had survived, and I dropped my towel on the sand and marched straight into the waves.

There are selfies in here, too, but not the kind I think Veronica or my mom would approve of. They aren't flattering or artistic; they're more to capture certain moments I don't want to forget. I've been taking rock-climbing lessons, and there's one I took from the top of a climb, my face sweaty and shining in the sun. There's one I took that day at the beach, just to prove to myself I could, that I wasn't afraid anymore. I was wet from the ocean, my hair plastered to my head, sunglasses a little lopsided, but, for the first time in my life, I felt brave and bold and all the things I've always longed to be.

After all, Nico is still out there. He could be back any day, with worse plans in mind than the ones he was forced to abandon. For the last six weeks, I've felt like I've been living in the eye of a hurricane, the hushed pause before a trigger is pulled. I think I'll feel this way until the police catch him, if they ever do.

And if they don't? Is this just how the rest of my life will feel?

I navigate to Instagram and open the years-old account I never use. It has a handful of photos with Liz from a couple years ago. I look like an infant in them.

I start uploading pictures. I caption them with *This was the day I went alone to the beach* and *Highest climb yet*. The captions are for me. I'm capturing my life, not for anyone else's eyes, but just to have it, and maybe even to share it with people who might like to be a part of it, like Veronica, or Claudia, or a few of the friends I've made on this new swim team.

Why does this sharing of pictures feel so different than when Veronica did it? Is it because I'm in control of my own story here?

When I'm done, I look at the grid, and it's so colorful. Bright blue water, bright blue sky, warm sun on tanned skin, the orange of a sunset.

I feel good. *This* is my story. The pictures of me that are going on tour—those are Veronica's story, they're the part I play in her life, but they aren't *me*. She can have them; she's allowed to own her side of the story. But I'm also allowed to own mine.

From down the hall, I hear Veronica let out a shriek, and then my phone buzzes with a text from her.

ARE YOU TRYING TO KILL ME, it says. An image pops up, a screenshot of the selfie I just posted, of me at the top of my recent climb. She's annotated it, drawing red arrows to the muscles in my shoulders.

I laugh out loud.

I write, *You're such a stalker, how did you even know about this account?*

Because I'm a stalker! Now come in here and take your clothes off.

I snort. *Your mom is home.*

A pause, and then *TANTRUM!!!!!*

Of all the colorful things in this new, precarious life, she is the most colorful.

CHAPTER FORTY-FOUR

◇◇◇

MICK

I PULL THE HONDA CR-V OVER ONTO THE SHOULDER of the too-familiar desert road. This is the used car Veronica's dad bought her for senior year. It was twelve thousand dollars. Claudia had said the words *it's only twelve thousand dollars* when she asked Veronica's dad to pay for it.

Veronica and I have been arguing about whether what I'm doing today is necessary, or if I should wait until she can come with me. I can't handle waiting anymore. As long as the photos are out here, they hang over my head, a threat waiting to be executed.

I grab the pile of rock-climbing gear from the back seat and lock the CR-V behind me. I don't bring my phone. It's off. No one can know I came here. The police have pretty much let go of the idea that Veronica and I might have been involved in Lily's and David's deaths, but it was touch and go there for a minute, with them thinking I may have killed both Lily and David despite Veronica's insistence that I didn't. Ultimately, the DA didn't think they had enough evidence to charge me, especially with so much evidence pointing to Nico. When the lawyer Veronica's parents paid for pointed out the impossibility of me pushing David, who was twice my size, off the bridge, they decided to pour their resources into the hunt for Nico.

But still. They could change their minds anytime.

The sun is so hot and bright, I feel like it's inside my skull, burning my brain. I'm already sweating through my T-shirt. It must be a hundred and ten. I pick my way carefully through the brush and cacti, trudging up the hill until I'm at the top of the cliff Veronica fell off of.

Damn, it's a long way down. I can't believe she survived the fall. She's so lucky. *I'm* so lucky.

I look back at the CR-V. It's completely alone, a solitary interruption in the desert and winding road.

Goose bumps stipple my forearms. This place feels like a fork in the road between a reality in which Veronica died and I was remembered as a stainless steel corpse and . . . and this. Just yesterday, I used the word *precarious* when thinking about my new life, and now I feel superstitiously certain that this life is wrong, that I stole it, that I cheated fate.

Stop. Enough. I need to get moving.

I find the little ravine I used to climb down last time. I strap myself into a harness and hammer some pins into the rocks. I'll have to be able to make my way back up alone, so it's important that I take my time and do this right.

I climb down backward, so much more confident now that I have the right gear. Rock climbing is getting easier and easier the more I practice, and this time, it only takes me fifteen or twenty minutes to get to the bottom. I disentangle myself from the gear and move carefully through the rocks and weeds; this is really a dried-up creek bed, now that I look at it without the distraction of wounded Veronica. It only takes a little while of scouting before I find the spot where she lay dying. The rocks where her head rested are covered in dried blood.

I walk past the rust-brown inkblot bloodstains. Twenty paces, heel to toe. I turn left and approach the wall of the cliff. At its base is a large, roughly triangular stone I immediately recognize. I squat down, get my gloved hands under it, and heave it up. With great effort, I shift it over six inches. The manila envelope comes into view. It's stained and dirty.

I shake grubs and spiders off it, remove my gloves, and pull out the contents.

There are the clear plastic negative sleeves with the negatives intact inside them and a stack of prints. I flip through them. There are photos of the tent, and there are David, Lily, and me lugging Christmas trees to surround it.

These people are dead. Lily, with her dark, sparkling intelligence, and David, with his uncomplicated good nature—gone forever.

I come to the picture of myself, torch in hand. Next to me, Nico looks at the camera with an exhilarated, smug expression that takes my breath away with fear.

It's kind of a shame to destroy it. I'll never do anything that reckless again, that destructive. For a moment, I'm sad, longing for the version of me that Nico inspired. It was powerful.

But no. That's a lie. With Nico, I only felt powerful when I was destroying something. Now I want to build things.

That's what I realize about Nico: He's not smarter than anyone else. He's not special, or a force of change. It's so *easy* to destroy. It's cheap and lazy and small.

That doesn't mean he won't come back for us. I know he will. It's only a matter of time. When he's set his mind on something, he does it. No regrets, no conscience, no second thoughts.

I pile up the photos and scrounge for twigs and dry leaves. I pull a lighter from my pocket and set them on fire.

I sit there and watch them burn. I add more twigs and leaves, and soon the whole thing is just a pile of ash. I stamp it out, afraid of starting another wildfire. I cover the ashes with dirt and rocks.

I return to the spot where I found Veronica. After staring at her dried blood for a while, I find myself sitting down and then lying back, putting my head on the rocks where hers rested.

I look up at the pastel-blue sky.

Birds flit around, back and forth, crisscrossing paths in front of the baby blue. Veronica is right. I've always noticed birds.

A silhouette appears on the cliff's edge.

My heart stops.

It's tall and slim. It stands there for a few seconds, looking down at me, and then it disappears.

I sit up.

It's Nico.

What do I do? I have no phone.

Did I lock the CR-V? I don't know.

He can either climb down somewhere I can't see him, or he can wait for me up there and kick me in the head when I climb up.

I'm safer down here. I should hide.

I grab the harness and other gear, throw it over my shoulder, and sprint down the creek bed. I make good time, jumping from rock to rock, dirt patch to dirt patch. The ravine winds around a little, but I'm not worried about getting lost. I can easily retrace my steps. The heat is taking its toll, though, and I'm excruciatingly thirsty. I think I might be getting heat stroke. I slow my pace and come to a stop.

I put my hands on my knees. I can't catch my breath. It's like exercising inside a sauna.

I walk past a crack in the cliff wall, and then I come back to it. It's really just the space between two boulders, barely wide enough for me. I grab a stick off the ground and poke around in there, worried about snakes and mountain lions and whatever other creatures might live out here. I can't find anything except more brush and rocks, so I turn sideways and slip into the crevice. It goes back about five feet and is just tall enough for me to stand upright.

I stand there for a long time, chest heaving, heart pounding, ears straining for the sound of footsteps.

My feet start going numb. How long can someone stand in one spot?

My ears are hypervigilant. Birds. So many birds. No footsteps.

It's cooler in here than out there, but I'm still sweating more than is probably okay, given how thirsty I am.

How long can I stay here?

He could just be waiting for me at the top of the cliff. He could wait there all day. All night. He probably has water. Knowing Nico, he has an arsenal of murder supplies in a car parked right there on the shoulder by mine.

To pass the time, I try to compile lists of things in my mind: all fifty states. All the algebra equations I can remember. All the movies I've seen. I try to count the times Veronica and I have kissed. I try to pin down my favorite moment between us. Maybe that first one, on the train. Or when she woke up in the hospital.

I can't stay here forever. At some point I have to go up there and find out what he has planned for me.

I'm not crying. I'm not anything. I'm blank with panic, an empty slate of pure adrenaline.

I have to face it.

I peek out of the crevice, half expecting him to be there waiting. It's peaceful, deceptively so. This desert is as dangerous as Nico. It will swallow me whole, and the birds will keep on singing.

I stay to the edge of the creek bed and make my way back on careful, quiet feet. I'm so thirsty, I almost don't care about Nico now. I'm desperate for water. The heat is alive, petting my skin.

I start worrying I've come too far, that I'm lost. I keep walking. Maybe I was running faster than I remember. I've lost my sense of time and direction.

And then there's my rope, dangling from the top of the cliff straight ahead.

I have to search the area. I can't have Nico leaping out at me while I'm trying to climb up.

With dread, I look all around, behind the next curve in the ravine, behind every bush and crack. I keep glancing up at the cliff's edge, searching for signs that he's watching me.

It seems clear.

I know it can't be.

He's probably got a sunshade and a picnic set up for himself. He's probably just going to wait for me to climb up and push me right off, so the cops will think it's a rock-climbing accident.

Trembling, I get back into the harness. I grip the rope. I have to clear my mind and climb carefully.

The climb is endless. I keep waiting for Nico to appear, for the rope to be cut. I clutch the rocks with desperation. Before I ascend the last bit, I say a quick prayer.

I pull myself up. I brace myself for an attack.

Hills. Rocks. Emptiness.

I scramble up the cliff and away from the edge. I detach myself from the rope and run down the hill, heart racing.

There's the CR-V, on the shoulder of the road. No other vehicle is parked anywhere in sight.

I climb back up the hill. From here, I can see the road as it stretches off on both sides for miles.

No cars.

Did I imagine the silhouette? Could I have been delirious from the heat?

On my hands and knees, I gather the rock-climbing gear into a pile and lug it back to the CR-V. I pop the back door and throw it into the storage compartment.

I shut the door, only now thinking—could he be in the car?

No. It's a thousand degrees in there. If that was his hiding place, he's dead.

Still, I drop down and check underneath it.

Nothing.

I fling the doors open, passenger's side front and back. No one is inside.

I'm losing it. I almost just got swallowed by the desert, and for what?

I shut the doors and go around to the driver's side. I open the handle, and just before I can hop into the car, I notice something on my seat. It's silver and shiny, like a stainless steel kitchen utensil.

I reach out and touch it with a fingertip. It's hot enough to burn straight through skin, like it's been sitting here for hours.

I pull my gloves back on and pick it up. It's heavy.

It's a silver rose, the stem about ten inches long. It's beautiful, but it's made out of steel.

Nico.

The rose has thorns, wicked sharp, all along the stem.

* * *

I get back to Veronica's house much later than I was supposed to. She and Claudia are in the living room with Erica, Veronica's new agent or manager or whatever. She's based in LA and is a striking-looking brunette with freckles covering her face, neck, and arms. The three of them are drinking coffee and laughing. Veronica looks good, like she spent some time primping. She decorated her wheelchair the second she got home from the hospital, and the wheels are all full of glued-on rhinestones. She calls them her "rims."

"Mick!" Veronica cries. "Where the hell have you been?"

"I'm sorry I'm late. I was hiking, and I took a longer trail than I intended to."

Veronica says, "Did hiking go well?" It means, *Did you burn the photos?*

"Yes."

"Good."

Erica says, "Well, we're planning the tour, in case you'd like to join us." She knows Veronica wants me to come with her on some of the trips if I can, but it's hard with my swimming schedule.

"Sure. Let me just clean up." I go down the hallway to the bathroom, shower off, throw on shorts and a tank top, and check every nook and cranny I can find in case Nico is hiding in the house somewhere. I come trotting back as they're examining something on Erica's laptop, which is open on the coffee table.

The silver rose from the desert is hidden in my bag. I don't know how to tell Veronica what it is, what it means, but there's no way around it. We're going to have to change the alarm codes, maybe add some new sensors or change security companies altogether.

Because on my pillow lies another silver rose.

CHAPTER FORTY-FIVE

◇◇◇

NICO

I RELAX BACK INTO THE LUXURIOUS WHITE COTTON
bedding. This is a nice hotel, even for downtown LA, but I'm
not an official guest here. I'm just occupying an empty room.

I check the news on my phone.

The Griffith Park wildfire is going well. That's good. The
Calabasas one is taking a little longer to get off the ground,
which is fine; we have until tonight. The Malibu fire is making news in a big way. All those celebrities tweeting about
their horses and mansions. I feel my mouth twist into a smirk.
The news outlets are barely covering the Mount Washington
fire, but that one's going to help shut down the 5 freeway once
it connects with the Sunland and Griffith Park fires. That's my
sleeper. The Sepulveda Pass fire by the Getty Center is doing
big things; it's crossed the 405 and is burning the hills in Bel
Air. Perfect. They're unable to keep it contained, not with so
much manpower deployed to other fires around the city.

That's the idea. Deploy all the manpower. Get every single first responder out there.

I check the time. Five o'clock. At six, the real fun will start.

Mick, I hope you're watching. This is all for you. My most interesting, unpredictable doll. My pretty little arsonist. I can almost forgive you for slipping away from your coffin. I suppose that's my best work: pushing you to jump up off the page.

And you gave me the idea for this, my best install yet. You're an actual muse.

Though, is it really an install? Is chaos something you can install?

You know what, Mick? I think it is.

CHAPTER FORTY-SIX

◇◇◇

VERONICA

MICK AND I GET HOME FROM SCHOOL AT A QUARTER to eight, since I had to wait for her to finish swim practice. Once I got used to seeing her in a bathing suit, watching her swim back and forth from one side of the pool to the other is incredibly boring. I mean, let's be honest. I can see her naked at home now. I don't need to thirst after her in a Speedo one-piece with her hair trapped in a rubber swim cap, getting yelled at by a masochistic middle-aged woman with unchecked access to a whistle.

Mick pushes my wheelchair in the front door, spinning me around so she can bump me up over the threshold. She's been doing this for a month and a half. She's getting good at it. I might even miss this when I'm cleared to walk again. Is it wrong that I like having her at my beck and call?

"Who were you on the phone with at swim practice?" Mick asks me. "Looked intense."

"Donna."

"Oh." She stops walking. Donna is our lawyer. "What'd she say?"

"Nothing new. They're still looking for Nico. We're good." I don't want to get her thinking about lawyers any more than I have to; she's been stressing herself out worrying about how she'll pay my parents back for her half of the bills. To change the subject, I tell her, "I don't know how you practice so much. Don't you get tired of soaking yourself in bleach and urine? Humans are land animals. Land animals, Mick."

She pushes the front door shut with her butt and wheels me toward the kitchen. "No one pees in a high school pool."

"That you know of."

"Isn't your arm almost better? You're going to be pushing your own self in this thing pretty soon."

"No!" I cry. "You're so good at it!" Before she can pull me inside, I say, "Hey. Mick. Come here."

She kneels down in front of me. "What's up?"

I reach for her face, run my good hand through her hair. "I'm worried you're allowing all this photo stuff, the tour and everything, because you're stressing the lawyer bills. You really don't have to do that. You have your whole life to worry about paying my parents back. I can take pictures of palm trees again if it makes you feel more comfortable. Or I can find a different model."

"I'm not. It's . . ." She looks at the scars on her palms. "It's therapeutic. It's showing Liz and my mom and everyone else that I really do not give a shit what they think." She shivers. "I don't like the way it feels, but I'm proud of myself for doing it."

I search her face for any sign of deception. She seems like she's telling the truth. "Okay," I say at last.

"Okay." She kisses me and hops to her feet. "Plus I have a feeling you're going to be an expensive prom date. I can't even imagine what you're planning. I'm already humiliated."

"Ooh," I squeal. I haven't even started thinking about prom yet. My brain launches into action. We could be the couple in *High School Musical*. Or, no. *Rocky Horror*. I could be Dr. Frank-N-Furter, she could be Janet. *Yes.*

Suddenly, I remember Nico's words. They come back to me in cruel, unexpected moments. He called me typical. He said I was boring, that I'm all show and Mick is the one with substance. I suddenly feel stupid for my *Rocky Horror* prom idea.

And then I slap the thoughts aside. Nico is a murderer. He killed our friends. He can eat a bag of dicks.

In the kitchen, my mom has something cooking on the stove and her laptop open on the counter. "Shhh!" she hisses as we enter.

"What?"

"Shhh!" She waves her hands.

Mick and I exchange a confused look, and she wheels me around the counter so we can see what my mom is watching.

"You're watching the news?" I ask. "God, you're getting old."

"All of LA is on fire." She turns the volume up.

A young newscaster stands in front of a screen on which are flashing pictures of massive wildfires. "Firefighters from all around the state are working on containing a series of fires consuming green spaces throughout Los Angeles, from Calabasas to Malibu to the Sepulveda Pass to Griffith Park. Authorities are requesting that everyone who is unaffected remain home; all freeways and major streets are needed by firefighters to—"

A picture of the logo from Universal Studios pops up on the screen behind him. "Hang on.

"We're getting reports of an active shooter situation at Universal Studios. The Universal Studios theme park is currently on lockdown. Again, reports are coming in that the Universal—" He touches his ear. "I'm sorry. We have a report of another active shooter situation. This one is on the USC campus, in the student center and in the— We also have one coming in from the UCLA Medical Center. And Pepperdine University, which is also affected by the Malibu wildfire. And Grand Central Market in downtown LA. Police are asking that everyone not affected by the fires or the active shooter situations remain—"

He stares at the camera blankly. Behind him, the screen flashes a picture of a bunch of different logos—NBC, Warner Bros., Disney, Nickelodeon. He says, "We're getting reports that a number of different studios are reporting active shooter situations as well. We're not sure—there seems to be indication that this is some sort of—"

The screen goes green. And silent.

CHAPTER FORTY-SEVEN

◇◇◇

NICO

THE LIGHTS GO OUT IN THE HOTEL ROOM.

The city had been humming around me, through the windows and through the walls. But now it's eerily silent.

I'm grinning. Laughter bubbles up inside me. I can't sit still. I hop up, take three long strides to the sliding door, and let myself out onto the balcony.

The city is blanketed in complete darkness.

Except for the fires. At the horizon, the hills shine orange light into the night sky. The headlights and taillights on the streets far below are like reflections of the stars you can't see beyond the smoke.

Good job, little nine-year-old Jessica, with your backpack at the Department of Water and Power.

Around me, some office buildings flicker with low yellow lights, the ones that have functioning backup generators.

I learned a valuable lesson during my last series. If

you go after a man, you create a martyr. If you want people to see the failings of a system, you have to attack the machine.

It's time to go to the roof. Time for the finale.

CHAPTER FORTY-EIGHT

◇◇◇

VERONICA

WE'RE HUDDLED ON THE COUCH, WATCHING TV. THE newspeople have gotten their generators working, and a frazzled-looking woman is saying, "We're reporting from downtown LA. The city is mostly without power. Authorities say an explosion at the DWP is to blame."

The screen flashes to an aerial view of Los Angeles. All the hills are glowing orange with fire. The downtown skyline is dark. The newscaster says, "Residents not evacuated are being warned to stay inside. The city is on official lockdown. Reports of active shootings at Universal Citywalk, Grand Central Market, UCLA, and USC have been declared a hoax. It appears that the sound of gunshots was simulated using explosive devices and fireworks placed strategically in high-traffic areas—"

A loud, shrieking sound interrupts her. She spins to look at the screen. As we watch, a series of fireworks explode above the downtown skyline.

"I'm not sure—" she begins.

The fireworks are red. Sparkling ones, spiraling ones, flashing ones. It's a magnificent display, huge against the dark silhouettes of buildings. My mom grips my good hand. Beside me, Mick's eyes are wide.

The fireworks stop.

The newscaster says, "We think that might have been unrelated, perhaps a previously planned display of—"

Another shriek and explosion. Silver fireworks blossom in the downtown sky. At first, I don't understand their strange formation, but then they expand into the shape of a long-stemmed rose.

"No," Mick whispers. Her hand is pressed to her mouth.

"What is it?" I ask.

She removes her hand from her mouth and whispers, "It's Nico."

CHAPTER FORTY-NINE

◇◇◇

NICO

I IGNITE THE ROSE FROM THE ROOF, AND I WATCH IT bloom over the dark, smoking city.

I survey the work I've done. The wreckage. The chaos.

Mick? Do you see me?

As the rose fades into the smoky air, I feel sad and nostalgic. They'll put out the fires; they'll turn the power back on. This day will vanish into history, like all days do.

I won't be photographing this series. I'm at a different level now. The world will document my work for me. Next stop: Manhattan. I feel like I'm standing on top of a mountain, looking behind me down at the climb.

I take out my phone and navigate to your new Instagram account. I stare at your photos and devour your words. I have them memorized.

I did that. I molded you—a human being—into something else. You're mine, and you're *glorious*.

Eventually, when I get tired of watching your shiny, brand-new life unfold from a distance, I'm sure our paths will cross again. When that happens, it will feel like fate.

I'm so glad I didn't melt you down with steel and turn you into a lifeless, shining doll. What a waste that would have been. You're too pretty to burn.

ACKNOWLEDGMENTS

This book would not exist in any form without the combined efforts of Jessica Anderson and Lauren Spieller. I owe these two a great debt of gratitude for their work on this project. They provided invaluable guidance and inspiration, and working alongside them has been an actual dream come true. Thank you, Jessica, for providing me the opportunity to tell this story and let it take its strange and winding course. I appreciate the creative freedom and the incisive direction; you're a master of words. Lauren, thank you for your infallible steadiness and wisdom. You are a rock, and these years of working with you have been better than I could have imagined.

My dear friend Kit Rosewater was my artistic coconspirator, planning Nico's antics alongside me. Without Kit, there would be no forest party, no Fishing for People. My critique partner, Layne Fargo, was, as always, an incredible sounding board for ideas and editorial eye on drafts of this book. Erica Waters, thank you for reading a broken early piece of this book and kindly helping to guide it. Of course, my mother was brought in to consult on art crime locations around San Diego; a mother's job is never done.

So many writer friends have provided a sounding board, a sympathetic ear, and a sense of community: Diana Urban; Mike Chen; Aiden Thomas; Hannah Mary McKinnon; Halley Sutton; Kristen Lepionka; Laura Weymouth; and all the writing colleagues who have encouraged me, providing a willing ear, and inspired me to do better, be better. JT Ellison, Kimberly Belle, Emily Carpenter, Jenny Hillier, Wendy Walker, Riley Sager—you've given encouragement and guidance freely and without reserve. How can I thank you for your mentorship and openness?

This book is dedicated to the memory of my grandmother, Veta Denton. She was the namesake of my only daughter, and she loved books more than anyone.

Above all, this book is for those who see themselves in its difficult moments. You're never a waste; you're so much more than pretty little things. Go forth in power and kindness.